MW01005655

Three and a Half Minutes

Minutes

A Novel

Caroline Fyffe

Three and a Half Minutes
Copyright © 2012 by Caroline Fyffe

www.carolinefyffe.com

Edited by Pam Berehulke – Bulletproof Editing
Cover design by Kelli Ann Morgan
Interior book design by Bob Houston eBook Formatting

Proudly Published in the United States of America

ISBN #978-0-9840146-7-5

Acknowledgments

My deepest gratitude goes to our dear friend, Father Peter, for his generous gifts of time, talent, and smiles spent with the Catholic portions of this novel, the tricky German dialog, and so much more—but mostly for the insightful spiritual guidance throughout the years. Also, to my girlfriend and fellow photographer, Cheryl Magoteaux Cody, for encouraging me to write the book in the first place.

Thank you!

Chapter One

Portland, Oregon

Camille Ashland breathed deeply and glanced at the clock on the wall. She ignored the slight queasiness in her stomach and handed a receipt to the young woman she was helping. No doubt about it, she loved *and* hated Valentine's Day. As owner of Chocolate Blossoms, a chocolate, flower, and perfume specialty store, Camille looked forward to the day created for lovers even though it meant utter exhaustion.

"What's wrong?" Suzie asked, touching Camille's shoulder gently. "You don't look well. Are you feeling okay?"

Camille rubbed her chest. "Just indigestion from that spicy shrimp scampi I had for lunch. I should know better by now." She laughed. "Actually, I'm thinking about Mom too. Today's the anniversary of my father's death. Every year around this time, she gets a bit melancholy. Even after all these years. I wish there was something more I could do for her…"

Suzie tucked a sprig of baby's breath into the bow on the package she was wrapping. "Go on and call her. Pam and I can handle this."

Camille mentally calculated the number of people still waiting to be helped. They'd be here for another hour at least. "That's a good idea. How about I take the next customer before I sneak off?" She leaned in and whispered, "He looks a bit impatient."

Chocolate Blossoms' tiny, yet charming display area was crammed with shoppers eager to find the perfect gift for their special someone. Camille smiled and waved the gentleman forward from the line that curled around the room. "Next."

He stepped forward in a rumpled blue suit.

She smiled. "May I help you?"

He nodded, then pointed to one of the display baskets on the counter. "That's nice."

"Yes. That's the Berry-Cherry Chocolate Basket. It's filled with milk chocolate hearts, chocolate-covered cherries, and blueberries. White roses and baby's breath adorn the center and handle. It runs forty-one ninety-five."

His lips tipped up. "I'll take it."

At his quick decision, her smile widened. "Perfect. Are you registered here?"

He looked through his wallet, then handed Camille his Chocolate Blossoms card. She swiped the pink and green card thinking how much he resembled her husband, Bret, deceased now for eight years. How she wished Bret could see her hard-won success. "Do you *ever* finish anything, Camille?" he'd asked her more times than she'd like to remember. "Just *do* it!" Bitterness threatened her mood. Even though spoken in jest, she knew his words were meant to hurt, just a little. He'd thought her a quitter. Had said it more times than not. *But it wasn't true.* As was her habit, she glanced at the Post-it note she'd stuck to the front of her monitor. FINISH IT! bolstered her resolve.

The customer's account flashed on her screen. "So, Mr. Snyder, how did Mrs. Snyder like the Sinfully Rich Chocolate Tower you purchased for her birthday?"

He chuckled softly and his brows rose in amusement. "She loved it. That's why I'm back today. I'm sure she'll be expecting something equally as wonderful tomorrow. You *do* have a racket going."

Camille's face warmed with the compliment. "That's the idea," she said as she hurried to the back room for a pre-made version of his selection. Back again, she took a few moments to check it over to be sure it was perfect, then nodded approvingly. "It's actually a personal favorite of mine."

Without warning, a white-hot pain seared through Camille's chest and sliced down her left arm. Terrified, she wheezed, and struggled to get even a thimbleful of air into her lungs. Before she was able to say a word, a crushing force from within, more frightening than the pain she still felt, slammed into her torso with the strength of a truck, making her cry out in shock. She clawed at the neckline of her blouse.

A collage of horrified expressions spun out of control before her eyes. She slumped over the countertop, knocking chocolate-laden baskets, flowers, and colorful bottles of perfume to the floor. She wished she could cover her ears, block the cacophony of screeching, incoherent voices, and breaking glass. A macabre kaleidoscope filled her vision. She thought she heard Suzie's panicked voice screaming for someone to call 911.

An awareness of her daughter, her beautiful, tenderhearted Kristin, flashed somewhere inside, followed quickly by an image of Bret and another of her parents. Bits and pieces of her life played out in fast-forward, flooding her heart with love, anger, joy, and sorrow. Compressed moments in time enveloped her, bringing with them the emotions she'd experienced and with whom. They shot through her at the speed of light, and she wondered how she could understand any of it. But she did. Every fleeting millisecond.

Was she dying? The thought of never seeing Kristin again produced an overwhelming agony, one far worse than the physical pain tearing her body apart. She wanted to live. There were too many things left to do. She wanted to find love again. Passion. She wasn't ready to die, ready to give up her dreams, ready to go before *finishing* any of it.

She slid to the floor. Everything went black.

Almost instantly, she was awake again and a slight snapping sensation cleared her thoughts. Her panic evaporated. The pain vanished and she suddenly felt wonderful—the best she had in her entire life. Light and breezy. The shop seemed brighter, different.

Suzie and Pam, as well as Mr. Snyder, were huddled together as if looking at something on the floor. She called to them, trying to get their attention. She needed to tell them she felt better now, and that everything was okay.

They couldn't hear her over all the commotion reverberating around in her small shop. People were whispering behind their hands. Others were crying. Customers left the store without completing their purchases. Camille tried to stop them, asked them to wait, but no one paid her any mind.

With a burst of frosty February air, two EMTs rushed in, one she recognized as Wade Moss, the other a stranger. They cleared the area where Pam and Suzie knelt.

Camille gasped. A woman was lying on the floor next to the display case. Her ghostly white face stood out sharply on the deep emerald and crimson of the floral tapestry rug.

Camille felt a resounding shock.

It was *her* face. *Her* body.

And yet, she looked different. Younger. Prettier than she remembered herself in the flat reflection of a mirror.

Was she dead? She must be.

Wade shook her shoulder. "Camille!"

He tipped her head back and pulled her chin up. At the same time, he placed his ear close to her mouth, listening. Putting a mask over her mouth and nose, he squeezed the air bag slowly once, then repeated the process. Placing two fingers on the artery in her neck, he checked for a pulse.

Camille watched with interest. These were people she loved. It hurt deeply to see them in such a state of distress. She needed to tell them she was okay. Happier than she'd ever been. It felt good and so natural to be rid of that encumbering coat of skin.

Wade's companion cut away Camille's blouse and bra in one quick motion. She was sure she should feel some embarrassment at being exposed to the bystanders like that, but she didn't. He proceeded to apply two round pads, one centered above her left breast and the other more to the left side, and lower. He hooked them to a small machine he'd brought in with him. Wade continued with the chest compressions he was administering.

"Still no pulse," Wade said, remaining steady and calm as he worked.

The other EMT flipped on a switch. His finger hovered over a button waiting for the signal. Wade nodded. A computerized female voice prompted, "Shock advised."

Wade never took his gaze from Camille's face as the numbers on the display raced up toward 300 joules. As the power climbed, an ascending hum of the machine mingled eerily with soft classical music that played in the background.

"Stand clear," Wade commanded. At the exact moment he pressed the button, Camille's body jerked violently as an electrical shock shot from one pad to the other.

Wade's partner pressed the analyze button again. "Shock advised."

"Charge." The red light glowed.

Pam cried out and Suzie turned into her arms, weeping openly.

Camille watched from the ceiling where her spirit floated weightlessly. Even though she felt no pain, she didn't like to watch as the electrical shock violated her body, making it react so abhorrently. It looked grotesque.

"Clear," Wade said again.

Camille squeezed her eyes tightly closed and covered her ears.

Chapter Two

A bright light pierced Camille's left eye, the intensity of it sending bursts of pain shooting throughout her brain. Ever so gently, the lid was lowered and the other eyelid was slowly lifted. Light now pervaded it.

"Camille, can you hear me?"

A voice. There was a voice calling to her. Camille cried out sadly as the voice chased away the wonderful sensation she was floating in. Like a dream, but a million times better. No, please, she thought, as she turned a full circle looking for the feeling that almost had a form. She was suspended in a sea of utter happiness, an embrace of overwhelming love.

Reluctantly, she opened her eyes.

Stephanie Ashland, her doctor and also Bret's younger sister, bent over her, worry shadowing her attractive face. Her blonde hair was pulled back in a taut ponytail and her white smock dangled loosely around her body.

"Hello, stranger," she whispered softly.

Camille looked at her for a few moments, then let her gaze wander around the room. She tried to make some sense of what had happened, why she was lying in a hospital bed with numerous tubes sticking out of her like a flattened porcupine on the side of the highway. Everything was jumbled in her head. It hurt to even think.

"I'm alive?" She struggled to smile but it felt more like a grimace.

"Yes."

Camille's eyes slowly lowered. "I'm so sleepy."

"It's the drugs. If you're still drowsy, let them do their job. Don't be frightened. You're in the hospital and I'm staying at your side."

The hum and beeping of monitors and machines in the ICCU *were* frightening. Lights blazed brightly. Nurses came and went, checking charts and equipment. Someone down the hall moaned.

"What happened?"

"You had a heart attack. As soon as your condition stabilizes, I'm sending you into surgery. It's a relatively easy procedure where they'll go up to your cardiac arteries through your groin and insert two stents."

Camille did her best to digest what Stephanie had just said. "Heart attack? But I'm only," she had to stop and think how old she turned on her last birthday, "forty-four."

"Shhh. We'll talk about that later. Right now you need to rest."

A sudden panic gripped Camille. "Kristin? Where is she? Does she know?"

"Yes. Your mom picked her up from school as soon as she was notified. They've been sitting here for hours. She's with Ellen now getting a cup of hot chocolate."

"Steph?"

Stephanie took her cool hand and warmed it with her own. "Yes?"

"I was dead."

Stephanie's expression was guarded. "Why do you say that?"

"I remember leaving my body and watching as Wade Moss revived me. It *was* Wade, right?"

Stephanie's thumb brushed back and forth across her hand. "Yes, it was Wade. As a matter of fact, he's been here too, pacing around the waiting room like a tiger, and sneaking in from time to time. He left only moments ago but said he'd come back to check on you a little later."

"How long was I—gone?"

Stephanie made a spot for herself on the side of the bed and sat for a moment, just looking at Camille. "Three and a half minutes," she answered gently. "But all this can wait." She smoothed Camille's hair back and then bent down and kissed her forehead. "Don't worry about anything. Just snuggle down into your covers and enjoy a day off. A novelty for you, I know, but you might surprise yourself and come to like it."

Camille sat with feet curled beneath her in her favorite cozy chair, a spot of late afternoon sunshine warming her face. She flipped through her day planner, noticing the seven days since she'd been home from the hospital with absolutely nothing penciled in. It was hard to believe. Valentine's Day had come and gone without her, and the store had survived. Suzie and Pam were handling the business just fine. Still, it wasn't in her nature to sit back and let someone else take the reins. There were decisions to make, advertisements to place, and window decorations and displays to be changed. *I need to get back to work.*

Kristin came bopping into the living room and, like most junior-high-aged girls, had her cell phone glued to her ear. Holes in her jeans showed both knees and her tee shirt was one size too small. Her glossy hair, a rich nut color, hung down her back in one long layer.

Kristin closed her phone and slipped it into her pocket. "That was Grandma. She's bringing dinner over. She's here now so I'm gonna go help her bring it in."

"Going. Going to go help her," Camille corrected softly, enjoying the sight of Kristin. Since her brush with death, Camille had learned to appreciate every living moment, regardless of how small or insignificant it seemed.

The doorbell chimed and Stephanie let herself in, passing Kristin on her way out. They gave each other a high five.

"Good news?" Camille asked as they hugged.

Stephanie held out a folder. "All the results are here."

"Fantastic. I'm half-crazy from sitting around this house. When can I start back to work?"

"Hold on, now. Not so fast."

Ellen and Kristin were back, their arms laden with bags and packages. Camille stopped her mother's progress across the room. "Let me take those."

"No, no. They're light. Kristin has all the heavy bags. You keep doing what you were doing with Stephanie, and Kristin and I will get dinner on the table."

Camille kissed her mother's cheek. "You're an angel."

When the kitchen door closed, Stephanie seated herself on the couch and patted the spot next to her. She began gently, "The tests aren't quite what I was hoping for, Camille. Your case is a little more problematic than I'd originally thought."

Worry chased away Camille's cheerful mood. She sank onto the sofa next to her sister-in-law. "I'm a case now, huh," she said with a forced grin, trying not to read too much into Stephanie's expression. "Why? I've been a runner for years. I've never smoked. I eat too much Ben and Jerry's, I suppose, but other than that?"

"Your dad passed away from the same kind of heart disease before he was fifty."

Stephanie reached around and gathered her hair over one shoulder, something she did when nervous. "It's in your genetics *and* your history and goes back to when you were a kid and eating Happy Meals and Ho Hos. However, tonight we start to turn back the clock. With the medication I prescribed, and healthy choices in diet and exercise, you should be fine."

"Then why do you look so pensive?"

Stephanie gave her a look. "How can you always read me so well?"

Camille shrugged, waiting for her sister-in-law to spit out what was weighing on her mind.

"Men's heart attacks are usually brought on by eating, or physical activity, whereas women's are typically preceded by emotional stress."

"Stress? How does that relate to me?"

Stephanie had the audacity to laugh, her brows rising in disbelief. "Bret's devil-may-care ways were always a big part of who he was. You had a hard time dealing with that. Now that he's dead, you're mad at him for being careless with his life. For leaving you a widow, and Kristin without a father. I don't blame you. I'm mad at him too."

Camille's face grew warm as those hard years after Bret's death resurfaced in her mind. Several risky business ventures had cleaned out their savings, all without her knowledge. And her with a young child to support—perhaps there were grounds for her anger. That wasn't all of it, though. She *did* grieve for Bret. But a man should take his role as the head and provider of a family seriously, not spinning his wheels looking for the next thrill, or quick gold mine. If he hadn't cared enough about her to settle down, he should have at least thought about his daughter. But she'd never tell Stephanie how destitute he'd left them. His little sister thought the world of him, even more now that he was dead. Camille never wanted to hurt her like that.

"It's true, Camille. We both know it."

Camille stood, then went to the fireplace where a framed picture of her and Bret was displayed. It was taken on their honeymoon, when they'd signed up for a white-water trip in the Rocky Mountains. Devil's Bend was just around the corner and his blond hair ruffled in the wind. He had that particular smile, the one that only appeared when he was doing something perilous, creasing his face. She'd given him her whole heart. Tried to make it work, cried more tears than she ever wanted to remember, when she had finally realized she and Kristin took a backseat to his danger-seeking ways.

"Camille," Stephanie said gently from behind her. "Hostility decreases blood flow and increases hormones that promote clots. It is possible resentment could have instigated the attack."

Resentment and hostility? *Really?* Camille almost laughed. Oh, it was a lot more than that. She gave herself a mental shake, knowing better than to let him so affect her life from the grave after eight years, even to the point of ruining her health. It galled her.

"Mom, dinner is ready," Kristin said from the doorway. Lines crinkled her forehead as she looked hesitantly between them, her childlike radar picking up on the tension coiling in the room.

"We'll be right in, sweetheart."

Stephanie waited until Kristin closed the door. "Camille, your daily work schedule has got to change. You're at that shop constantly. Since Bret's been gone, you haven't been out on a single date. Put nicely—you don't have a life."

"Steph, shhh. I don't want to upset Mom and Kristin any more than they already are."

Stephanie smiled apologetically. "If you don't change your ways," she continued in a hushed voice, "you're twice as likely to have a repeat episode. And this could be the one that *really* kills you. Is that what you want for Kristin? For her to grow up without any parents at all?"

The implication that Stephanie thought she, like Bret, would put her ambition before her daughter's needs, was outrageous. She'd worked night and day to keep a roof over their heads and food on the table. Now that the shop was actually turning a fabulous profit, she felt compelled to keep it going. As she'd found out, things could change quickly. She never wanted to feel that vulnerable again. The urge to strike back at Stephanie was strong.

"And having a self-righteous, know-it-all sister-in-law? Does that heighten my chances?"

Stephanie's expression tightened with disappointment. "Not fair. I'm your doctor. If you want it sugarcoated, I can do that. I'm only trying to keep you alive."

"Dinner is getting cold," Ellen called. "And Kristin is starving. I won't be able to hold her off much longer."

Years of pain, disappointment, and loneliness jumbled up inside Camille. Bitterness too—in spades. Stephanie was right in her diagnosis and she was being a stubborn fool not to admit it. Taking out her pain on her best friend wasn't what she wanted to do.

"That's not how I really feel." She held out her arms and Stephanie stepped into her embrace. "You're the sister of my heart more than a sister-in-law. I love you. I don't know what I'd do without you."

Camille caught their image in the mirror. Stephanie's straight blonde hair contrasted with her own wavy chestnut. Four years younger, her sister-in-law was taller by three inches but that didn't stop them from embracing, heart to heart. They smiled and stepped away.

"Will you forgive me for being a nincompoop?"

Stephanie's smile widened. "Nothing to forgive. I love nincompoops. But I *am* relieved to hear you say it because, like it or not, you're stuck with me."

"That may not be as long as you think." Camille rolled her eyes and clutched her chest playfully as she started toward the kitchen.

"Not funny at all."

Almost to the kitchen, Camille turned back abruptly. "By the way, just *who* am I supposed to be dating? I haven't seen a host of men beating down the door to this house."

"Wade Moss has been trying to catch your eye for the last two years. Unfortunately, he's just too shy to do anything about it. Maybe now that he's seen you bare-chested, he'll be inspired to give you a call."

"Steph!"

"What?" she replied innocently. "One can only dare to dream."

After dinner, Stephanie set her napkin beside her plate and gave a satisfied sigh. "That was delicious, Ellen. Thank you."

Kristin finished the last bite of fruit salad on her plate, then asked, "Grandma, if you could go anywhere in the whole world, where would it be?"

"I don't know. Before I could answer that, I'd have to give it much thought and consideration."

"Okay, then tell me, what was the best trip you ever took?" Kristin had a mischievous twinkle in her eye.

"Now *that's* an easy one. My honeymoon. Your grandfather and I were young and so in love that it didn't matter that we only rented a shabby little cabin in Tahoe. It was heaven."

"That's so romantic," Kristin crooned. "How about you, Aunt Stephanie? Do you have someplace special you'd like to go?"

Stephanie smiled. "Tahiti. I've seen pictures where they have huts right over the water. I can see the sunset now and taste the Chi Chi in my hand. Maybe I can talk your mom into joining me when I go the second week in May."

Camille wiped her mouth with her napkin, and then set it beside her plate. "That's right before Mother's Day, one of the busiest days in the year. You can send me a postcard."

Undeterred, Stephanie continued. "That's understandable. But if you *could* have a dream vacation, Camille, what would it be?"

Camille sighed. "If I was going to take the time, there's only one place in the whole world that I've ever dreamt of going. You know how I've worked teaching myself German with CDs and tapes? Well, I'd go to Vienna and study at that school I've been taking an online course from the past two years. I even know one of the instructors a little. He's really very nice, and with his help, I've improved dramatically."

At the thought of Günther Christove, a smile crept onto Camille's face. His attention to her studies was, well…indescribable. She loved his comments pertaining to her work, so full of amusement and yet thoughtful. He'd come to feel like a friend, though they'd never met.

"I wouldn't stay in a hotel, but with a host family, to get the whole European feel," she went on. "Students attend from all over the world. That's where I'll go someday—when I have the time."

"That *does* sound special," Stephanie agreed, covering her slight smile behind her hand.

They all nodded. Kristin was the first to break into an ear-to-ear grin.

A niggle of unease settled in the pit of Camille's stomach. "How come I feel like you know something that I don't?"

Kristin jumped up and ran out of the room. She returned with a manila envelope and handed it to her mom.

As Camille stared at the packet in her hands, a strange sensation came over her, much like the one she'd felt in the hospital when she'd been first waking up. It was beautiful, making her almost giddy with joy. She'd forgotten all about it until now and desperately wanted to remember, to feel, but the harder she tried, the more remote it became. She just couldn't grasp what it meant. She looked up, disoriented.

"Mom, open it," Kristin cried excitedly.

With shaky hands, Camille opened the large envelope and pulled out a glossy pamphlet from the Vienna School of Language. Concentrating on the beautiful color pictures became impossible because she knew she was about to break Kristin's heart.

"This is very sweet of you," she began slowly.

"Before you say anything further, look at the rest of the contents," Stephanie instructed sternly.

She didn't want to look. It could only get worse.

Stephanie took the packet from her hands. "Okay, if you won't look, I'll just have to show you." She reached inside. "What's this?"

"An online ticket with"—she searched the itinerary—"Austrian Airlines."

"Very good. This?"

"My passport."

Panic took over. "Stephanie, you *know* I can't leave the shop." She looked around, trying to find some support. "Kristin needs me," she said, her voice ascending an octave. "Mom, help me out here." Camille looked to her mother pleadingly.

Ellen reached over and patted Camille's hand. "It'll be good for you to get away. Stephanie came up with this wonderful idea, and now it's all settled."

"What about my heart attack? It won't be safe for me to travel abroad at this time."

"Nice try," Stephanie said. "It just so happens one of my colleagues has a very good friend who lives in Vienna and has a practice there. I've sent him your file and he's agreed to take you on as a patient throughout your stay. He's excellent with a worldwide reputation. Even better, he also has an extra room in his flat in the city. He's expecting you."

Camille stood in one swift motion. "This is where I draw the line. I'll go, if I'm forced to. The tickets have been purchased and I'm sure they're non-refundable. That said, I won't stay with your friend. I don't know him and I refuse to put him out."

Stephanie's face glowed in victory. "That's fine with us, Camille. You can stay wherever you like. Kristin, go get the cake. It's time to celebrate."

Resigned, Camille slowly took her seat, turbulence swirling within. She looked from one happy face to the other and wondered how in the world she'd been manipulated into this. To be honest, wasn't this what she'd been dreaming about doing for years? Well, wasn't it?

"How long will I be staying?" she asked.

"Two months."

Chapter Three

Three Weeks Later, Vienna, Austria

Günther Christove clapped his hands together several times and blew into them with a force that would stop a train. He'd forgotten his gloves this morning and his fingers were as frozen as the *Wurst* he'd pulled from his freezer last night.

"Günther," the boy at his side called, "I can run to the corner and get you hot coffee. Holding the cup will warm your hands."

Günther ruffled the scruffy black hair of his little companion and smiled. "And how would you pay for this coffee, Johann? Your good looks?"

They laughed and Johann bowed eloquently. These shenanigans left the boy ten paces behind as Günther's stride took him quickly across the narrow cobblestone street and through a wrought iron gate. Günther's hair swayed with each step, brushing the collar of his supple leather jacket. Johann ran to catch up.

"Almost there." Günther's breath came out in a frosty cloud. They rounded the corner of *Schweinfußstraße* in full stride. "We must hurry. We don't want you to be late to class. Did you have any breakfast this morning, Johann?"

"Yes, sir. *Brot und Käse*." Johann's tattered hand-me-down coat all but enveloped him.

"Ah, bread and cheese. What is that American saying? Breakfast of champions?" *At least that uncle of yours saved something back from the pub to feed you.*

Johann stopped abruptly. "Günther?"

Günther turned back, the anxiety in Johann's voice stopping him in his tracks. "Yes?"

The boy's expressive green eyes held his. "A woman from the agency came to our apartment early this morning looking for Uncle Bernhard. When he wasn't there, she got upset."

The troubled look on Johann's face tore at Günther. "Did she say what she wanted?"

"No."

Günther patted his back. "No worries on this new morn, my young friend. I will look into it. All will be well."

They turned onto a small street and had to hop quickly to one side as a shopkeeper hosed down the sidewalk. "That was close," Johann laughed, his eyes bright with excitement.

"Your English is excellent, Johann. I can tell you've been studying very hard. I'm as proud of you as if you were my very own son. You're what we call 'gifted'. Especially in language." At his words, an overwhelming sadness threatened to drop Günther to his knees. A vision of Nikolaus, barely three years old, flashed into his mind. His son was laughing and pulling on his hand. Similarly, Johann's face beamed with pleasure at his compliment, coaxing a smile back into Günther's heart.

It was a few moments before Günther was able to speak. "English is very important for your future," he went on. "It will open many doors, and give you opportunities that you wouldn't have otherwise. I can see in your eyes that you will leave your mark on this world." As Günther spoke, his enthusiasm spilled over to Johann, making the boy skip along even more eagerly, if it were possible. Günther liked the impact his words were having.

A motorbike sped by at top speed and he quickly grasped Johann by the shoulder, holding him back. "Now, we are late and must hurry." Günther proceeded across the intersection.

Johann soaked in his praise like a sponge. Günther chuckled and continued, "How I wish all my students learned as quickly as you do." The clock tower chimed once, signaling quarter till the hour. Günther hitched his head. "Come on, let's run."

Somewhere above Western Europe

"Would you like anything else?" The flight attendant held out a tray of scrumptious-looking pastry creations. The accent and her dark velvety hair, coifed into a beautiful French twist, bespoke her Western European heritage. "We'll be landing soon. This will be your last opportunity."

"No, thank you." Camille whispered, trying not to disturb the man sleeping beside her in the aisle seat. The young lady smiled graciously and continued down the aisle.

Camille's stomach turned over for the hundredth time and she pushed aside the twinge of fear that threatened whenever she felt anything strange happening inside her. The thought of a repeat heart attack loomed constantly in the back of her mind. Stephanie had reassured her that those feelings were natural and would become less frequent with each passing day.

Searching through her bag, she found her bottle of antacids and placed one on her tongue. She checked her reflection in her compact only to find her face pale and drawn. Discreetly, she applied a dab of moisturizer to her face and a light coat of lipstick. Not much could be done for her hair, so she brushed it quickly and let it fall naturally around her shoulders.

The grueling ten-and-a-half-hour flight to London had her nerves frayed and body aching. After stretching her legs at Heathrow, she'd boarded the flight to Vienna for the final two and a half hours in the air.

Camille yawned to open her ear passages as the plane began its descent. Deep and articulate, the pilot's voice thanked them over the intercom for choosing Austrian Airlines and wished them a pleasant and romantic stay in Vienna. The local time was five fifty p.m. and the temperature cool at three degrees Celsius.

She glanced out the window. Even at this altitude, the rolling hills, just greening up for spring, were prettier than she could ever have imagined. Excitement pushed away anxiety. Austria. In her estimation the most beautiful country in the world. She had dreamed of this day for years, and now she was actually here.

She was alone.

She was single.

She was allowed to do any little thing she pleased.

"Have you been to Vienna before?"

At the sound of the voice, Camille turned to find the man next to her awake. His thick brown hair had a sprinkling of silver around the temples and his face was interesting.

Eyes that had been closed for most of the flight, she now saw, were the same shade as the coffee she'd had with her dessert. Funny how some people waited until the very last minute to strike up a conversation.

"No, this is my first time. You?"

"I come often." He tried to stretch his legs in the cramped area, but ended up crossing them at the ankles. "It's an intriguing city. Are you staying long?"

"Two months."

His eyebrows rose. "That's a long time. You must be visiting relatives."

"Actually, I'm attending the Vienna School of Language. It's been a dream of mine for some time. And now," she lifted her hands palms up, "here I am."

He sat up straighter, clearly interested. "I know the school well." He smiled for the first time, displaying straight white teeth. "My office is right around the corner from *Brandstätte* and *Tuchlauben*." He laughed. "Not that that would mean anything to you. However, it's extremely close to the institution. Perhaps when you get fed up with *Diphdonge* and *Umlaute* exercises, you would consider having lunch with me."

Heat surged inside Camille and she hoped her face wasn't turning red. *Is he asking me out?* His expression told her that was indeed the case.

"I'm sorry, but…I haven't any idea yet what my schedule will be like."

"Of course. Of course." His smile widened. "I'll drop by sometime and look you up. Then, if time allows, I'll show you the city. Stephen Turner." He held out his hand until she had little choice but to take it in her own.

"Camille Ashland."

She felt like a treed cat. Who would've thought? It wasn't as though dating was unthinkable. She'd worked hard and kept her shape, hadn't let herself go. It was just…

A buzz of quiet conversation erupted in the cabin as passengers began preparing for landing. If she wanted to go to the ladies' room, she'd need to hurry. The seatbelt sign illuminated with a subtle *dong* but if she went quickly, no one would stop her.

She unbuckled her seatbelt and half stood. "Excuse me."

Hurrying toward the lavatory, Camille couldn't get her mind off their conversation. The young man directly in front of her turned around. Before she could stop, a woman plowed into her back and sent her vaulting into his arms. Horrified, she tried to pull away, but not before a scalding sensation made her gasp. She grabbed at the hot material burning her chest.

Looking up, Camille winced as the fellow's face contorted in pain and a long hiss slithered from between his teeth. For one brief moment, he was too startled to speak. His cup of coffee was now one big splotch on the front of his starched white shirt and running in rivulets down his expensive-looking pants.

Laughter erupted from three teenage girls seated nearby. Their giggles and snorting seemed to go on forever.

"I'm *so* sorry. I'll get something to wipe it off." Camille waved at the flight attendant.

Her victim, who looked to be nineteen or so, stood rooted to the spot. He had a high, intelligent-looking forehead on a very round head. His crimson face stood out next to his white-blond hair. Blotches appeared like two flags on his cheeks amid an array of freckles, and in his embarrassment, they darkened like a chameleon's.

The sympathetic flight attendant handed Camille paper towels. Camille began wiping at his shirt.

He angrily grabbed the towels from Camille's hands.

"Somebody ran into me. It was an accid…" Camille's voice trailed off as she looked around for the person who'd shoved her into him. The aisle was empty behind her.

"Please," she tried again. "Let me get some cold water. I think I can get most of this out."

He raked her with his eyes.

The flight attendant interrupted. "I'm sorry, you'll have to take your seats now. We'll be landing soon."

Camille went back to her seat and waited as Stephen Turner unbuckled and got up, letting her in.

She refastened her seat belt feeling sick. Her silk blouse was ruined and the coffee had soaked through to her bra. She was thankful she had brought a jacket that she could use to cover up the mess.

"Too bad," Stephen Turner said quietly. "But don't beat yourself up over it." His smile was understanding. "As they say, stuff happens. Even to the Prime Minister's so—" He closed his mouth and shrugged. "To important and unimportant people."

That was a rather odd comment but Camille was too upset to give it another thought. Under normal circumstances, that young man was probably a very nice person. She snuck a quick look back. Seated one row in front of the laughing girls, who to Camille's horror were *still* carrying on, he stared out the window.

Vienna, Austria

Camille's mouth watered. She stood before a vending machine staring at a Kit Kat bar with utter longing. She was exhausted. And hungry. Her host family had failed to show to pick her up and she was without a single euro. Without any difficulty at all, the fine thread of self-control that held off panic could snap at any moment, turning her into a blubbering mess.

The overhead intercom crackled once before a smooth female voice announced, "*Lassen Sie Ihr, Gepäck nicht unbeaufsichtigt. Nehmen Sie keine Pakete von Fremden an.*" The voice repeated in English, "Do not leave your bags unattended. Do not accept packages from strangers." The almost vacant airport had an eerie feel.

Camille sank onto a nearby bench and pulled her luggage up close. Getting through Customs had been the last straw. She'd been shuffled from one agent to another trying to explain that the Canadian tags on her bag contradicting her United States citizenship were not part of some sort of treacherous espionage plan, but the brainless advice of her travel agent.

Mr. Sterns had assured her he routinely encouraged his clients to conceal their US citizenship from anti-American extremists with a smoke screen, so to speak. Canadian luggage tags were an easy way to do that. Americans were not the most popular tourists these days. He'd banned visors and fanny packs, tacky tourist red flags he'd called them, and coached her against reading maps, speaking loudly, and asking too many questions in public places.

Finally past the Customs gauntlet, she'd hurried over to the ATM only to have it reject her PIN number twice. Gone were the days of traveler's checks, Mr. Stern had assured her.

"Before leaving the airport, just make a withdrawal from the ATM. You get the best exchange rate and you only withdraw what you need. It's perfect."

Perfect, indeed.

On her third try, the cranky machine ate her card, leaving her alone in a foreign country with only fifty US dollars. Emergency money of sorts. At eight twenty p.m., the exchange office was closed until tomorrow.

Taking a deep breath, she squelched the overwhelming urge to call home.

"Camille, is everything all right?"

Stephen Turner stood before her, concern in his eyes.

"Stephen." She almost winced at how desperate she sounded.

"I saw you sitting over here all alone. Isn't anyone here to meet you?"

"There was supposed to be. I've called my contact number but there's no answer. Maybe they're just late."

"It's been almost two hours since we landed. Customs was slow and then the car rental agency screwed up my paperwork, adding another thirty minutes. If they're not here for you by now, I don't think anyone's coming."

He was right. She'd have to take a bus or taxi. Would she have enough cash? Would they even take American money? Without her credit card, she felt naked.

"Come on. I'll give you a lift."

Is he serious?

Lunch in a public restaurant was one thing, but going off alone in a foreign country with a total stranger was quite another. How many times had she made Kristin swear she'd never do something like that?

She must have had uncertainty written all over her face because he smiled his understanding. Folding the paperwork he held in his hands, he put it in his briefcase.

"I know the city well, Camille, so it won't be a problem finding the address. I promise I'll drop you off anywhere you'd like. Just friends."

What choice did she have? Spending the night on a cold bench in a foreign airport held no appeal.

"Well...okay." She stood and straightened her stained and rumpled clothing, and gathered her things. She looked up into his attractive brown eyes and prayed she was doing the right thing. "Lead on."

Chapter Four

Stephen, true to his word, delivered Camille safe and sound. Now, early Monday morning, she descended the stairs and met Helene, the wife and mother of her host family, at the front door. The house smelled of freshly baked apple strudel and coffee. A small candle on the knotty pine entry table winked at Camille, as if to say good morning. Petra and Patrick, Helene and Wolfgang's eight-year-old twins, and Sasha, their three-year-old daughter, were still asleep.

"Have a good first day," Helene said, hugging Camille. "Do not worry about anything."

Helene looked darling in a red and yellow frock resembling the hippie styles of the sixties. Her reddish hair, cropped one inch from her scalp and spiked out in all directions with the help of a fragrant hair gel, was cute. She had an appealing oval face with translucent skin.

"It will be enjoyable, and…" Helene struggled with her English, "before you know it, it will be time to come home."

Camille's heart did a somersault. She'd said those same words to Kristin on her first day of kindergarten.

Helene gave Camille a long look. "You are nervous?"

In truth, she was petrified beyond words but preferred not to worry her hostess. "No. Only excited."

Helene didn't look convinced. "If you change your mind about walking home, call my number and I will send Wolfgang to get you. Or tell one of the instructors, and they will call for you."

"I'm sure I'll want to walk." The school was only a bit over three kilometers. Since she'd be living here for the next two months, she figured walking was the best way to get some of the exercise Stephanie had prescribed. "It's part of my therapy. But thank you so much, for everything."

Camille closed the door behind her quietly and stepped into the frosty morning air. Not knowing what to expect on the first day, she'd agonized over what to wear. If possible, she wanted to blend in with the other students. Feeling silly for having changed three times, she'd finally decided on a neutral calf-length skirt, cream tights, and a brown lightweight sweater. She wore sneakers for her walk, but carried a pair of casual loafers in her backpack next to her ultra-sleek laptop. She didn't want to look like a fuddy-duddy, but trying too hard to look trendy was a sure ticket to disaster.

She smacked her gloved hands together and set off at a brisk clip. She took deep breaths and forced the air out through her nose without breaking stride. Like always, she expected a jolting pain to pounce on her at any moment, as it had before. With determination, she pushed her fear away. She was on her way to recovery, stress free.

It surprised her she hadn't thought about Chocolate Blossoms once since landing in Austria. She'd thought of Kristin, of course, and her mom and Stephanie too. But always with a smile. They were excited she was here. Thoughts of Bret tried to sneak in and ruin her joy, but she pushed them aside. She'd not let him spoil her adventure.

She'd married for the wrong reasons, hadn't taken the time and discernment needed before jumping into a short engagement. They'd hardly known each other. They had never discussed anything important, and she'd paid the price. After the glow of the honeymoon had worn off, it was like waking up next to a stranger.

Camille placed two fingers on the top of the watch she had purchased before leaving Portland. It was a remarkable contraption, designed to check her heart rate simply by touch. She was walking swiftly and the blinking red light said her pulse was slightly elevated. She hadn't yet called Dr. Williamson but intended to do so later today.

As Camille drew closer to the heart of Vienna, the sidewalks buzzed with inhabitants. Motorbikes sped by at alarming speeds. Cars and busses jockeyed for position on the narrow roads, honking noisily at each other as if they were the only vehicles permitted to be there.

She liked it. The feel of the city wrapped around her. The people were gracious and the experience was so European. Rounding the corner, Camille saw the school straight ahead. The building stood proudly in the early morning light, students bustling here and there.

"Camille."

Glancing back, she saw Stephen Turner loping in her direction. She had the sneaking suspicion he'd been waiting for her to arrive.

"Camille. How are you? I've been wondering how things are going at the Eberstarks'." His words came out in great puffs of frosty air. "After the look on their faces when you knocked on their door that night, I couldn't help but wonder."

He was wearing rich brown corduroy pants and a wool jacket over a patterned shirt. His shoes were expensive, and slung over his shoulder was the same computer pack he'd had at the airport. Freshly showered and shaven, he looked younger, mid to late forties. "Stephen. Hello. The Eberstarks are extremely nice. I couldn't have picked a nicer family. They felt horrible about the mix-up. Their paperwork had me arriving the next day."

"Ah, mystery solved. How're your accommodations?"

"Lovely. My room is the only one upstairs. It has a private bathroom, albeit very tiny, and a darling spiral staircase that comes out in the back of the kitchen. It's comfortable and cozy."

"Good. Sounds like you're all squared away. After I dropped you off, I realized I hadn't gotten a contact number, you know, so I could see how you're holding up. I hope you don't mind that I decided to find out in person." He continued, not giving her a chance to answer. "Are you ready for your first day?" He looked her up and down and then smiled into her face. "Excited?"

She laughed, enjoying the easy, struggle-free conversation with an American. "Panicked, is more like it." She glanced at her watch, then around at the people and bustle. "I'm surprised it only took twenty minutes to get here. That's quicker than I expected."

"What time does your class start?"

"Eight. It's good to know that I won't have to leave the house quite so early from now on."

"Or, if you were so inclined, you could still leave early and we could share an espresso before the day begins. If you haven't noticed yet, everything in this city revolves around coffee." He laughed deeply. "And pastries. The best in the world."

"I guess we can sometime, but not today. I'm much too nervous." She switched her backpack to her other shoulder. "I'm sure I'd spill it all over myself."

He raised an eyebrow, then broke into laughter when she realized too late exactly what she'd said. "You make a habit of that, do you?"

They began walking toward the school. "You're going to be fantastic. I thought about you all day yesterday and what you're accomplishing and I think it's quite courageous. In my estimation, Camille Ashland is a brave woman."

"Brave or stupid?" she responded easily, now thoroughly enjoying the conversation. "I'll let you know which after I get through this first day. I feel like I'm back in senior high and have my first speech to give."

They laughed again as they walked past cafés and shops.

"I remember those days. Feels like yesterday."

She admired his enthusiasm. He was congenial and so self-assured. With his thick wavy hair and brown eyes, she figured most women would consider him a handsome man. More importantly, he was incredibly nice and friendly. God knew she needed a friend right now.

"Stephen, thanks for coming out to meet me on my first day. I appreciate it a lot. But if you don't mind, I need to get going. I only have ten minutes to find my class."

"Of course. Oh, your phone number. Do you mind if I take it now?" He handed her a business card. "Just write it on the back."

She hastily scratched out the long, alien-looking number she'd committed to memory.

He took the card from her gloved hand. "Have a great day," he said. "Knock 'em dead."

Camille hurried up the wide flagstone steps leading to the main entrance of the school. Two huge double doors, constructed with thick, iron-covered wooden beams, stood fifteen feet tall. A remarkable conglomeration of different levels and styles, the building looked worn and old like the pictures she'd seen in history books of medieval monasteries. The bell tower donged loudly, telling her she was late on her first day. Once inside she felt tiny in the gigantic hall, with its musty smell and cool air.

Students sat at their desks as Camille hurried down the hallway, passing each room. She was looking for D-14. The numbers above each door all began with the letter *E*. E-6, E-7. A young woman hurried in her direction.

"Please, can you tell me where D-14 is?"

The girl looked at her blankly. Camille held out her paperwork and pointed to D-14.

"Ah, *ja*." She pointed up.

"Upstairs?"

The girl took her by the shoulders and turned her around. She pointed to the end of the corridor where she saw a flight of stairs.

"*Fahren Sie zum dritten Stock.*" The girl held up three fingers.

Camille nodded. "*Danke, danke*," she called over her shoulder as she hurried away.

By the second story landing, Camille's heart was thumping frighteningly in her chest.

At the top of the third floor, she stopped to catch her breath and let her heart rate slow down. If she were late, so be it. It was better to be safe than sorry. Once she felt better, she continued on, counting the doors as she passed them. Finally at D-14, she hurried inside and assessed the situation.

The instructor hadn't arrived. Seeing only one vacant seat, she made a beeline for the front of the classroom. She willed herself to relax.

The talking stopped as the professor entered the room. Of medium height, he walked with purpose. Well-built, with a chiseled, masculine chin and defined nose. His shiny chestnut hair moved with his stride and his blue eyes shone brightly.

He went directly to the front of the room.

Willkommen in Vien, he wrote, welcoming them to Vienna. He turned back to the class.

All five senses in Camille went on red alert. Her heart, which had so recently slowed down, took up the familiar thudding, surprising her that it could happen with no exertion at all.

"Welcome to Vienna. My name is Günther Christove. My colleagues and I are delighted to have you here to study the German language and experience the splendor of our magnificent city." He rolled the piece of yellow chalk back and forth in his fingers.

"As you know, this is conversational German. There will be some writing assignments, but most of our time will be spent talking, either here in the room, or out in the field." He pointed out the open window to the sounds of the city. "We will be studying the formal usage of this language. Most of you are beginners to intermediate."

Günther Christove! Exhilaration flooded Camille as her cheeks tingled with warmth.

He continued. "A few of you have been here before and are returning for a second or third term. I've assigned each of you a study partner so you won't feel overwhelmed with your assignments."

A beautiful young woman raised her hand.

"Stena?"

"Can I be *your* partner?"

Laughter erupted.

A brief smile pulled at the corner of his lips as if this was a well-known joke, then he continued without giving an answer.

"As I call your name, please stand and find your partner. Rearrange your seating so you will be in close proximity to each other. *Verstehen Sie*?"

All nodded in understanding.

"*Gut*. Now, Niclas *und* Lena," he called out in a strong voice. "Timm *und* Maria."

One by one, each student stood and found the person *Herr* Christove had assigned to them. "Mark *und* Stena. Konrad *und* Scott." The young man beside her stood and moved away, leaving his seat empty. "Hanna *und* Angie. Camille *und* Branwell."

Everyone began mingling, making their way to their new spot. Being in the front of the class had kept Camille from seeing the other students sitting behind her until now. She rose and looked back. All students had paired up, leaving one young man standing alone.

He was very tall.

Blond hair, cut razor short, hugged his exceptionally round head, accentuating its bowling-ball shape. His large, projecting forehead still looked intelligent, and shadowed a nose that was too small for his face.

Their eyes met in equal shock.

Locked in disbelief, neither could look away.

After several long moments, blood rushed to his face producing splotches of deep crimson on both of his cheeks. Out of all the people in Austria—they were destined to collide again.

Chapter Five

Oh, no. Not him. Camille's mind screamed as the young man made his way to the front of the room and folded his large frame into the remaining seat next to her, making the chair look as if it were made for a child instead of an adult. Impeccably dressed, his countenance shouted authority and position. Without so much as a by-your-leave, he turned and hung his backpack on the back of his seat, ignoring her completely.

This couldn't be happening. She struggled to think of something to say but nothing came to mind. Everyone else in the room chatted and exchanged information. She darted a quick look over to the two men seated to her left. She guessed one to be in his late thirties and the other closer to sixty. *Oh, why couldn't I have gotten one of them?*

But she hadn't—so she better just accept it. "Fate would have us meet again." She held out her hand. "My name is Camille Ashland."

He just sat there, looking at a schedule he'd pulled from his binder.

Herr Christove walked over to his desk and waited for the class to quiet down. "Now that you have met your study partner, we will begin with our first exercise. I'd like everyone to introduce themselves to their partner."

Chattering erupted again.

He held up a hand. "*Natürlich, auf Deutsch, bitte.*"

Silence ensued.

"It is important to try. Do not to be afraid to make mistakes."

One by one, students sputtered and laughed as dialogue in German began to flow.

Recognizing she was older than Branwell by quite a few years, she therefore was more mature. Somehow she would win him over, and they would become friends. The time for timidity was over. She would take control.

"*Ich bin* Camille Ashland. *Ich komme aus* Portland. *Und Sie?*"

He glanced at his watch, checked his phone for messages, then began texting.

When *Herr* Christove started in their direction, he slipped his phone back into his pocket turning to Camille.

"*Ich heiße* Branwell. *Ich komme aus* London."

"Branwell," Günther said to him as he approached. "Good to see you again. How have you been?"

"Very well, *Herr* Christove."

"I was surprised to see your name on my attendance sheet again. This is your third term." Smiling, *Herr* Christove looked between her and the young man. "But it's always good to have you back in class."

"Thank you. It's good to be back in Vienna."

"And you are Camille Ashland. The same Camille Ashland who has been studying through our online correspondence course all the way from Portland, Oregon?"

"Yes, that's me." A flurry of butterflies burst open inside her. "It's nice to finally meet you in person, *Herr* Christove."

"Likewise. But I am more than surprised that I didn't know sooner that you were coming."

Camille could feel the depth of study from his dark blue eyes.

"It was a quick decision. I barely had time to pull the whole thing together." She wouldn't go into the details of her heart attack here in front of Branwell.

"Well, I'm happy that you have come all the way from America to meet me in person. I think you will love Vienna. Perhaps, you will like it so much you will end up staying."

He was kidding, of course, but Camille couldn't help but respond with an inane display of schoolgirl shyness. To her horror, she giggled.

"*Bei wem wohnen Sie?*" he asked her slowly.

She shook her head, disappointed to have failed her first test.

"With whom are you staying?" he repeated in English.

"*Die Eberstarks. Ich wohne bei den Eberstarks.*" She corrected the response, putting it into a full sentence.

"*Sehr gut.*" He nodded his approval as he moved on to the next pair of students.

Two months of this? Forget killing Stephanie, she'd kiss her instead. It was wonderful to be here, and very exciting to be alive. She ran a shaky hand through her hair and realized she was almost relieved that he'd moved on to somebody else. She watched as he chatted and interacted with the next student, now giving him his undivided attention.

She turned back to Branwell, feeling ready to take him on. "Wie alt sind Sie, Herr Branwell?" She asked him his age knowing she had him over a barrel. Herr Christove was still within hearing distance.

"*Zwanzig.*" He said it as if the word was distasteful in his mouth.

"Twenty," she responded in a low voice. "That's considered an adult in America. I'm twenty-four years your senior, so I'd say you'd better shape up and show a little respect."

His eyes bulged.

Her courage fortified, she continued. "*Was ist ihr Nachname?*"

"Rothshine-Millerman."

"Rothshine-m-m-man." She said, trying to get the long surname right. Even though she couldn't say it, it sounded a little familiar.

He repeated it curtly.

He was so pompous she could hardly stand it. Still, she refused to let him ruin any more of her wonderfully exciting first day in class.

"I have some handouts," *Herr* Christove said, "simple conversations that you are to memorize before tomorrow. There are also some stickers to put on your things where you are staying. All the host families know that this is an assignment and it won't be a problem. Affix them to your alarm clock, mirror, bed, and anything else they pertain to. Even if you already know these words, it is a good review exercise. When you see them, say out loud. *Wo ist der Wecker?* Where is the alarm clock? Then answer yourself out loud, *Dort ist der Wecker.* And so on. For the next two months I want you to speak, think, and dream in German—not only when you are here in class, but everywhere."

"*Fräulein* von Linné," Günther said, as he held out a stack of handouts. He pulled his hand back quickly before she had a chance to brush his fingers with her own, and ignored the little pout on her lips.

Stena von Linné, twenty-four, was from Uppsala, a medium-sized town directly north of Stockholm. She was intelligent and quick. Attended the University of Uppsala. This was her second term in his class. She was classically Swedish, with pale blonde hair and cobalt eyes. Her voice was clear and soft, pleasing to the ear, made for laughter and singing, if nothing else. She moved with graceful actions, very well aware of her great allure to the opposite sex. Her willowy body would tempt the strongest of constitutions without the slightest effort, and she had men young and old falling at her feet, pleading for the slightest morsel of her attention. Her energy was inexhaustible and she was truly fun to be around, making other women like her too. He would have to be blind not to see that she had a huge crush on him, and although he wasn't interested, he was flattered.

"*Vielen Dank, Herr* Christove," *Fräulein* von Linné purred, her eyelids lowering suggestively as she took a packet of the papers and passed the others to her partner, Mark Marslino.

"Class, *Fräulein* von Linné is a language student working toward her doctorate degree. German is her fourth language."

An "ahhh" of appreciation rippled through the class. "If you find yourself stuck and I am unavailable, I'm sure she could be of help to you."

He went to his desk and sat down. This was going to be an interesting class. But then, he thought the same of every class, enjoying each for its uniqueness of individuals. Smaller by a handful, this group would be easier to take on field trips and outings and make it possible to get to know each student on a more personal level.

He remembered the American woman quite well from the assignments he'd overseen online, and considered her bright and determined. She'd work at something until she got it exactly right. Upon meeting her in person, she surprised him with her youthful zeal. He couldn't help but smile as she tried to draw Branwell out of his self-absorbed shell.

Yes, Branwell was back. Again. Still the enigma. Günther hadn't heard that his father, *Herr* Crawford Rothshine-Millerman, the prime minister of England, was sending his son for his third term. It was a mystery to Günther why, because Branwell's conversational German was, on the whole, quite fluent. Perhaps fluent was not good enough, and the prime minister expected perfection in regard to his only son. The young man was studious and intelligent. But his aloof behavior, together with his strange looks, unfortunately kept him on the outside of most social circles in his class.

As promised by Helene, the day passed quickly. Soon three o'clock had arrived. As other students hurried by laughing and talking, Camille found herself standing alone at the top of the school's wide flagstone steps. The air was chilly and the sun, barely peeping through a thin layer of low-hanging clouds, lit up the golden and silver hues of the many different architectural façades that encompassed the perimeter of the square.

The view overlooking *Michaelerplatz* was spectacular. She stood mesmerized, unable to draw her gaze away. How lucky she was to be here. How lucky she was to be alive.

A café with its green-and-white-striped umbrella-topped tables drew her attention. It was an exhilarating feeling— being free. She decided that it would be a nice welcome-to-Vienna treat to have a cup of coffee before heading back to the Eberstarks'.

The café was smoky, crowded, and lively. Every table was occupied and the overflow of people stood crammed into every nook and corner in animated conversation. No one seemed to notice her as she made her way up to the counter.

The man behind the bar turned. *"Kann ich Ihnen helfen?"*

"Kaffee, bitte."

He looked at her for several seconds. Camille quickly held out her hands and formed a paper cup. "To go?"

He nodded. She felt triumphant. The barista promptly set about making her request as she dug through her backpack for the euros the Eberstarks had lent her until she got her money situation squared away. Moments later he handed her the drink, along with a little tray that held sugar, a spoon, and some sort of condensed milk. She gave him the money before doctoring her drink.

In the square again, Camille shaded her eyes and looked around. Opposite from where she stood was St. Michael's Church, its bell tower standing majestically above the busy square in quiet survey. She assumed she must have passed it this morning but hadn't noticed because of her conversation with Stephen Turner. That already felt like a lifetime ago.

She shouldered her backpack, feeling twenty years younger than her age. Sipping the rich, hot coffee, she made her way toward the church and rounded the corner. People were everywhere enjoying the nice afternoon and Camille felt overwhelmed to be a part of it. It wasn't five seconds before she heard her name called. Totally expecting Stephen Turner again, she was entirely taken aback when she saw Günther Christove waving to get her attention. He had a backpack too and fit in nicely with his surroundings.

"Mrs. Ashland, over here." He was on the side of the church in a narrow passageway.

Nervous and excited, she made her way over to where he waited. His smile warmed her insides so much she wondered if the barista hadn't secretly slipped a little brandy into her drink.

"I was just wondering if you'd had a chance to see this. It's amazing. I come here often to meditate."

"What is it?" She looked at the sculptural drawing on the side of the church.

"Look more closely. You tell me."

"Christ?"

"Yes, on the Mount of Olives. This relief dates back to 1480."

Camille looked closer. The artwork was chiseled directly upon the side of the wall in earth tones, not immediately obvious. If one were not looking for it, they might walk by without notice. With closer inspection, the figure of Jesus, shrouded with his face unclear, was in a prayerful position.

"Fourteen eighty? That's incredible." She regarded Günther's forthcoming countenance. "I can't thank you enough for sharing this with me."

They turned and began walking toward *Michaelerplatz* side by side.

"So tell me, how did you like your first day?"

"It was so much more than I expected," Camille said. "And that's a lot because I've been dreaming about doing this for a very long time."

"I'm pleased again, to hear that. And you are staying with the Eberstarks. They're a good family and host a student for the school each term. I'm glad that you're there, for they will make you feel at home. Are you married?"

"Widowed," she said, taking a sip of her coffee.

He tipped his head in sympathy. His gaze swept up to the church steeple, an odd longing written on his face. "I'm sorry to hear that."

"Bret liked to live on the edge. But that's another story entirely and was a long time ago. I have my teenage daughter, Kristin, and my mother, and my sister-in-law, Stephanie, to keep me busy. I'm not lonely. Actually," she laughed, "I don't have the time to be."

Camille was astonished at the things she was sharing with *Herr* Christove. It was just so natural with him.

"And you work?"

"I have a business that keeps me running full speed. I started it four years ago. Chocolate Blossoms."

He smiled at that.

"A silly name, I know," she agreed, enjoying his nearness very much. "It's a floral, chocolate, and perfume shop. Other than my daughter, it's what I live for. Every investor told me it was retail suicide to specialize in only three items. They said I needed to diversify, and attract the interests of all. But I can be very stubborn when I set my heart on something." Camille laughed and nervously took a sip of her coffee.

"And…" he prompted.

"Well, I kept my vision throughout. The run-of-the-mill, generic gift store was not in my business plan. Anyway, that's where I was able to take the online course from your school. When it's slow, either early in the morning or an hour or two before closing, I work on my assignments. It's perfect because it never interferes with my time at home with Kristin."

He looked at her as if taking her measure. "It suits you."

"Really?"

He nodded.

Laughing softly, Camille shook her head. "I can't believe I just went on about all that."

He shrugged, a most appealing look sparkling in his eyes. "And why are you here with us studying German?"

That was the million-dollar question. Everyone always wanted to know why she spent her time poring over books and listening to tapes and CDs. Any time in a bookstore was spent admiring all the new arrivals in the language department.

"My great-grandmother was from Germany, but—that's not the reason. I've just always had an attraction to its language—fascinated by its sounds and combination of letters. But it wasn't until I started my shop that I actually had time to start studying. I'm sorry, but it's a mystery to me too. I can't say."

They were in the square now and it was time to part company.

"You don't have to have a reason," he told her. "Your desire alone is enough. I will be looking for you bright and early tomorrow. It is hard on the nerves, skidding into class at the last minute, yes?" He laughed at her surprised look.

"Now watch the motorbikes on your way home. They stop for nothing."

Chapter Six

Pfarrer Florian Christove sat at his desk staring at his computer monitor. The middle-aged priest was working on his sermon for the first Sunday of Lent, but his thoughts kept getting in the way. Absently, he pushed his reading glasses up the bridge of his nose and reread what he had already written.

His intercom buzzed, and after listening to his secretary's question, he flipped open his appointment book and scanned his calendar.

"I'm not free that night. Have him call *Pfarrer* Schimke. He might be available. If he is not, I can do it the following weekend, or the one after that."

"*Danke, Herr Pfarrer.*"

He placed the phone back in its cradle and returned to his computer.

Within moments, the intercom buzzed again. Trying not to feel irritated, he pressed the button. "*Ja?*"

"*Herr Pfarrer, Frau* Kleimer wants to know what you would like for your supper this evening?"

Dinner? That was the last thing he had on his mind right now. *Frau* Kleimer had a talent for cooking and baking.

Everything she made was delicious. "Whatever is convenient."

Sitting back in his chair, he stretched his legs and closed his eyes for just one moment of rest. He'd passed the night in the hospital, praying with a longtime parishioner as she'd died. He'd anointed her and given her Viaticum. A cancer patient, she'd lingered in and out of consciousness for the last three months.

Opening his eyes, the picture of his younger brother, Günther, with their little friend, Johann, came into view. It was taken on the boy's First Holy Communion and Johann beamed with happiness. The parentless child had flourished this past year with Günther's aid. The boy even assisted them with the class that he and Günther gave every Saturday morning in the rectory hall, teaching underprivileged children English. They had started the class three years ago, and Florian couldn't imagine a weekend without it. From there, he glanced to another favorite photo taken when he was only twenty-one and served in the Austrian Army.

Enough. He gave himself a mental shake and turned back to his computer. But before he was able to type a single word, his phone rang again. This time it was his private line.

"*Herr Pfarrer* Christove," he said into the receiver.

"*Herr Pfarrer* Christove!" The excited young voice screeched through a clamor of people on the other end, making it difficult to hear. A whistle blew somewhere in the background and then a whooshing noise he couldn't identify.

"Yes, this is *Pfarrer* Christove. Who is speaking?"

The childlike voice hastily began rattling off details, but Florian could only grab bits and pieces because another announcement blared out, obscuring the caller's words.

He tried again. "Who is speaking?"

"It is Johann. *Johann*," the boy repeated.

He straightened. "Yes, Johann. What is wrong?"

"Come get me. My uncle, he is high again and—"

An announcement giving times and destinations drowned out what Johann was saying. "*What?* I didn't get that last part."

"We are leaving Vienna right now. He is taking me away. Please, I don't want to go with him."

"Just tell me where you are."

"We are at the subway station on *Kagraner Platz*. We will be boarding soon."

"Do you know how soon, Johann? Or where he is planning on taking you?"

"I don't know where we are going but we will be boarding in fifteen minutes. Only fifteen minutes."

Johann's voice cracked and Florian could hear him crying.

"No crying. You must be strong. Go into the bathroom and stay in there as long as possible. Say you are sick. Try to miss your train. I will get there. Don't worry. I will get there."

"Hurry. I am afraid that—" An inbound train shot through the tunnel making it impossible for Florian to hear the rest of what Johann was trying to tell him, and then the line went dead.

Florian bolted from his chair and grabbed his motorcycle helmet. He ran through the rectory office, drawing shocked stares from *Frau* Blutel, his secretary, and *Frau* Kleimer, his housekeeper and cook.

In the garage, he lifted the old wooden door and hopped on his motorcycle, then pulled on his helmet in one fluid motion and fastened it. Lifting the kickstand with the toe of his shoe and turning the key, with a blasting roar he was out the door and down the street. He swerved between cars like a madman and prayed that there were not any policemen in the vicinity.

He slowed for a red light but punched the accelerator when it turned green. He rode fast, but carefully, not wanting to hurt anyone on his way. When he passed on a double line, he silently asked God to forgive him this trespass, but the driver of the vehicle wasn't as charitable and stuck his arm out the window and shook his fist, cursing.

Five minutes had passed and he still had several miles to go to reach the subway station. Ahead, vehicles crammed the intersection. He had two choices. Ride the sidewalk. Or take the alley.

A quick glance at the sidewalk revealed it was as overcrowded with bystanders as the intersection was with cars, so without a second thought, he downshifted two gears and with a belligerent shriek from his engine, leaned left and swerved into the alleyway, punching the gas. A black cat scrambled to get out of his way.

The pavement was slick, sending the bike skidding dangerously close to a brick wall. Straining, he muscled it back securely under him and continued through the dark passage. Slowing as he approached the end of the alley, he looked right and then left, then shot across the sidewalk. The subway station was directly ahead.

Driving right up onto the sidewalk, he beeped his horn at a woman to let her know he was driving into the no-parking zone where she was walking. Her head jerked up. When she saw the big bike careening directly at her, she stumbled forward and dropped the cup of coffee she was carrying.

Florian jerked the bike to a stop several feet from the subway entry. He hopped off and unbuckled his helmet as he ran. For a brief moment he turned and called out to the woman, "So sorry." That was all he had time for before running into the station.

The station was dark and it was several seconds before Florian's eyes adjusted. There were two trains parked on the far side of three sets of tracks. One set of tracks was empty.

He glanced at his watch. Sixteen minutes had passed. Johann must be on one of the two remaining trains in the station, getting ready to pull out.

The first train's doors swished closed, startling Florian into action. He looked quickly around the area. No Johann. Running over the grease-covered rails, he began looking into the windows of the train. He banged on the Plexiglas to get the passengers' attention.

No Johann.

For some unexplained reason, he didn't feel that Johann was on this train. He would have to follow his instincts, because there was no way to get the automatic doors to open up now, anyway.

His only chance of retrieving Johann was if he was on the second train. He ran to the entrance and boarded just as the doors closed.

This train was almost empty. With only a handful of passengers, it was easy to spot Johann's scraggly head above a seat at the end of the car. The other train pulled out, gently rocking the one he was in. An automated voice came through the speakers announcing they were ready to depart.

He walked up the aisle slowly toward Johann, whose eyes were red and puffy. The boy didn't budge from his seat.

The train surged forward and Bernhard opened his bloodshot eyes and swiped his hand across his face. Florian took the seat opposite the boy and his uncle.

"Let me take the boy to school, Bernhard. It will go a lot easier for you if you do."

"So, *Herr Pfarrer* Christove," he slurred, as he tried to sit up. "You are after my Johann again. You know he is the only reminder I have of my dearly departed brother."

"Look at you. Can't you see that you need help? I will help you get straight, my friend. You shouldn't keep endangering your nephew in this fashion. He is only a frightened little boy."

Bernhard pulled Johann close with the grip he still had on his coat. Johann's pleading eyes tore at Florian's gut.

"At the next stop, we are all getting off," Florian said. "I'll take you to rehab and get you checked in. Where were you going?"

Bernhard jumped up. "I'm not getting off," he bellowed.

The few passengers turned around and stared. Some got out of their seats and moved as far away as possible. Bernhard saw their reaction and, with a belligerent expression and a few colorful expletives under his voice, slumped back into his seat.

The train began to slow, and the voice on the speaker announced its arrival at the next station.

"Come here, Johann. Get your things and come over to me," Florian said in a steady and commanding voice. Johann's uncertainty clouded his face. "Come, now," he repeated.

The train stopped. Bernhard just stared forward as Johann got up and did as the priest asked. "Go out and wait for me on the walkway."

When Johann was safely out the door, Florian took Bernhard by the arm and pulled him up. "We don't have much time to get off. Come on, now. I will help you." He pulled the bulky man along the aisle and barely made it off the train before the doors closed.

Johann waited for them, looking like a little ragamuffin much younger than his seven years. Fear and uncertainty replaced the child's normal smile and dancing eyes.

An attendant had seen the odd threesome getting off the train and came over to see what the problem was.

Florian explained that he had boarded at the last station without a ticket, and asked how much he owed. The attendant assessed the situation of the slouched man, the frightened boy, and the white collar around Florian's neck, and shook his head.

Bernhard was hardly able to stumble along on his own. When they reached the street, Florian sat Bernhard on a bench and took Johann aside.

He hunkered to eye level. "Are you all right?"

"*Ja.*" As the barely audible word tumbled out of Johann's mouth, his resolve crumbled and he broke into tears. He vaulted into Florian's embrace and the priest wrapped his strong arms around him. Johann sobbed, his fear real, and clung to him like a vine.

"Shhh. Don't cry, my brave little Johann. God loves you. You are His bravest soldier. He depends on you very much." That statement usually brought a smile to the boy's face but now it was as if he hadn't heard a word.

Florian tried a different tack. "I left my motorbike at the other station. Illegally parked on the sidewalk, no less. We should go back and retrieve it—before I get a ticket." Johann loved his motorcycle.

Johann pulled his head back and wiped his nose on the sleeve of his coat. "Let us go."

"Okay. Let's."

When they turned around to the bench, Bernhard was gone. Scared little eyes looked up into Florian's. "I will find him, Johann, and get him back into the rehabilitation program. We must pray for your uncle and do our very best to love him and help him. Do you understand?"

Johann nodded. They walked along in relieved silence, Johann's hand tightly gripping his.

Camille's hand shook violently as she inserted the key into the front door lock. That motorcycle had almost run her down in cold blood. Its driver didn't even seem to care. He'd jumped from the bike and ran like a wild man for the station. He'd turned back for an instant, long enough for her to see the depth of passion in his eyes.

Günther had warned her, and he was right. Motorbikes *didn't* stop for anything. And too bad too. That cup of coffee, before she'd dropped it, had been the best she'd ever tasted. Now it was splattered down the front of her tights. From now on, she would be much more watchful as she walked. This was not the United States.

The house was warm and quiet, and smelled of something delicious cooking. The soothing aroma calmed her rattled nerves. She laughed at herself, remembering her funny scream when she'd seen the motorcycle bearing down on her. Tomorrow she'd buy a journal. She'd call it "My Disastrous Adventures Abroad."

Unhurriedly, she made her way into the kitchen and up the back spiral staircase to her bedroom, feeling a bit like an intruder. Above the threshold to her room, she noticed a little sign she'd missed before, carved in knotty pine, and done in sweetly scripted writing. Little etched flowers decorated the border.

"EDELWEISS ZIMMER," she read, feeling as if she'd stepped into a dream.

The sunshine-yellow room, with white crown molding and baseboards, filled her with joy. It had been tidied and a vase of fresh flowers had been added to the table next to her bed. A note saying she'd received a phone call from her mother leaned on the vase. Since her mom was a very early riser, she picked up the phone and dialed but the line was busy. She removed her skirt and sweater, hung them in her closet, and pulled on her sweats. She filled the bathroom basin to soak her tights.

Digging through her backpack, she pulled out her address book. Flipping to the entry for Dr. Williamson, she dialed the number.

"*Guten Tag.* Dr. Williamson's *Büro.*"

"Hello. I was referred to your office by Dr. Ashland, my physician in the United States."

"Your name?"

"Camille Ashland."

"One moment, please."

The line clicked, followed by classical music playing softly on the line. She swung her feet up onto the bed and reclined onto the fluffy pillows.

The woman came back on the line. "Your information is already in our system. Would you like to make an appointment?"

"Yes."

Camille heard another phone ringing in the office.

"One moment."

The music was back so Camille closed her eyes. A relaxing moment passed, then Günther Christove popped into her mind. Günther and his all too charming smile. His charming smile *and* his expressive blue eyes. His expressive eyes *and* his soothing voice…

She sat up, surprised. She hadn't thought about a man, any man, *like this*, not since Bret's passing. On reflection of her late husband, a powerful band of bitterness gripped her chest and threatened to come up into her throat.

The line clicked again. "My next available appointment is this Wednesday at ten a.m."

"That soon?"

"There was a special notation in your file that you were to be seen right away."

"I see."

"Will Wednesday work for you?"

"Yes, thank you," she responded. With the appointment made, they said their good-byes. She returned the phone and lay back into the pillows.

It was quiet. She loved this cheery little room. Her gaze meandered around slowly until it landed on a book on the nightstand that she'd seen before, but hadn't looked at yet.

She picked it up and was surprised and happy to find it written in English. The Eberstarks were so thoughtful. She let the book fall open.

"If a soul is seeking God, its Beloved is seeking it much more… He attracts the soul and causes it to run after Him." (J.C. LF, 3,28)

She thought about the words she'd just read for several seconds, letting them seep into her mind. "Lord, are you looking for me now?" she whispered. "Were you looking for me all those years ago? No, I'm sure you weren't because I wasn't looking for you. I was too busy. Caught up in my life. Caught up in my work."

An especially hurtful memory popped into her head. Bret, angry because she'd gotten pregnant. A time of joy had gone so bad. "Thought we agreed we'd wait," he'd said, angrily bumping past. "Now you'll be ready to deliver at the exact time of the Indy 500. Nice going, *Camille*."

So much heartache at what was meant to be the happiest time in their life. They should have talked about important things before getting engaged. Things like beliefs and expectations. Instead, they'd partied and went about as if it were no big deal.

Time slowed. Somewhere outside a bird trilled, and Camille felt a semblance of peace descend into her heart about her past marriage, and the turbulent years that followed. Her eyes grew heavy after her emotionally charged day. She yawned and settled back into her pillow.

Chapter Seven

With several turns of his wrist and a quick tug, the wine cork slid easily from the expensive bottle of cabernet. Günther filled his glass, deriving pleasure from the little splashing sounds the dark burgundy created.

He appreciated a nice glass of wine now and then, and this fine bottle, of a very good year, was a gift from a former student.

"Hello, Flocki," he said to the small black and white cat that wound through his legs in an affectionate greeting. "I've been saving this bottle for a special occasion, but since that time has not yet arrived and I don't see it arriving anytime in the near future, we'll enjoy it together tonight. What do you say?"

He swirled the wine around the glass several times with finesse then took a sip, holding the liquid for a few moments in his mouth to savor its exquisite flavor. Swallowing, he welcomed the warmth spreading through his body.

The cat's insistent purring was loud. "I'm happy to see you too, my furry little friend." He picked her up and stroked her velvety coat. "Now, where are my glasses?"

The purring cat in one arm and his glass of wine in the other hand, he went in search of his reading glasses. The one-room flat didn't have many places to lose something, and he soon found them under the newspaper haphazardly draped on the divan.

Exchanging the cat for his mail, he sank into his recliner, clicked on the freestanding lamp, and flipped through the stack of envelopes. The cat hopped onto his lap at her first opportunity and in the process of getting comfortable, tickled his nose with her tail.

He waited for her to get completely settled. "Are you quite finished?" She seemed to be, so Günther took a drink and continued with his mail.

Bills. Three solicitations. A postcard from the electric company announcing an interruption in service next Monday. Ah, an envelope of interest. Small, handwritten, heavy. Return address from Spain. He opened it and was surprised to find a key enclosed.

Lieber Herr Christove,

Thank you for your dedication and creative teaching style that so delighted and inspired Falicia. She enjoyed her term with you at the Institute and still talks about it all the time. She has blossomed from a shy girl into a beautiful young woman. We are very pleased and cannot thank you enough.

As a small token of our appreciation, please accept the offer of our second home in Switzerland. It is located in the tiny alpine village of Champery. It's cozy and within walking distance to the main street.

We have enclosed the key for your convenience. Our vacation plans this year don't include Champery and we don't let it out to others, so it is readily available to you. You can plan an extended stay or just drop in for a day or two. It will please us greatly if you find time to use it.

Our deepest thanks,

Antonio and Maria Bandier

Günther folded the letter and slid it back into its envelope. He looked at the key for a few moments and then sipped his wine. When was the last time he'd taken time off? He tried to remember. Not since Katerina. He pictured her as she reached up to stroke his face. A three-day vacation they'd taken the year before Nikolaus was born. Off the coast of Italy, where they'd stayed holed up in their room the entire time.

A small smile pulled at the corner of his mouth as he remembered the concierge of the tiny inn, and how embarrassed he'd been when he tapped on their door to see if everything was all right. They'd laughed for hours about that and then went out for a late supper, dining in a tiny café that overlooked the twinkling lights of the shoreline. They'd finished with chilled tumblers of Limoncello and walked the beach until dawn.

Günther stroked the cat. "Ah, how I miss her. And my little boy too. I can't imagine myself anywhere but back then. Or with anyone but her." He took a deep breath. Life was good and had much to offer, he reminded himself. He had much to atone for.

There was a rap on his door.

Setting the mail on the side table, he stood, tossed the cat into the warm cushion, and went to answer the door.

"*Bitte, kommen Sie*," *Frau* Handler said, requesting he follow. "*Schnell!*"

"What is wrong?"

"Aggie *ist krank*."

Sick? He'd just looked in on Katerina's mother this morning before going to the academy and then again briefly on his way home tonight. She'd been fine then. Thin and weak, but relatively the same as she'd been for the last five years.

Günther grabbed his coat and locked the door. The nursing home was only a block from his flat so they walked quickly, side by side in silence, until they came to the house.

She was sleeping. The hospital bed all but swallowed up her tiny broomstick body. Her gray hair stuck out in tufts and her sunken eyes pulsated as her shallow breathing trudged on. The right side of her face pulled down in a grimace and her claw-like right hand retracted stiffly upon her flat chest.

Günther leaned over her bedside, taking her frail hand into his own. "*Kannst Du mich hören?*" He asked if she could hear him, his face close to hers. He tenderly smoothed the hair back from her forehead. "Aggie?"

She opened her eyes for one moment, looking at the ceiling.

The doctor attending the nursing home, a resident of the hospital across the street, came in and put his hand on Günther's shoulder.

Günther straightened.

"She seems to have suffered another small stroke, Günther," he told him. "We won't know anything for certain until tomorrow when we run some tests. That is, if you want to have the tests run. Knowing if she has indeed had another stroke is irrelevant at this point and won't really change anything we are doing now for her, or her therapy."

"I just saw her two hours ago. She seemed fine then."

"Well, you know how these things happen. I do believe this was nothing major, like before. Tomorrow she may be fine. Only time will tell."

"We will pray for that."

"I'm sorry," the doctor said, "I have an appointment and need to go. Rest assured that they'll call me if there are any changes in her condition during the night."

The doctor stood eye to eye with Günther. "You are doing all you can, Günther. Your mother-in-law is comfortable and comparatively speaking, other than her strokes, quite healthy. There is nothing more to be done for her."

Günther nodded. "Thank you, Doctor."

He knew that. But it didn't make it easier to see her like this, day in and day out, month after month, year after year. He'd tried keeping her with him at his flat when he'd first returned to Vienna, five years ago, but that proved impossible. Her condition demanded supervision twenty-four hours a day. He would have had to quit his job to accommodate her and then he wouldn't have the funds to pay for the therapy she needed.

He pulled up a chair alongside her bed.

The cloying aroma of the room was a smell Günther was long used to, and at the same time, one he would never be used to. The staff did what they could with meticulous housekeeping and sanitation, but four elderly, bedridden human beings, living in the same house, was enough to keep the air pungent.

His heart broke again for Aggie. He didn't want her to be here anymore than she wanted it. As often as he could, and as much as the weather permitted, he'd dress her warmly and take her out in her wheelchair for strolls through the park.

She liked being outside, where she could see the sky and the trees and grass. They would sit for an hour just watching the children play. He imagined her lungs hungrily sucking in the fresh, clean air. Then when she tired, he'd take the robe from her lap, fold it, and push her home again, closer and closer to the confinement of this bed and this room.

Günther took her hand and closed his eyes. "Give her peace. Bring happiness into the days she has left. Ease her pain and anger." Emotion surged within him and he was unable to stop his eyes from filling. They had been thrown together, Aggie and him. They were a strange pair. He was doing his best for her, but sometimes that didn't seem like it was nearly enough.

Günther dug in his pocket for his rosary. He kissed the crucifix and made the sign of the cross. Leaning toward her and in a voice just loud enough for Aggie to hear, he began with the Apostles' Creed. "I believe in God, the Father Almighty, Creator of heaven and earth."

Chapter Eight

Camille, awakened by the jangle of pots and pans, listened to the prattle of Sasha's endless questions. The kitchen was directly below her room, making it possible to hear a muffled conversation between Petra and Patrick. The twins were bright and well-mannered. Both were fair-haired and slender like their mother, with blue eyes.

Sasha, the baby, favored her daddy with thick curly hair and big brown eyes. She had an incorrigible smile that could draw in even the most steadfast grump. She was fast on her sturdy little legs.

Groggily, Camille looked to the nightstand. It was six p.m.. Camille forced herself up and moved quickly into the tiny bathroom and brushed her teeth. She splashed her face, dried it, then applied moisturizer and the minimum of makeup.

She rummaged through her earrings choosing silver dangles, subtle but attractive. No pendant. Donning a pink sweater and a nice pair of jeans, she felt presentable. She descended the stairs and greeted Helene and the children in the kitchen.

"Hello," Camille offered as she picked Sasha up, giving her a brief hug.

"All was well today?" Helene asked.

"Yes. It was lots of fun."

"Good. I knew it would be. Remember, the scooter is always here if you need it. Use it for sightseeing or shopping. No need to ask. Consider it yours." She opened one of the cupboards and several keys hanging from a snow-covered chalet key holder swayed with the motion. "It is the blue key."

"Thank you."

"I'm sorry we were out when you returned. Patrick had an appointment and then I had to stop at the market. But not to fear, I have a nice supper planned and we will be eating shortly."

"Please, no fussing over me. Just do what you normally do." Camille pulled out a stool and sat.

Helene looked to her older daughter. "Petra, please set the table. We will take supper in the dining room tonight in celebration of Camille's first day of school." She took plates out of the cupboard and set them on the counter. "Come see, Camille." She opened the oven door and cautiously lifted the lid of a large cast iron pot. Inside, boiling in broth, was a good-size roast. The origin of the heavenly smell.

"Now I add the carrots, celery stalks, and leeks." Retrieving the vegetable-laden cutting board, she started placing them carefully around the meat in the hot broth. "*Tafelspitz* is boiled beef with vegetables and dumplings. It's a typical Viennese recipe and was a favorite of *Kaiser* Franz Josef, the Imperial Emperor."

Finished, she wiped her hands on her apron and handed Sasha a carrot to chew on. "And is also a favorite of *Herr* Christove, too," she added. "How was Günther today?"

"*Herr* Christove?" Camille asked, surprised that Helene had brought him up.

Helene nodded.

"Good. I knew him online a little but putting a face to a name helps."

The phone rang. Helene answered with her singsong, "Eberstark."

There was a pause. "Yes, one moment, *bitte*." She handed the receiver to Camille.

"Hello?"

"Hi, honey. I wanted to check to see how everything is going. How are you?" Camille's mother said.

"I tried to get you earlier, Mom, but your line was busy. I meant to call you right back but I dozed off. Right now, I'm learning how to prepare *Tafelspitz.*"

"How exciting. So, you're enjoying yourself?"

"Very much. I can't tell you how relaxed I'm becoming. You won't recognize me when I get home."

"That is such good news. I'll pass it on to Stephanie."

"Tell her too, I already have an appointment with Dr. Williamson day after tomorrow. The receptionist was very nice and spoke wonderful English."

"Wonderful."

"It's so beautiful here, you just wouldn't believe it. The family I'm living with is amazing, and their home is so nice. I can never thank you enough for insisting I come. I love you."

"That's what moms are for, silly. I love you too. I'm going to let you go now since this is a very expensive time to call—and I don't want to interrupt your cooking lessons. Kristin is fine and sends her love. Keep in touch, please. And have fun."

"I will."

They said good-bye and hung up.

Camille knew Helene's courteous manners would never allow her to ask why she was seeing a doctor. Rushing off to a medical center upon arriving in a foreign country was a peculiar thing to do. She hadn't wanted to bring this up so soon but since the subject was now broached, she may as well get it out in the open. At least the children were out of the room.

"About the doctor's appointment," Camille began.

"*Nein*, you don't have to say anything."

"I know. I want to tell you. I had a heart attack before coming to Europe."

She wouldn't mention that she'd actually died and had to be resuscitated. That was too disturbing. She didn't even like to think about it herself. "I've been recuperating, but my doctor felt I needed a complete change in everything to get my mind and worries off my business and family life. She is sending me to a doctor here just to keep an eye on things."

"A heart attack," Helene said slowly. "But you are young for that, yes?"

"Young, but not too young. I'm forty-four. It runs in my family, lucky me."

The front door opened and Wolfgang entered, his arms full of files. He stopped in the hall and swept the police hat from his head, tossing it onto the closet shelf in one fluid motion. As the files he was carrying began to totter, he heaped them onto the kitchen counter.

Wolfgang was in his late thirties and had a face that might worry you if you didn't know him. It was stern with straight lines and a moon-shaped mouth that pointed down. But that was only when in a relaxed state. In actuality, he was a happy man, always laughing at something, but mostly at himself. He talked with expression and used his hands extensively, entertaining the children and making them giggle.

When their conversation had been interrupted by Wolfgang's entrance, Helene's expression told Camille that her secret was safe with her for as long as she chose to keep it quiet. A pact between women.

Wolfgang smiled charmingly at Camille. He kissed Helene before loosening his tie and unbuttoning the collar of his shirt. He looked to his son. "Patrick, help your papa, *bitte*." They gathered the files from the counter and left.

Petra was back gathering the utensils. "Why does Patrick not have to help?"

"Because he is your brother. He will do other help after dinner. Right now he is helping your father who's had a long day at work. You know better than to complain about chores, Petra," Helene scolded.

Petra blushed.

Laughter erupted from the other room. Chanting rattled off an unfamiliar song.

"*Der dicke Dachdecker deckte das dicke Dach.*" Over and over, faster and faster. The baby came out of the room dancing around in circles and clapping her hands. Her faced fairly beamed.

"What are they saying?" Camille inquired, chuckling.

Wolfgang and Patrick were back, punching at each other playfully as they tried to make the other mess up their recitation.

"It is what you would call a tongue twister. It means in English, 'the fat roofer roofed the thick roof.' Not nearly as fun as it sounds in German. Or as difficult."

The laughter was contagious and soon Camille was as hysterical as the rest of the household, trying to get the confusing words right.

At last, Helene clapped her hands for attention and wiped the tears from her cheeks with a corner of her apron. "Enough now. Dinner is ready. Children, run and wash up quickly." She gave them a stern eye as she pulled the heavy pot from the oven. "I will be very unhappy if Camille's first taste of *Tafelspitz* is cold."

Chapter Nine

"**A**chtung!" Herr Christove called the class to order. Camille watched as he tossed a look to Stena von Linné, who was chattering incessantly with her partner, Mark. The woman's platinum hair draped her shoulders like a mantle and her bodice stretched tautly across her ample breasts, leaving more than a hint of cleavage showing. Turning to the board he wrote, *Heute ist Mittwoch.*

Today is Wednesday, Camille read silently. Tuesday had come and gone without any big surprises or calamities, much to her delight and relief. She sat relaxed at her desk in a knobby periwinkle sweater with rolled collar and cuffs, worn Levis, and a backpack filled with things needed for her trip to the doctor's office today. A plastic bottle of coconut water, map of Vienna, power bar, written directions from Wolfgang, and a handful of Tibetan goji berries for energy.

Before class had begun, she'd had a brief conversation with the older gentleman, Scott Wilkins. Since he actually was from Canada, she'd had fun relating the fiasco that her Canadian luggage tags had caused her in Customs. He'd gotten a big kick out of her story and laughed enthusiastically, completely oblivious to the stares of curiosity from the other members of the class. He'd been on the same plane with her flying in from Heathrow, and had seen the unfortunate collision with Branwell.

Herr Christove handed out a worksheet and the students began working at once. Camille raised her hand and *Herr* Christove approached.

"Yes, *Frau* Ashland?" he asked with a small disarming grin she felt all the way to her toes. His casual tan and blue plaid shirt was open at the collar, revealing a tan tee shirt underneath. A brown sports jacket hugged his wide shoulders over a pair of Levis. It created a look totally his own that Camille thought was incredibly handsome.

"I have an appointment at ten this morning," she said softly, trying not to disturb anyone. "It couldn't be helped." As she fidgeted with the corner of her paper, her pencil rolled from her desktop, bounced twice, and landed at his feet.

He picked it up and handed it to her.

"I'll try to be back by one at the latest," she said quickly, as she felt her cheeks heating up again.

"Do you know where you are going?"

Camille reached for her backpack. "Yes." She took out the directions Wolfgang had given her and handed them to Günther.

"Wolfgang said it was easy. Just catch the train at *Enkplatz* and get off at the third stop. From there it's only three blocks to the medical center." Darn. She hadn't meant to let that slip.

His eyebrows raised a fraction in question. He looked over her directions and gave them back to her. "You should be able to do this easily. It's in a good part of the city. Branwell." At the mention of his name, Branwell set his pencil down. "I'm giving you an extra credit assignment. You are to go with your partner, Mrs. Ashland, to her appointment, have lunch at some place of interest, then give a detailed report to the class tomorrow."

Camille straightened. "No." She held out her hands, palms out. "*Herr* Christove, please. That's totally unnecessary."

"No argument. Branwell knows the city well."

She couldn't bear to look at Branwell. How embarrassing. She didn't want him along. How could she get out of it? She looked at her watch. It was already eight twenty-five and she needed to leave soon.

"Isn't that so, Branwell?"

"Absolutely, *Herr* Christove. Not to worry. I will take good care not to lose Mrs. Ashland."

"Good. It's settled. Go ahead and get going. You don't want to be rushed."

There was no help for it. Camille folded her worksheet and put it in her backpack. Branwell stood when she did and proceeded to the door. For one brief moment, he stopped by Stena's desk and whispered something into her ear. They both laughed. Her gaze swept Camille quickly. She said something back and gave him a knowing look. Camille tried not to be suspicious. The two were friends, for heaven's sake. They had this same class together last term. Even if they were meaning to hurt her feelings, she wouldn't let their tomfoolery disturb her.

Camille and Branwell walked down the hallway side by side in silence. She wondered if she should apologize or just keep quiet. He had a way of just looking at her that set her teeth on edge. She brushed her hair back off her shoulders and smiled at a passing girl, as if she didn't have a care in the world. On the wide school steps, she stopped for a moment and looked around, pretending to enjoy the view. She wanted to break this icy wall of silence but was uncertain of how to go about it.

"So. Where are we going?" he asked in a pleasant voice.

His unexpected question startled her. All her defenses flashed on alert. "The *Enkplatz* station." She had a general idea where the *Enkplatz* station was, but nothing concrete.

"This way," he said over his shoulder as he started off.

Two blocks from the school, they came to the station. Branwell fed a couple of euros into a tall ticket machine and when the ticket popped out, he handed it to her. "You owe me," he said, repeating the process. They proceeded to the platform to wait for the train's arrival.

This was a good time to try to talk. He seemed receptive for the first time. "Branwell, I'm sorry you got sucked into this."

"Not a problem," he answered, casually glancing at his watch.

She chose her words carefully. "But I thought you couldn't stand me. After what happened on the plane."

"That?" he said in surprise. "Don't be silly. Accidents happen."

A flicker of apprehension wiggled through her. What was this all about? Something was not right. She preferred knowing who her enemies were.

When the train arrived they boarded, sat in silence, and in a handful of minutes were at the third stop, where they got off. There were shops and boutiques everywhere and many interesting things to see. A man stood in the doorway of an art gallery and motioned for Camille to come inside. Camille looked at her directions. "We want *Rosenbursen Straße*," she said.

Branwell glanced left and then right. "Not sure where that is. I'll go ask." He strode over to the open-air farmers market and disappeared into the crowd.

Camille looked at her watch. It was already nine twenty-five. The square teemed with people. She wished Branwell would hurry. When ten minutes had passed, she knew he wasn't coming back. *Fine. I'll go it alone—like I'd planned in the first place.*

"Can you tell me where the medical center is?" Camille asked the first woman she saw.

The woman shook her head. "*Ich spreche kein English.*"

Camille tried again. "*Können Sie mir...mir,*" she struggled with the words, "*S-sagen wo das Medical Center ist...bitte?*"

Now the woman smiled. "*Ja. Gehen Sie rechts auf Hollandstraße und dann links um die Ecke.*"

Camille caught some of her directions but must have looked confused because the woman now employed the universal language known by all. She pointed.

"*Hollandstraße,*" she said again, jabbing at the air.

Camille thanked her and hustled in that direction. On her route, she came to a bridge that crossed the Danube. Halfway across, she paused and gazed at the fairy tale-like city beyond. It was breathtaking. She wanted to see it—drink it in. The river hurried past, unimpressed with her presence, winding and lapping its banks.

Slowly, a sensation slid through her body and a shiver traced up her spine. Someone was watching her. Her skin grew prickly and the cold air seemed suddenly constricting. *Branwell.* She was sure. He was back in the crowd thinking just how funny and clever he was.

The nurse called Camille into the examination area five minutes after she'd signed in at the office window. Straight off the cover of some fashion magazine, Daniela, as her nametag said, placed a thermometer into Camille's mouth with a showy display of her long nails, beautifully manicured in French white. She took Camille's blood pressure and pulse without saying a word, and entered the data into a razor-thin laptop, after which she left Camille sitting on the end of the examination table to wait for the doctor.

Dr. Williamson was very nice. The exam took forty minutes and he finished by giving Camille a good report. Everything looked as it should. She need not come back until next month unless she had some sort of problem. He gave her his private phone number just in case, with an invitation to call him anytime, day or night.

By the time Camille exited, the sun had disappeared behind some clouds, putting a chill in the air. She took her power bar from her backpack and took a bite.

Before leaving the office, the receptionist had explained where Camille needed to go to catch the train back to *Michaelerplatz*. She glanced up the street. Was Branwell still around? Perhaps he'd gone back to class without her. She wasn't anxious anymore, more perturbed at him than anything. It was only a few blocks to the U-Bahn station so she started to walk.

The lunch crowd was out in force, cramming quaint cafés and eateries everywhere. People jammed the walkways and congested the streets. Businessmen in Armani suits sat drinking martinis, and businesswomen sipped mineral water while talking on cell phones that never seemed to leave their ears. It was chaotic.

Purposely, Camille steered clear of the most crowded areas, skirting the hustle and bustle. She veered onto a winding street with a tiny shop that reminded her of Chocolate Blossoms. It was darling and resembled something straight from the pages of a children's storybook. Since she was in the candy business herself, curiosity won out.

A silver bell tinkled as she stepped inside. A sparkling glass display case greeted her, filled with every kind of confection, surely delectable enough to please the most finely honed palate while their artistic beauty would satisfy the most discerning eye. Camille felt a pang of nostalgia for Chocolate Blossoms when the scent of warm milk chocolate wafted from the back room, where something was cooking.

A voice greeted her. "*Grüß Gott.*"

Camille had thought she was alone in the shop. She looked around. "Oh, *Grüß Gott,*" she replied, spotting a small woman wavering precariously off the side of a wall-sliding ladder as she restocked a highly placed shelf. She smiled broadly at Camille and hurried down.

"Can you please recommend something special?" Camille asked.

"Yes. *Die Mozart-Kugeln* are our specialty." Her eyes gleamed passionately. "You may try one." The woman reached into the case, took out a foil-wrapped ball, and handed it to Camille.

Camille unwrapped it and took a small bite. Her senses exploded in a rainbow of tastes the likes of which she'd never experienced before. "Delicious."

"*Natürlich.* The famous *Mozart-Kugeln* are made with only the finest of *Schokolade.* The center is pistachio marzipan and has a hazelnut nugget. You like?"

Camille couldn't speak yet. She was still in euphoria. Finally she said, "I love it. I've never tasted anything quite like it in all my life."

"*Ja*, that is what most people tell me."

"I will take a small gift bag, please."

Camille made it back to *Michaelerplatz* without too many problems. She was curious as to what *Herr* Christove would say when she showed up without Branwell. She didn't care that Branwell had gone off and left her, she was capable of navigating on her own; it was just such a weird thing for him to do. Ignoring her because he didn't like her was one thing, but actually disobeying *Herr* Christove was quite another.

She hurried up the steps to the school feeling comfortable and at ease. She was happy about her prognosis. The doctor wanted her to just keep on doing what she'd been doing for the last few weeks, but most importantly she was to avoid all stressful situations.

Class was in session when she rounded the corner of the hallway and went into the room. *Herr* Christove's face lit up when he saw her.

"So, you are back," he said. "How did it go? Did you have a nice lunch?"

Camille was about to answer when a voice behind her said, "We had no trouble finding it. And we lunched at Sardino's."

Stunned, Camille spun around. She had not heard him approach. Branwell was not two feet behind her. He towered over her, making the back of her neck prickle. How could he? She glanced down at his big feet to see he wore soft-soled shoes. She stared at him in disbelief. *What* was his game?

"Camille?"

She turned back to *Herr* Christove at a loss.

He looked worried. "Are you feeling all right?"

"Yes," she sputtered. "I'm fine."

"Is something bothering you?" Concern was written all over his face.

She glanced up at Branwell. "No. Nothing."

"You are sure?" His look said he didn't believe her. "Well, I am glad you are back safe and sound."

They took their seats and began working on the paper *Herr* Christove handed them, but Camille couldn't concentrate on the vocabulary lesson before her. She couldn't decide if she should say anything to *Herr* Christove or not. He knew Branwell—and seemed to be his friend. It was her word against his. Branwell could just say he went off shopping and then lost her accidentally. She knew better. She'd felt his stare on the bridge.

"Mrs. Ashland, could I speak with you for a moment," *Herr* Christove called.

Camille approached his desk. He had one of her papers lying on his desk. He motioned for her to take a seat in the chair facing him with her back to the students.

He began in a quiet voice. "I want to thank you for spending the day with Branwell. I should have told you this earlier, but he's the son of the prime minister of England. Don't let that bother you, though. They like to keep his identity quiet for security purposes, you understand. I know he's kind of a different young man, so I appreciate your kindness toward him. His uncle is a benefactor to this school and serves on the board."

Branwell really *was* the prime minister's son. Stephen Turner had almost said that on the plane. In jest, she'd thought at the time. Sometimes truth really *was* stranger than fiction. "I see," was all she could manage to get out.

He looked at her questionably. "That won't be a problem, will it?"

"Is there a problem?" Branwell said, from behind her.

Chapter Ten

"This is a private conversation, Branwell," *Herr* Christove said in a flat voice. Camille noticed the instructor's mouth harden and pleasant expression vanish.

"Sorry," Branwell said politely. "I thought I heard you say there was a problem with something. I wanted to help if I could."

Herr Christove stared up at Branwell from his desk, his gaze steady over his steepled fingers. "It's nothing that concerns you."

Camille wanted to laugh. Branwell was afraid she was going to snitch on him, tell *Herr* Christove about his shenanigans. Well, she should. It would serve the egotistical brat right.

She forced herself to turn around and look at Branwell. His eyes were dark, unreadable. "No worries, *Bran*well," she said. "It's not always about *you*."

"Fine then. I'm just trying to be accommodating," he said with a shrug.

Herr Christove watched him go back to his desk, a perplexed expression on his face. "You're *sure* everything is all right?"

She nodded. Felt empowered. She weighed Branwell's audacity. Was his interruption his way of warning her not to say anything? His boldness was creepy. He was far more connected with the school and *Herr* Christove than she'd previously thought.

An hour later, Günther put his lesson planner away in the top drawer of his desk and stood. "I'm ending class a little earlier than usual today. Put your papers on my desk as you leave. This evening, go over the conversations I gave you yesterday. There will be a quiz tomorrow." He walked over to the windows and glanced out before twisting the blinds closed.

"As most of you know, today is Ash Wednesday," he continued. "For those who are interested, I'm walking over to St. Elizabeth's Church. You are welcome to join me." He shrugged into his coat as the students prepared to leave.

He held up his hand. "I'm sorry. One more thing. Tomorrow evening we will meet at *Spatzennest*, Sparrow's Nest. It's not fancy, but is known for its classic Viennese cuisine. We'll gather at six for before-dinner refreshments. It's a good way to get acquainted with each other. If you don't feel like it, that's fine. It's not mandatory—but you will be sorry if you miss." He grinned.

Scott Wilkins, Timm Zalzamaci, and Lena Eezer left immediately. Branwell and Stena talked quietly and exited the door. Mrs. Ashland still sat at her desk as she looked through her backpack. After she found what she was looking for, she approached with something in her hand.

"I forgot about this. It's a small thank-you for letting me off the hook today."

He glanced at the bag of *Mozart-Kugeln*. "Thank you so much. I really like these."

She smiled warmly. "You're welcome."

"Are you coming along?" He watched her face as she considered the idea. "Are you Catholic?"

"Uh, yes."

Mark Marslino, Angie Dirabelle, and Konrad Larroux brushed past, talking animatedly about the dinner at *Spatzennest*. Hanna Lodyard and Niclas Shiollière stood back, and he presumed they were waiting.

"I am, but I haven't been practicing for a very long time."

"Good. All the better reason to come now since we are beginning Lent." He could see by her expression she was torn. "It's okay. Come."

She shrugged. "All right. I just hope the walls don't cave in on me."

He couldn't help the happiness her decision caused him. "And it's a nice, brisk walk, I'm sure you'll like it."

"It's not the church next door?"

He shook his head.

"Why not?"

"You'll see. Hanna and Niclas, you are coming along too?"

"*Oui, Herr* Christove," Hanna Lodyard replied. She was a seventeen-year-old Frenchwoman from Clermont-Ferrand, in the region of Auvergne. Her layered dark brown hair, merry brown eyes, and engaging smile were captivating.

Niclas, nineteen, and also from France, gave Camille and Günther a cool nod. Günther could see a romance in the making as sure as the day was long. "This is a fine group. Let us depart." Günther stepped aside, and with a wave of his arm ushered the three through the doorway. He locked the door, slipped his key back into his pants pocket, and they started down the gigantic hallway, four across.

Niclas and Hanna were making eyes at each other and laughing as they exited the building, descending the flagstone steps. At the bottom a man waited, watching their approach with interest. A ball cap covered his dark hair, a computer case slung across his shoulder, and a cup of coffee in his hand.

The man stepped forward as they were about to pass. "Camille."

Surprised, Camille jerked her attention away from Günther, who was explaining to them how *Michaelerplatz* got its name.

"Stephen. Hello." She paused and greeted him with a friendly grasp of her hand.

"Hi. I was waiting for you. How's it going?" His gaze took in the foursome and landed on Günther.

"Very well. Let me introduce you to my instructor. *Herr* Christove, this is Stephen Turner. We were seated next to each other on our flight from Heathrow to Vienna." She looked to the teenagers. "This is Hanna and Niclas, students also." The teenagers, who were now holding hands, nodded.

"Pleasure to meet you." He glanced around the group of faces and returned to Camille. "And I was afraid you'd be lonely not knowing anyone in Vienna," he said jokingly.

"Not to worry," Günther assured him. "She has many friends already, and has captivated the whole class with her American charm."

Camille's eyes grew wide and her face began to darken in color at his familiarity.

Stephen shifted his weight to his other leg, then straightened. "I can see that."

Stephen Turner was not going to give up easily. Niclas and Hanna were already walking away in the direction of St. Elizabeth's, bored with the adults' conversation.

"We're on our way to St. Elizabeth's," Camille told him. "For Ash Wednesday. Would you like to join us?"

He glanced at his watch and then repositioned the cap on his head. "Think I'll pass this time, but thanks. You go on, I'll catch you later."

"Okay, I'll see you later."

Günther watched Stephen as he crossed the square, upsetting a flock of pigeons hunting for crumbs in front of a café. They caught up with Hanna and Niclas who were waiting for them on the corner.

"Now where?" Hanna asked.

Günther rounded the corner. "This way. We have a couple of blocks to go."

He took out his phone and punched in a number.

"*Hallo*, it's Günther," he said as they walked.

Camille could hear a very happy female voice on the other end talking away in German.

He barked out a laugh, making the teens giggle. "*Ja, und* Sasha?" He responded to the woman on the other end of the line, laughing again.

"Hold on, Camille wants to talk with you." He handed the phone to Camille.

"It's Helene."

Camille explained to Helene that she would be home later than normal and not to worry about her. After a friendly conversation, she hung up and handed the phone back to him. "Thanks. I would have forgotten."

He folded the phone and slipped it into his inside coat pocket. "Helene and I are old friends. Her sister and I were sweethearts, back in gymnasium, our equivalent to America's high school. We've stayed in contact on and off throughout the years. She and Wolfgang host a student for the academy every term. They added that cozy second-floor addition specifically for that purpose." They crossed the empty street in the middle of the block and turned into an alley. "Do you like it?"

"What? The room? Oh, yes, very much."

He grinned, the smile going all the way up into his eyes. "I helped them build it," he said proudly.

"You're a carpenter, too?" she replied in surprise.

"No, not really." He smiled at her look of pleasure. "Come on, we're here." The four went up the steps to St. Elizabeth's and Günther opened the door for the group to enter.

The interior of St. Elizabeth's blushed ambient illumination cast from two rows of chandeliers. It was a gorgeous church, very old, with a personality of charming elegance. There were two side altars, each with its own giant fresco, one of the Transfiguration and one of Mary, Queen of Heaven. A bevy of saints adorning the walls gazed down on the carved pews. Stained glass windows glittered in a multitude of colors and the ceiling, as most churches of old, had cherubim and other angels portrayed everywhere.

Günther led the three up the left side aisle, past a confessional, past the side altar of the Transfiguration, and past a metal tray of prayer candles, with flames that swayed and blinked in the draft. Soon they were close to the front, stopping at the pew of the third row. They all genuflected and filed in.

Günther lowered the kneeler and they knelt, making the sign of the cross. With Günther to her right and Hanna to her left, Camille struggled to calm her inner self, and center her thoughts. All the sights and sounds assailed her senses and she felt a deep regret for having stayed away so long.

An altar boy went about lighting candles on the back altar with a tall silver lighter. Finished, he looked out into the growing multitude of people as if searching for someone. His face brightened. He descended the steps from the sanctuary coming toward them, then stopped and whispered into Günther's ear.

After he left, Günther glanced over his shoulder at the filling church and leaned over to Camille. "Everyone comes for their ashes. It's one of the most well-attended days of the year. Too bad it's not always like this."

A family of four joined their pew, scrunching them toward each other. Günther's shoulder brushed hers. She appreciated his nearness as she knelt in prayer for the first time in many years. She looked at the tabernacle. She'd been bitter for too long. She was tired of it. Was it possible to pick up where she'd left off, as Günther said?

A woman seated next to the microphone stood and greeted them in German and they all stood.

Camille opened her hymnal and sang along the best she could. Günther glanced her way and gave her the slightest nod of support as he sang.

Up the aisle came the same altar boy that had whispered to Günther, this time gripping a long pole with a crucifix at the top. Next was a staunch-looking man, carrying a big book high over his head, followed by the priest, his chasuble, long, flowing, and purple. He sang in a deep clear voice.

Something about the priest caught Camille's attention. She looked closer as he ascended the steps of the sanctuary and kissed the altar. Bending low, he added three spoonfuls of incense to the thurible, the device the altar boy now held. The priest proceeded to circle the altar, swinging the thurible back and forth on its long chain, creating a small billow of smoke. Finished now, the priest handed it back to the altar boy, who hung it on a stand. Facing the congregation for the first time, the priest greeted them.

Camille sucked in a quick breath of surprise. Günther turned to her in question.

"I have seen him before. I think we've met."

"Really?" he whispered. "Where?"

She shook her head slowly. "I can't put my finger on it. But I *know* I've seen him *somewhere*."

Mass progressed and after the psalms were sung, Günther slid from the pew and ascended the pulpit. He reached in his pocket and slipped on his glasses. Flipping the page, he flattened the purple ribbon to the side and began reading.

Camille listened in awe. Günther's voice rang throughout the church, his pronunciation and inflection a work of art. Happiness filled her. This was exactly where she was meant to be at this time of her life. She was sure of it. It was amazing how she'd gotten here and why. Her life had changed so much in the last month.

Günther finished and returned to his seat. He offered Camille one of the smiles he was so generous with. She'd never realized, before meeting Günther, the power a smile held and the happiness it could convey.

Now came the distribution of ashes, so Günther stepped into the aisle and let Camille, Hanna, and Niclas out in front of him. As Camille drew closer to the sanctuary, she could not take her eyes off the priest and his vivid blue eyes. She was sure she had seen them before. It was exasperating not being able to remember where; she hadn't been to that many places since arriving in Vienna.

She thought about the airport, the Eberstarks' home, *Michaelerplatz*, the café, the school. She knew she should be thinking about what was about to happen and Lent and God, but darn, this was driving her crazy. Had she seen him somewhere back home?

Almost there. Only two people ahead of her. The U-Bahn station, the candy store, the doctor's office. *Where was it?*

She stood before him. He rubbed his thumb in the small round canister of black ashes and traced down from her scalp line to her eyebrows, a shower of particles drifting over her cheeks and nose.

Where?

He made the horizontal line crossing through the first mark. "Remember, man, that you are dust, and unto dust you shall return," he said in German, but she knew what it meant from her childhood.

Afterward, out front in the courtyard, the four of them admired each other's crosses, delighted that the priest had been heavy-handed. Everyone's marks were big and black.

"Come on, there's someone I want you to meet," Günther said, escorting them around the side of the church. They reentered St. Elizabeth's from a side door and Camille found herself in the sacristy.

"Are you sure it's okay that we're in here?" she whispered. It was quiet and cool. She felt like a trespasser.

Günther laughed. "Of course. The Swiss Guard won't be thumping on the doors to arrest us."

She glanced out into the church. Most of the parishioners were gone. Camille's gut tightened realizing that most likely Günther wanted to introduce her to the priest.

"Here he is now," Günther said, as the priest came into the room, followed by the altar boy and some other parishioners.

"Ah, Günther, I hoped you would stop in and visit. It's good to see you. How have you been?" The men embraced and something strong and tangible passed between them.

"I have no complaints."

Günther lifted the boy and hugged him too.

"Let me see your ashes," the boy said. He lifted the hair off Günther's forehead and laughed. "*Pfarrer* Christove got you good."

Günther put him down and turned to Camille. "These are a few of my new students, Camille, Hanna, and Niclas." An outbreak of murmurings ensued as everyone became acquainted, but Camille only concentrated on where she'd run into this man before. "This is my brother, *Pfarrer* Florian Christove."

Had he said *brother*?

They were both grinning like fools from ear to ear.

"The father is your brother?" At her silly-sounding question, everyone laughed.

"*Ja*," they both said in unison.

Well, this solved her mystery. "That must be why I keep thinking I've seen you before. You two look and sound very similar. We haven't met somewhere else, have we?" She asked, looking straight into the priest's sparkling eyes.

"Not that I recall."

"Camille comes to us all the way from Portland, Oregon," Günther said proudly. "Isn't that something? Camille, since I understand your American way is a little less formal, you can refer to *Pfarrer* Christove as Father Florian. I'm sure he won't mind."

She nodded. "Thank you."

Father Florian proceeded to pull the chasuble over his head, and hang it in a closet. Actually, the priest's resemblance to Günther was striking. They had the same build, although Father Florian was a bit taller. Same hair, same smile. He looked a year or two older.

"Welcome to Austria. Are you enjoying your stay?" he asked, as he removed a colorful sash that hung around his shoulders and down his chest. He kissed it and placed it neatly into a drawer.

"Very much. Your country's beauty is beyond compare."

"Very true words," he replied.

An older gentleman moved about the sacristy, ignoring them completely as he tidied up and put things away.

"Wait, so I can walk you out," Father Florian offered.

Camille squelched the impulse to close her eyes when he reached for the thin white under gown and pulled it over his head. The priest's usual black clothes were underneath.

They exited out the opposite side door and walked toward the back lot of the church, which was now almost empty.

"I have an appointment in a few minutes at the Eberstarks'. Will you see Johann home to *Frau* Weissman's?" Father Florian asked Günther.

"Of course." Günther wrestled Johann playfully as they walked along.

Father Florian was visiting the Eberstarks? What were the odds of that? Seemed the world was getting smaller by the second.

"Wolfgang is investigating Bernhard's case," Father Florian said quietly.

They stopped by a Volkswagen sedan that Camille assumed was the priest's car.

"It was a pleasure meeting you," he said. "Günther, I will see you Saturday morning, correct?"

Günther nodded. "The lesson is prepared." At her confused look he added, "My brother and I give an informal English class for disadvantaged neighborhood children here at St. Elizabeth's every Saturday morning. Johann helps too."

Father Florian turned and walked around the old car to a motorcycle parked on the other side. He went to the back and unfastened the helmet hanging from the trunk, and slipped it easily over his head.

Camille's eyes widened as she sucked in her breath.

Chapter Eleven

" *You*!" Camille gasped as he swung his leg over the big bike and sat deep into the seat. "It was you. You almost ran me down."

Father Florian jerked up his head and looked at her through the visor of his full-face helmet, a puzzled expression in his eyes. "Excuse me?"

"I knew I'd seen you somewhere before, and now I remember. I'd thought your resemblance to Günther was the reason for it, but that's not the case at all."

The group had stopped talking and had gathered around at her excited tone. Johann stepped protectively between Camille and Father Florian, his chin tipped up defiantly.

"*Tut mir leid*, Camille," Father Florian apologized. "I'm confused. What are you saying?"

"I was walking home in front of the train station on Monday and a motorcycle almost ran me over. Shame on you for riding into the pedestrian zone at such a fast speed. I almost had anoth…" she stopped herself just in time. "Never mind."

At her first accusation, Father Florian had taken off his helmet. He covered his mouth with one hand. "That—was—you?"

She stood there accusingly, waiting to hear what he had to say for himself. "You bet your booty it was," she said angrily.

He slowly got off the bike. "I cannot apologize enough for my irresponsible behavior. But I am thankful God has brought us back together so I can tell you in person how sorry I am for scaring you. I felt horrible about it."

"Not so bad to stop and say anything to me. My stockings are ruined, you know."

Johann looked back and forth from his beloved friend to the woman who was verbally attacking him. His little hands balled into fists at his side.

Günther held up his hand. "Florian was the biker you told me about, Camille? The one who almost ran you down in cold blood?"

Camille could see he thought the situation was extremely funny and could hardly keep from laughing.

"I don't see what's so amusing."

"You don't? God works in mysterious ways. I'll tell you about it on our walk back. There was no harm done. Right, Camille?"

Günther was right. And Father Florian *had* apologized. She felt a smile tugging at the corner of her mouth. "Yes. Of course."

The priest took her hand. "Thank you for forgiving me. But your stockings were ruined?"

Embarrassment radiated through her and she looked away. How childish of her to cause such a scene. "Well, not actually. I washed them immediately and the stains came out." She wished she could go back and do it over. She had handled everything horribly.

The priest bid them all good-bye and a good night, and rode off in a rumble.

By the time they reached *Michaelerplatz*, Günther had told Camille everything about Johann and what they were trying to do for him. And about Father Florian and why he'd scared her so badly. Why he couldn't take even one moment to inquire and apologize.

With each word he spoke, her guilt grew more vivid, causing her acute anxiety. What on earth had she been thinking to attack the priest in such a manner? And her heart ached for poor little Johann; he was such a darling child, in spite of the things he'd already endured in his young life.

It was six o'clock and the five friends stood in the center of *Michaelerplatz* and said their good-byes. A throng of businessmen and women filled the cafés, bistros, and bars, harried after a full day in the office. Hanna and Niclas left Günther, Johann, and Camille laughing at some skirmishing pigeons.

"I guess this is where our paths split," Günther said, smiling at Camille. "You will be okay on your walk home? It is starting to get dark."

Johann stood by his side, still eyeing Camille suspiciously, probably waiting for her to launch into another angry fit. She was sure he would not soon forget how she had treated his champion. She'd tried several times to strike up a conversation with the boy, with no luck.

"I'll be fine. All the streets are well lighted."

"And no more tangling with motorcycles," he teased, making a surprised face.

"That's not funny in the least," she said, trying to remain stoic, when she really wanted to laugh. "*Herr* Christove," she began.

"*Please*, you *must* call me Günther. After today, I feel we are fast friends. Is that all right with you?"

"Of course," she replied, wondering at how open and honest he was. No pretenses or games. He just said what he felt and thought and wanted. She had an uncontrollable urge to hug him, but she held her ground.

"Günther," she continued, "Thank you so much for taking me today. I'm so glad I went. I enjoyed it very much."

"Then I am happy you are happy." He stood in his casual, boyish way, resting his weight on one leg. "And, most importantly, I know that *God* is happy too. Love demands a presence. Yes?"

The cool March breeze lifted a few wisps of his hair, and he combed it down with his fingers.

She couldn't help but smile.

Johann tugged on Günther's hand. "It is getting late, Günther, we should start home."

"Of course. We are going now. I will see you then tomorrow in class. Have a restful evening."

"You too."

"*Servus.*" He pressed his cheek to hers, and the warmth of his skin was heady, despite the chill in the air.

She was a good half block away when she heard him call to her. She turned.

"Go straight home, don't dally."

He was walking backward and he bumped into a café chair and almost fell. His embarrassment quickly turned to laughter, joining Johann's.

The walk passed quickly and before she knew it, Camille was at the Eberstarks' house, standing under a streetlight at the corner of the driveway. The ominous motorcycle stood, parallel to the house, off the narrow street.

She'd forgotten completely that Father Florian had said he was coming over to talk with Wolfgang. As embarrassing as it was going to be to see him again, passing the night standing in the street until he left would be even more uncomfortable. She proceeded to the door and let herself in.

The house was quiet except for murmurings coming from Wolfgang's den. The family must have already eaten, but Helene had left her a nice place setting on the counter, complete with cloth napkin and wineglass.

She unbuttoned her coat and hung it in the entry closet, then placed her backpack on the first step of the staircase that led to her room. She went back and peeked into the oven. Helene came into the kitchen at that moment, a cobalt-blue sneaker in one hand and a rolled-up sock in the other. She had ashes on her forehead also.

"It's just tomato soup," she informed Camille as she washed her hands, then took the covered tureen out of the warm oven, removed the foil, and placed it at Camille's spot.

"Thank you. Actually, that sounds wonderful."

Camille felt very pampered. "Please don't go to so much trouble for me. I can help out around here and most definitely serve myself."

"It's no trouble. The children are studying and Sasha is in with Wolfgang and *Pfarrer* Christove." She retrieved Camille's salad from the refrigerator and placed it next to her soup bowl. From the bread keeper she brought a small plate with two rolls, the kind with a hard, stout crust and dreamy, soft center. The whole thing looked like a feast.

"It's Sasha's bath time. If you hear screaming and carrying on, you'll know why," she said, chuckling. "If I let her, she'd go a month without bathing."

She uncorked the half-full bottle of red wine and poured Camille a glass. "Fortifies your blood," she said knowingly.

Camille thanked her and sat down to eat. This was the first time she'd taken her meal sitting at the counter on the high barstool. It gave her a good view of the kitchen.

Camille loved interior design. After the second year of Chocolate Blossoms' wild success, she'd sold her small tract home and bought a brick colonial in one of Portland's older, more established neighborhoods. It was elegant and large, and she'd painstakingly gone room by room redecorating, playing off the home's personality and her love of yellows, creams, and periwinkle. She'd taken extra time with Kristin's bedroom, making it every girl's fantasy.

At the thought of her daughter, a pang of homesickness rolled through Camille. As soon as she was finished eating, she'd get online and say hello. It had only been four days since kissing her good-bye, but she missed her daughter terribly. On the other hand, Kristin wouldn't be missing her much, since she adored spending time with her Aunt Stephanie. They were like two peas in a pod.

Helene's kitchen was tiny compared to hers at home, but the ambience and feel of it was comparable. The cabinetry was white, offsetting the black, caramel, and white countertops. Two of the cabinet doors were paned glass, letting their contents act as accessories to the room. Over the stainless steel cooktop and recessed into the tile, an intricate design of a flowering fuchsia in a tall vase drew one's eye. *The heart of the room.* A built-in hutch, directly across from where she sat, held Helene's random collection of colorful plates, pitchers, and knickknacks. All were classically European.

Just as Helene had predicted, several high-pitched screeches echoed from down the hall. Coincidentally, at the same time, the door to the study opened and the men appeared. Camille was just bringing her wineglass to her lips.

Upon seeing her, they both stopped mid-stride and smiled. She felt her face flush.

"This is our friend, *Pfarrer* Christove," Wolfgang said. "And Camille is our new houseguest."

Camille lowered her glass. "Actually, we've met."

"You have?"

Father Florian grinned. "Yes. Twice."

His eyes smiled into hers and his voice was a mixture of humor and something else, atonement? His helmet dangled conspicuously from his hand as he stood next to Wolfgang, his lean frame a contrast with Wolfgang's stouter, more muscled physique.

"Oh, that's right," Wolfgang, answered. "Helene mentioned to me that you had gone to church with Günther this afternoon, and of course you'd go over to St. Elizabeth's and meet *Pfarrer* Christove."

"Yes. I enjoyed it very much, Father," she offered.

She wanted to make up for treating him so poorly only the hour before. She was still in shock over the fact that this priest was indeed not only Günther's brother, but her motorcycle assailant, and now, friend and confidant to her host and hostess.

Another ear-splitting scream pierced the air. Sasha, dressed in her pajamas, darted from the hallway and ran through the room, hiding behind Father Florian's legs. Her crimson face peered through his legs and her damp chestnut curls bounced with enthusiasm. She squealed and laughed nervously when she saw her mother in pursuit.

When the distance between them had shrunken past Sasha's comfort zone, she turned to make her escape, but Father Florian reached down and took hold of her arm.

"*Halt, bitte schön*," he requested. He restrained the child until Helene could catch her.

Excitedly, Sasha gibbered off a conglomeration of sentences and words, none of which any of them could understand. She strained and pulled, trying to get away.

"*Nein, nein*," Helene scolded her daughter, and picked her up. Sasha writhed and cried. Then in a quick, fluid movement, the child reached back and struck Helene across the face, causing her mother to gasp in shock.

All activity in the room stopped instantly and dead silence pervaded. Everyone stared in disbelief, especially Helene, whose face was frozen in surprise. Sasha knew immediately she had made a huge mistake and buried her face against her mother's shoulder.

Without a word, Wolfgang took the now quiet child from Helene and carried her off to her room with his wife following, her hand pressed to her cheek. The door clicked quietly behind them.

Father Florian stood next to Camille watching the retreat of the three.

He turned to Camille. "So," he said, trying to relieve the tension.

She smiled sympathetically and shrugged. "She must be overly excited with all the company in the house. Or, maybe she didn't nap today. My daughter, Kristin, used to get totally wired and out of control if she didn't get enough rest."

"Perhaps you are right. We will pray for that."

He took his coat from the closet and put it on, taking care to button it all the way to his chin for the ride home.

"Father?"

He stopped with his helmet halfway over his head, took it off, and lowered it.

"Günther explained to me about Johann and what really happened the day at the train station. I can't tell you how sorry I am for the way I treated you. You never even once tried to tell me what had actually happened. I'm so sorry. Can you ever forgive me?" she asked softly.

"There is nothing to forgive. I am only sorry that I scared you so badly."

They stood face to face, assessing each other.

"Thank you," she said, and slowly put out her hand. "Friends?"

He took hers and held it firmly. "Of course."

Günther unlocked his door and threw his keys over to the side table as he crossed the threshold. Flocki appeared mewing tenaciously. She trotted to her empty bowl in the kitchen.

"Patience," Günther said, and pulled the shades closed. He turned on the kitchen faucet and let the water run a few moments before filling a glass. Next, he fed the cat and then clicked on his television. The news was just finishing, and *Sports Report* with Bryant Sanderson was on. Uninterested, Günther clicked it off and pushed the button on his answering machine.

Beeeep.

The caller hung up without leaving a message.

Beeeep.

Another hang-up.

Beeeep.

The machine clicked again and a voice said, "I want Johann back." Bernhard, his voice gravelly and low. He slurred his words between heavy breaths. "Tell your brother to get him for me." He hung up without leaving a number or place where he wanted them to leave the boy.

Günther leaned on the counter and pushed his fingers through his hair. That was the last of the messages. He went to the cupboard and looked at the meager selection, realizing it had been some time since he'd been shopping.

"No meat today," he said as if he needed to be reminded. He pulled down a can of French onion soup and warmed it over the flame on his stove. Luckily, there was a section of a French roll left over from yesterday's dinner that he'd wrapped up in plastic wrap. It was still soft.

It was ten p.m. and still Camille felt edgy. She'd been trying to settle down, to relax after such an event-filled day. She blew on the hot tea she'd brewed in the empty kitchen and carried up to her room.

Comfortable in the chubby, floral-patterned chair, she sipped her tea. She snuggled her feet under her robe-covered bottom and opened her journal to the first page.

"My Disastrous Adventures Abroad." She chuckled. Entry one was a recap of the dinner with Stephanie, Kristin, and her mother and how they'd tricked her into leaving her shop and taking such an extended holiday. The next summarized her first meeting with Branwell on the flight into Vienna. Entry three, the first day of school, and her near-miss collision with the motorcycle. She read that page again. Now that she knew Father Florian, it was actually pretty darned funny.

She smiled, remembering how he'd looked when she'd dressed him down about scaring her to death. She picked up her pen to write the next entry into the journal when there was a light tap at her door.

She knew it would be Helene. The woman looked tired. "I'm sorry to disturb you, but I brought you a hot water bottle."

"Hot water bottle?"

"It's supposed to get very cold tonight. Your room stays a little on the cool side." She went over to Camille's bed and turned the comforter down. She fluffed the pillows and then lifted the blankets, unwrapped the towel from around the rubbery bottle, and placed it between the sheets at the foot of her bed. There," she said smiling. "You will be glad it is there later on when the temperature begins to drop."

Her hostess meandered toward the door, straightening a photograph of the Tyrolean Alps hanging on the wall. She hesitated.

Camille thought there must be something she wanted to say. "Helene?"

Helene brought her tortured eyes up to Camille's, woman to woman. Her voice was soft and barely audible as she said, "I'm sorry for the scene Sasha caused tonight. I hope she didn't embarrass you too much."

Camille stood. She crossed the room and put her arms around her new friend. "It didn't embarrass me at all. You're forgetting I have a daughter of my own. Raising a child is not easy."

Helene hugged her back. "I don't know what got into her," she whispered unsteadily. "She's been a handful lately, but she's never hit me before. Or the other children."

They sat down on Camille's bed side by side.

"Perhaps she's just tired, and got too excited with all the company. Did she nap today?"

"She did, but not very long. She's almost too old for napping anymore. I'm lucky if I get her to sleep for fifteen minutes."

Helene already looked a little steadier as they talked. Sometimes just sharing a problem was enough—even short of figuring out a solution.

"Does she have any allergies that you know of? Did she eat anything new?"

Helene slowly shook her head. "Not that I'm aware of."

They sat silently for a moment, thinking. "I'm sure it's just a stage," Camille said. That's what her own mother always told her. "She was exploring her boundaries and got caught up in the excitement of the moment. She was sorry after she did it. I wouldn't let it worry you too much since it's never happened before."

And that was probably true. Some children were just harder than others. Hopefully it wasn't a foreshadowing of what the Eberstarks had to look forward to with their youngest daughter in the years to come.

Helene reached out and squeezed Camille's hand. "Thank you for listening." Absently she reached up and rubbed the cheek that Sasha had struck. "If you get cold during the night, there is an extra blanket in your closet."

"I've seen it. Thank you."

"Can I get anything else for you?"

"Not a thing. I'm as cozy as can be."

"I am glad. Sleep well."

Helene began to close the door behind her.

"Helene," Camille called to her.

Helene paused in the doorway, the little wooden sign above her head.

"I'll pray for Sasha tonight," Camille said, surprising herself. It had been so long since she'd thought in those terms—about praying. Her mother was always praying for her and her friends and the world and anything else that needed God's help, but the words felt strange crossing her lips.

Chapter Twelve

From the center of the bar, Camille pulled out a stool and sat down. She arranged her skirt around her legs comfortably, hooking the heel of her boot over the second rung of the bar stool as she crossed her legs. She was the first to arrive at *Spatzennest*, but that didn't bother her. As a matter of fact, she was beginning to like this newfound feeling of independence.

After the bartender took Camille's drink order, she looked into the reflection of the opulent mirror. Six o'clock was early for European dining, so there were only a few patrons. Each table had a white draped tablecloth and a vase holding one large periwinkle flower. Alluring aromas of garlic and sizzling butter floated on the air, making her mouth water.

She had her euros waiting when the bartender set her glass of burgundy in front of her.

"*Danke, sehr.*"

"*Bitte, sehr,*" he replied. He must have realized from her halting speech when ordering, that she was from the school. Surely Günther brought many students here. She saw a challenge in his eyes.

"*Wo kommen Sie her?*" He asked her where she was from as he set her change on the bar next to a little Wedgwood bowl of cashews and peanuts. He picked up a glass from behind the bar and began to polish it with a white linen napkin.

Camille sipped her wine for courage and then smiled, taking up the dare. "*Ich komme von den Vereinigten Staaten.*"

This is exciting. She was actually keeping up with an easy, slowly spoken conversation.

He smiled, patiently waiting for more. The glass went around and around in his hands. She could see he was well practiced at playing along with the students.

One of the tapes she frequently listened to popped into her head. It had easy German phrases set to familiar tunes to make memorization and recall easy.

"*Ich bin Ausländer und spreche nicht gut Deutsch,*" she rejoined effortlessly, without a single stumble, telling him she was a foreigner and didn't speak German well.

He nodded his approval of her statement and its intonation. "*Nein, Sie sprechen sehr gut Deutsch.*" He contradicted her, complimenting her skill. "*Wo haben Sie Deutsch gelernt?*"

Liking him enormously for asking her the exact questions from her tape, she answered keeping her voice soft and unrushed, "*In einem Abendkurs, mit Liedern und Gesang, in der Schule.*"

He chuckled when she told him she learned her German in an evening course, by singing songs, and at school. *Well, that's what the tape said.* She couldn't help but laugh at herself. The evening course part wasn't exactly the truth, but it just popped out. Thankfully, a waitress called him over to the cocktail station and he left her with a wink and a promise to return.

Somewhat rattled, Camille straightened the collar of her white blouse and retied the maroon sweater she had draped across her shoulders for warmth. She looked into the mirror to check her reflection and saw Günther standing behind her.

He smiled when their eyes met. "I can see you are enjoying yourself."

She swiveled around, thoroughly happy to see him. His hair was combed back, still a little damp from a shower. He had a small grin on his face as if he had a secret.

"I am. Here, sit," she said, offering him the stool next to hers.

"How long have you been waiting?" he asked, resting his hands on the bar top and looking around. "I hope not too long."

"Only long enough to order a drink and lose my appetite trying to make conversation."

He laughed heartily, his eyes darkening with pleasure.

"That's not true. I was listening. You did very, very well. I give you an A."

She could feel her face warming and she knew it had nothing to do with the wine she was sipping. She fought the urge to look away.

The bartender was back. "Günther, my good man, what will you have?"

"Sean. Good to see you," he replied, pointing to Camille's wineglass. "The same."

Stena von Linné entered and took the seat next to Günther. Seated between the two women, Günther swiveled his position so he wouldn't have his back to either woman.

"*Guten Abend, Herr* Christove," Stena said in her naturally sultry voice. She took her time with every syllable as if each was an intimate friend. "I've been looking ahead to this evening with anticipation." She ran her hand slowly down his arm.

He nodded.

"*Hallo*, Camille," she added, allowing a few moments to pass so her greeting to Camille fell after the fact.

"Stena," Camille replied. With Günther blocking her, Camille couldn't see much of the young woman. At that point, several other students appeared and Günther suggested they move to the table he'd reserved.

He picked up Camille's wine glass and carried it along with his as they followed the maître d' to a big round top table next to the window, set up for nine. It had a beautiful view of the street and a fountain across the way.

"Unfortunately, a few of the others won't be here tonight," Günther said as they seated themselves. "Branwell is not feeling well and Hanna and Niclas have other plans."

Stena appeared after a trip to the ladies' room. She swished closely past Günther and Camille couldn't help but notice the sheerness of her body-hugging white dress, impudently displaying the outline of her thong underneath.

No menus were offered, for *Spatzennest* served only house specialties that the waiter rattled off too quickly for Camille to understand. Most of the others looked a bit confused too. Stena, on the other hand, was questioning the waiter in German, laughing and flirting candidly.

"I will summarize for you," Günther said. "There is a grilled pork medallion dish served with rice and butter *Gemüse*, that, as you know, are vegetables. Very tasty and healthy for those of you who are conscious of that kind of thing. Maultaschen, which is a German ravioli filled with vegetables and well-seasoned meat. It's exceptional and I recommend it highly. *Käsespätzle*, an egg noodle dish covered with a thick cheese sauce and sautéed onions. *Forelle Blau*, a fresh blue trout sautéed in a lemon butter sauce, is served with vegetables and boiled potatoes. And last, but not least, *Wiener Schnitzel* and *Bratwurst*."

Everyone ordered an entrée and a drink. Bread and butter were delivered to the table and Camille took a piece, broke it apart, put a small bite into her mouth, and the remainder on her bread plate.

"Scott, would you please tell us something about yourself so we can get better acquainted," Günther said when everyone looked content and settled.

Scott Wilkins, the bald-headed man from Canada began. "I've lived in Beaumont, Alberta, Canada, my whole life. I'm a semi-retired contractor, divorced, and want to spend some of my hard-earned money while I'm still young enough to enjoy it. I have a son and two daughters. My grandparents, on my mother's side, came to America from Stuttgart in 1898."

Camille could tell he was totally comfortable talking about himself and would probably go on for half an hour if he were given the chance.

Günther held up his hand and stopped him. "*Sehr gut, Herr* Wilkins, thank you." He looked at Angie Dirabelle, giving her the go-ahead.

"I'm seventeen years old and live in Ravello, Italy, on the Amalfi coast. I have two brothers and two sisters. I am the middle child."

Angie Dirabelle's long dark bangs, streaked with honey-blonde highlights, hid her right eye entirely. Her silver hoop earrings swung softly as she spoke, almost caressing her shoulders.

"My family comes from a long line of lemon farmers. We make Limonchello. I'm taking this class for extra credit to graduate early." She smiled and breathed a sigh of relief.

"Thank you, *Fräulein*. I have enjoyed the Limonchello from your region and can say it is the best that I've ever tasted."

The waiter was back with a full tray of drinks for the table. He passed them around and asked Camille if she'd like another glass. She shook her head no.

"*Herr* Larroux, you are next."

Konrad Larroux, the man Camille figured to be in his mid-thirties, was sturdily built, with medium-length brown hair and brown eyes. His large features made him stand out, but in an attractive sort of way.

Konrad set his bottle of *Gösser*, an Austrian beer, on the table and began. "My family owns and operates the resort of *Königsschloss*, Kings Castle, in Lucerne, Switzerland. It was built two hundred and fifty years ago by my great-great-great-grandfather and has remained in our family line ever since." He looked straight at Stena von Linné, who was swirling her glass of wine, not paying the least bit of attention to what he was saying. "I'm the Director of Tourism for the corporation, and fall in line to be the next General Overall."

That got Stena's attention. She glanced at him and smiled saucily. *Oh, brother.* Camille had to look into her wineglass to keep from rolling her eyes.

A team of waiters delivered the entrées. Keeping in line with her low-fat diet, Camille had ordered the *Forelle Blau* with new potatoes. The plump little fish, with its head still on and eyes wide open, looked up at her as if to say, *I really don't taste all that good, so you need not waste your time eating me.*

"Lena, your turn," Günther said, after swallowing a bite of his *Wiener Schnitzel* and wiping his mouth.

Lena was from Turkey and the quietest student in the class. She was paired with the boy, Niclas, who liked Hanna from France. Very thin, her weight, or lack of it, bordered on alarming, and Camille wished the young woman had ordered the *Wiener Schnitzel* with potato salad and a chocolate milk shake. Instead, she picked at her *Forelle Blau* and pushed her vegetables around on her plate; little, if anything, made it to her mouth.

"My home is Antalya, Turkey. My family farms also, but wants me to go into the tourism trade that is flourishing in Antalya. That is the reason I'm taking this class," she said, looking at Warner. "Antalya gets approximately two million tourists in the summertime to our Mediterranean coast."

"*Danke, Fräulein. Herr* Zalzamaci."

"I'm from Prague, in the Czech Republic," Timm said. "I'm nineteen years old. I am here because my father says I *have* to be here, and no other reason." That was all he offered and shoveled a huge fork full of ravioli into his mouth and started chewing.

The waiter was back with another glass of wine for Stena, a beer for Konrad, and a scotch on the rocks for Scott. "Can we hear from Camille?" Stena asked.

Günther looked at her. "Camille?"

"As some of you know, I'm from Portland, Oregon. My teenage daughter plays on the basketball and tennis teams for her school. I'm the proprietor of a gift shop in the downtown area, which I started four years ago. We're now online if anyone is interested. It's called Chocolate

Blossoms," she added after the fact. "I'm here because I enjoy learning, and seeing different parts of the world. And meeting new people."

"Are you married?" Stena asked boldly. Her sharp eyes flickered with interest.

When had this turned into a question-and-answer session? Camille pushed away a jab of irritation. "No."

Stena wasn't finished yet. "You had fun with Branwell yesterday?"

Camille and Branwell had been asked to give an accounting in class about the outing they'd taken. She'd let him do all the talking, which he fabricated with ease. When Günther had asked her what she'd liked best, she'd described her time in the candy store and the walk on the bridge.

"It was quite the adventure," she said truthfully.

"Thank you, *Frau* Ashland. Let's see. Who has not yet spoken?"

Mark raised his beer. "I'm Mark Marslino. I'm twenty-four. I'm an importer-exporter for a company in Rome. Attending a language school at least once every five years is a requirement of my job."

Mark was Stena's partner and he was totally smitten. It was easy to see she had him wrapped around her little finger, as tight as could be. From the looks Konrad had been giving Stena all evening, there was certain to be some stiff competition between the two men vying for her attention.

Camille glanced at Maria Glibrov, who hadn't yet introduced herself. She dressed modestly, almost mannishly, had long, straight brown hair. She wore very little make up, if any at all.

"I'm Maria Glibrov and I am eighteen years old." She looked around the table, touching each person with her gaze.

"I come from the Republic of Macedonia, which gained its independence from Yugoslavia in 1991. My family, men and woman alike, fought in the war for freedom. Many died. I was too young to fight then, but would do it now if I had to."

Her voice was hard, her expression defiant, as if she had something to prove.

Obviously interested in the girl as an oddity, Stena asked, "And why are you here?"

Without pause, Maria answered, "Knowledge is power."

Everyone looked a little uncomfortable.

Günther nodded. "*Fräulein* von Linné, you are last. Will you please tell us about yourself and afterward we will order dessert. *Spatzennest* is famous for its strudel and I hope everyone will try it."

"You all know my name, Stena von Linné," she began, unrushed and confident, brushing her silky hair over her shoulder with her right hand. "I'm twenty-four, and come from Uppsala, Sweden."

Mark and Konrad sat transfixed by her melodic voice, content to stare at her even if she were to go on all evening. It was evident she was used to center stage. She worked the table with animation, eye contact, and pauses, smiling at just the right moment, and by no means giving anyone the opportunity to break in. Camille wished she had a tenth of the confidence Stena possessed.

"There are four girls in my family, of which I am the youngest. My grandfather, Aaron August Linné, was a Swedish chemist and one of the founders of the science of physical chemistry in Sweden. My uncle, Fran Smale, is a Swedish diplomat and politician. He was the Swedish Minister for Foreign Affairs and now is the head of the

United Nations Monitoring Verification and Inspection Commission. He controls…"

"Ahh, *here* is our waiter now. Thank you, *Fräulein*." Günther said, breaking her long-winded, pretentious decree. "We will have nine strudels mit *Schlagsahne, bitte*," he said to the waiter. "Whipped cream."

"Certainly, *Herr* Christove," the waiter replied, as he cleared away the dinner plates and, with his small silver tool, scraped the crumbs from the white linen tablecloth. After dessert and Günther had paid the bill, some of the students left and some returned to the bar area. Camille had the maître d' call for a taxi.

"Your taxi," the bartender said, when a long black Mercedes cab stopped in front. She looked to the group and said her good-byes, thanking Günther for the lovely evening. The friendly bartender gave her a wave.

The driver got out and opened the back door of the cab. When she glanced back at the restaurant, she noticed a tall figure standing in the shadows between the restaurant and the adjoining building. In the evening darkness, splashed with lights from the restaurant, the whole thing looked surreal and foreboding. A niggle of apprehension slipped up her spine. "*Fräulein?*"

Camille should have felt flattered that the driver thought her that young. Instead, a dark premonition unsettled her thoughts. She glanced back. Whoever it was, was now gone. "Uh…district three, *bitte*," she said. "*Hollandstraße* 7688."

The cab started off.

Chapter Thirteen

Before Florian opened his eyes, he ran through the Divine Praises in his mind. *Blessed be God. Blessed be His Holy Name. Blessed be Jesus Christ, true God and true man…*

When he was finished, he thanked God for another day and consecrated himself to the Holy Spirit, asking for assistance in sanctifying everyone and everything he came into contact with this day.

Now fully awake, he rolled out of the warmth of his covers before his alarm sounded and he was tempted to lie there an extra five minutes. He looked at his clock. Five a.m. He twisted the knob on the radiator along his bedroom wall, and then glanced at his calendar. First Friday of Lent. He was on the schedule tonight for the Stations of the Cross and to head the soup and bread dinner put on by the *Jungschar*, the very active youth group in his parish. Then on Saturday, he and Günther had their English class for underprivileged children, something he really enjoyed. He pulled on his sweatpants and sweatshirt, then donned his running shoes. In the bathroom, he splashed his face once and was out the door quietly, so as not to wake anyone else.

The neighborhood was dark and still asleep. A dog barked a couple of blocks over. He looked at his wristwatch, gauged his time, and turned left, beginning the course he ran three times a week.

He warmed up slowly and then settled into his rhythm, sucking the cold, crisp air deep into his lungs. Joy for life filled his heart. He offered a few morning prayers of thanksgiving for his life and this new day, his vocation and his parish, as he lengthened his stride in order to cover the six miles in fifty-five minutes, no longer.

If he could choose, Wolfgang and Helene Eberstark would be his first choice as parents for Johann, he thought as he ran down the street. But they had already been blessed with three children and were on a very tight budget. Especially since Helene had given up her lucrative art curator's position at *Galerie der modernen Kunst*. Supporting a foster child would be very difficult.

Rounding the corner, the awesome sight of St. Peter's Church stood before him. He came this way often, just so he could see the dramatic baroque structure in the rosy light of dawn. It was gorgeous and he offered a thanksgiving for it as he took in the banquet of splendor. Its façade of angled towers, elegant steeples, and blue-green domes was awe-inspiring. He crossed *Peterplatz* in only a few strides, and turned onto Der Graben. He jumped a puddle of greasy water on the uneven cobblestone street.

Ahead, between the *Hauptpost* Building and VKB Bank, were two provocatively dressed women. They laughed and smoked cigarettes, looking very out of place in evening attire, with tall heels and black stockings. The length of their skirts left little to the imagination. Besides Florian, they were the only two people on the street. They watched his approach with interest.

"*Guten Morgen*," he called to them politely when he was within hearing distance.

They smiled and nodded.

He stopped beside them breathing hard, his hand on his side, his forehead moist.

"*Hallo*," the younger one said, blowing smoke coyly into the air. Her bleached blonde hair was stringy and her eyes were heavily shadowed.

"*Hallo*," he responded. She didn't look a day over sixteen. The older woman had short jet-black hair and looked around eighteen. She eyed him suspiciously.

"*Polizei*," she whispered into her friend's ear.

They would probably prefer he was a police officer rather than a priest. "*Ein Polizist*," he repeated, laughing. "No."

"*Wie heißen Sie?*" He asked their names.

"*Ich bin* Hilda," the youngest said. "*Sie heißt Rosa.*"

"*Ah, Hilda und Rosa, Freut mich sehr Sie kennen zu lernen*," he said, very pleased to meet them. Now that he was closer, he could see that their clothes were tattered and worn. If a wind came up, it would blow them away for their thinness.

Before either one could proposition him in any way and embarrass everyone concerned, he hurriedly invited both to join him for coffee and dessert, something scrumptious and all they could eat, at his place tomorrow morning, at seven thirty.

It must have been the best offer they'd had on this cold March morning because Rosa asked for the address. He reached into his pocket and drew out two business cards, giving one to each girl. He always carried his cards for precisely this reason. He never knew when God would drop a golden opportunity right into his lap—or running route.

They looked at the card and then into his face. The younger of the two started to back away slowly.

"*Nein, nein*," he pleaded low. "*Bitte kommen Sie.*" He put out his hand in supplication as he told them he hoped that they would come for Mass at seven, but if they didn't want to do that and only felt like coffee and sweets, to arrive at seven forty-five. That his English class was more fun than work. There would be other kids their age there too. He gave a wave and started down the street at a jog.

Camille's alarm sounded at five thirty, waking her from a fitful sleep. She lay in her warm bed for a few minutes, listening to the breeze as it pushed a branch against her windowpane.

She was tired today after her night out on the town. She stretched, remembering the whole evening of enjoyment. Even Stena's behavior hadn't spoiled the two and a half hours sitting next to Günther and listening to him talk. When the alarm sounded again, she switched it off and pushed back the warm, downy comforter. It was time to get up.

Nothing but quiet below. *Am I the first one up?* Slipping on her robe, she descended the steps admiring the yellow walls. She would paint the inside of Chocolate Blossoms the exact same shade when she got home, to remind herself of her time spent here.

About halfway down the staircase, Camille heard someone in the kitchen. Must be Helene putting on the coffee. She rounded the corner and stopped. At first glimpse, she wasn't quite sure what she was looking at. Then as she stared in disbelief, her senses quivered, not recognizing if what was before her was a natural phenomenon.

There was a tower in the kitchen.

A pillar of cans and boxes, cups, plates, saucers, and silverware, a queer-looking obelisk that pierced the room's cozy charm with an unearthly sense.

Sasha stood on tiptoe on a chair that was placed on the countertop. She reached up as she tried to place a round spice shaker on the top of a can of beets. The tower she'd created was taller than Camille by several feet, and eerie in its steadiness. Intent on her mission, Sasha hadn't noticed her entrance, or the small sound of distress that escaped from Camille's throat.

Günther checked his watch as he took the steps to the nursing home two at a time. He let himself in with a key, walked down the hall, and entered the third room on the right.

Aggie had been attended to already this morning. She was awake and looked as if she'd come through the effects of the small stroke, as was her pattern. Her gray hair was combed back from her face and hooked neatly behind her ears. A fresh pitcher of ice water sat on the table by her bedside. The pillows behind her were plumped and fluffed, the blue eyelet coverlet folded neatly at the foot of the twin bed.

Breakfast would arrive soon.

"*Guten Morgen, Mutti*, I'm glad to see you are doing better today," he breathed happily to the old woman as he stopped at her bedside. He leaned down and placed a kiss on her warm forehead.

"Look," he said, holding out a small cluster of flowers in his hand. "Aren't they pretty?" He didn't expect an answer as he went about filling a vase with water from the sink in her bathroom.

"There." He placed the daisies on the windowsill directly in line of her view after he'd drawn the heavy curtains open.

"*Frühstück*," the nurse called in a singsong voice as she came in with a tray of hot porridge, coffee, and a little pitcher of milk.

Günther clapped his hands together cheerfully. "*Wunderbar. Danke sehr, Frau* Blitter."

The nurse set the tray on the nightstand and looked at Günther with an expectant expression. When he had time, he preferred to feed his mother-in-law himself, giving him something to do and talk about during his visit. It could be a challenge thinking up things to say in a one-sided conversation. Food was always a big help.

He pulled a chair next to her bedside.

"*Du bist nichts als Dreck*," she murmured under her breath, calling him nothing but dirt.

"Ah, so you can speak." He ignored the content of her address. He was used to it, and worse. "I've been wondering about that."

"*Dreck*," she said again with distaste. She turned her head and looked at him through shrewd eyes.

She'd been holding out, a trick she liked to use to confuse the nurse and doctor. One she'd used many times over the years.

"Not so," he said matter-of-factly, refuting her claim of him.

He picked up the small pitcher of milk and added some to her porridge. Next, he opened a package of sugar and sprinkled it on, then stirred well with the spoon. He added sugar and milk to her coffee, blew on it a few times to cool it down, and held the cup to her lips.

Aggie tried to hold out. Stubbornness was her best quality. But as the rich aroma danced up into her nostrils, her will crumbled and her lips opened just a crack, and took the warm liquid in.

He smiled and nodded. "Good."

She took another sip.

The nurse stuck her head in the room, smiled at Günther, and asked him if he'd like a cup of coffee. He declined and tried giving Aggie a spoonful of the porridge. Her hunger always won out sooner or later over her mulish determination, and she'd end up eating.

He scooped a small amount of the hot cereal onto the spoon and was able to get some into her mouth through her lips.

She made a face and stuck out her tongue, letting the porridge fall to the towel he'd placed on her chest. "*Beschissen.*" She called it shitty and gave him a chilling smile.

Günther looked away and counted silently to five. If he gave in to the temptation of a response, her distasteful behavior worsened. He'd learned to keep his cool. Katerina would expect that of him.

He scooped up another bite and held up the spoon. "*Bitte, Mutti?*"

She just looked at him.

It was no use. Bitterness filled her heart. She'd not oblige him in the least just because he said please. "Okay, suit yourself," he said in English, knowing perfectly well she understood. "It's time for me to go. *Frau* Blitter will finish up here."

He stood and kissed her forehead. As he left the room, he passed *Frau* Blitter in the hallway and shook his head, telling her she'd have to finish feeding Aggie her morning meal.

Outside on the stoop, Günther buttoned up his black wool overcoat. He looked up and down the street and then ran across, jaywalking.

He longed to believe Aggie's malicious display toward him was a result of the many small strokes that had followed her big one. That she couldn't help it or didn't know the filth that she spewed. He'd read of such cases. Some patients, after suffering a stroke or a series of seizures, could do nothing but utter foul language and curses. It was a condition of the brain and nothing intentional.

Unfortunately, this was not the case with his mother-in-law. Aggie hated him. She had ever since he and Katerina ran away and married, squelching all Aggie's dreams of Katerina becoming an actress. Katerina had begged and pleaded with her mother to understand that acting wasn't her dream at all. She loved Günther and wanted nothing more than to be his wife. He'd hoped after Nikolaus was born, Aggie's ugliness would wane and she'd take to him and her grandson. Unfortunately, that was not to be.

Chapter Fourteen

Wolfgang, Helene, and Camille stood in the threshold of the kitchen in stunned silence.

"What?" Helene finally managed to get out through her strangled throat. The single word was high-pitched and terrified. "W-What is it?"

Sasha moved in a trance-like state, unmindful of being watched.

"I have no idea," her husband whispered back. His police training dictated his ability to maintain calm, a disciplined control, but the wobble in his voice gave him away. "It's like she doesn't know we are here or…"

Sasha climbed down from the chair, interrupting his statement, and now stood on the shiny surface of the granite countertop. From her hands and knees, she reached down into the open drawer and grabbed a handful of spoons. Serenely, she went about carefully and with calculation, sticking them here and there into her unnerving creation, like a music box's spindly-pronged mechanism.

Chills ran unchecked up and down Camille's spine. She knew she was witnessing something exceedingly abnormal and in no way a typical three-year-old prank. Why this spectacle made her so frightened, she didn't quite know, except that it was like something in a science fiction movie, completely off the chart for normal behavior. She shifted her gaze over to Wolfgang and Helene.

Wolfgang took a step forward. "Sasha?" His hair was rumpled from sleep. Fire engine red pajama bottoms hung loose around his hips and his feet had a sparse covering of dark hair over his toes. A small butterfly tattoo stood out on his left shoulder.

Sasha gave no reply.

"*Liebling*," he called again softly, but the spoken endearment still brought no response.

When Wolfgang took another step, she stopped mid-reach, suspended in time, holding her pose for several seconds while never taking her eyes off the tower. Then, as if someone flipped a switch, she continued.

Helene, who wore only her pink camisole top and short tap-pants bottoms, reached out and took Camille's hand in her own. Camille felt her quiver and heard the shallowness of her breathing.

Wolfgang reached out. "Sasha." It was low, barely audible. He was a couple of steps from the tower, in direct line of Sasha's vision.

She looked past the tower at her father.

"*Vati?*"

Camille let out a breath. It was as if the trance-like state evaporated, and the Sasha she knew was back. Her eyes sparkled. "*Vati?*" she said again in question, her voice high and uneven.

Wolfgang stepped forward, lifted his daughter off the counter, and carried her into the living room. Cradling the child in his arms, he sat on the sofa. Helene and Camille followed and sat on either side of them. Helene reached out and took Sasha from his arms to hold her close. The look that passed between husband and wife spoke volumes.

"I'll ask around the department for the name of whom she should see," Wolfgang said, watching as Helene rocked her back and forth.

Petra came into the room, her brow marred with worry. "*Mutti, was ist los in der Küche?*"

"I will tell you later," Helene replied. "Just go get ready for school. And tell Patrick to get ready quickly. *Vati* will drop you off early."

Camille sat on the sofa as the family dispersed, leaving her with Helene and Sasha. Sasha got up and followed her sister out of the room. "What can I do to help, Helene?"

"I don't know. I don't know what is going on. I'm frightened. I didn't hear anything this morning, or any noise in the kitchen as she made that detestable thing." Tears slipped from her eyes and ran down both cheeks. She wiped them away with the back of her hand.

"I'll take it down," Camille said.

Helene shook her head in protest. "No, you have your class to go to."

"I want to help," Camille replied firmly. "I'll take care of the kitchen. You go get your shower and get ready for the day. I'm sure you'll want to be ready if Wolfgang can get an appointment with someone today."

Patrick walked by the kitchen slowly, looked in, and his eyes grew round. His sister must have filled him in with the little information that she'd gotten from her mother.

Helene got up and returned to her bedroom, and Camille went into the kitchen to make the coffee. She tried to ignore the looming object as she filled the coffeemaker with coffee and water. Helene appeared and the tension in her voice showed how shaken she was still. "I'm going to go in with Wolfgang now. We'll take the kids to school and then see about Sasha right away. Thank you for doing this for me."

"It's not a problem at all," Camille responded. "Things will all be where they should when you get home.

It took Camille several hours to disassemble the tower. It was tricky and Camille still couldn't understand how Sasha had built it so tall and balanced all by herself. As careful as Camille had been, more than a few cups and plates had fallen to the ground, smashing into hundreds of hazardous shards. At the moment, a rainbow of bright colors covered the tile floor.

Camille startled at the sudden ring of the phone. She picked her way carefully across the littered kitchen floor and got to the phone on the third ring. "Hello?"

"Camille, it's Günther."

She glanced at the kitchen clock. It was already ten thirty.

"Is everything okay?" he asked.

"I'm sorry. I should have called you to let you know I wouldn't be in class today. The time just got away from me."

"Are you all right?" His voice sounded guarded.

"Yes. But something really weird is going on with Sasha. I stayed home to help Helene as best I could."

"Sasha?" The concern in his voice was thick. "Is she hurt?"

"Not hurt. But she's acting bizarre and doing strange things. Wolfgang and Helene took the children and left early this morning. They're trying to talk with someone today, a doctor, and maybe even get her seen by a specialist. With

Wolfgang's connections, they felt sure that they would be able to. Hopefully get some answers."

"Acting weird? Like what?"

"Last night she slapped Helene in the face. That alone had them upset. This morning was worse. When I came down for coffee, I found her alone in the kitchen. It was very early and she must have been awake for hours. She was in a dreamlike state and had built a tower almost to the ceiling from anything and everything she could find in the kitchen. I couldn't have done it the way she did, very balanced and symmetrical. No way. Just taking it down was difficult. That's what I've been doing this morning. Trying to get it down without breaking every dish and cup they own. I'm not doing a very good job, I'm afraid."

He was silent for a few moments. Finally, he asked, "Do they have any ideas what could be the cause?"

"Not yet. I'm waiting to hear."

"How are you?" he asked her. "Is there anything I can do to help?"

His phone call had helped already. Just the sound of his voice calmed her roiling stomach and brought back some sort of stability. A warm, wonderful sensation started to warm her insides.

"I'm okay. I'll be better though when they call or come home. I'm really worried."

"That's understandable. I'm giving you my cell number. Let me know what they find out."

She found a pencil in the desk drawer and took his number.

"Don't worry. You can call anytime. Day or night. For anything."

She smiled. "Thank you."

"The morning break is almost over so I better get going." His voice was easy on her heart, calming. "Remember to let me know."

"Okay, I will," Camille promised. "And thank you so much for calling."

"You're welcome. *Tschüss.*"

They hung up and Camille went in search of a broom and dustpan. If she didn't hurry up, they might get home before she had it all swept up and put away. She found what she was looking for in the hall closet that led to the garage, and set to work.

Finally finished, Camille ran upstairs and took a five-minute shower. She donned a clean pair of jeans and a sweater. She applied the minimum of makeup to her face and ran the brush through her hair.

It was almost lunchtime, but the thought of food of any kind made her stomach queasy. All she had to do was to think of that *thing*, and everything flew out of her mind and shivers ran up her back. She glanced around. *I need a distraction.*

She plunked herself down on the sofa and clicked on the television.

A cooking show flashed on. The chef spoke so swiftly Camille only caught a word here and there. He must be a comedian, for the audience was laughing at almost everything he said. Amidst one uproar of laughter and applause, Camille almost missed the ring of the doorbell.

She ran to the door and looked out the peephole.

Stephen Turner? She looked around the room as if there was something that could circumvent his visit. He knocked.

Camille opened the door. "Stephen, hello."

His expression said he knew that he was calling at an inopportune time.

"Camille? I'm sorry to surprise you like this. I was in the neighborhood and decided to stop on the off chance you might be at home. Actually, I didn't think you'd be here. But I'm glad now that you are."

He was rambling and she was embarrassed for him. She stood in the doorway like a sentinel, not knowing if she should invite him in or not. Finally, pressure to be polite won out over her caution, and she stepped back in invitation.

"Would you like to come in?"

"Oh, maybe for a moment, if you have the time."

"Of course."

She showed him into the living room and clicked off the TV. "Can I get you something? I was about to fix myself a cup of hot tea."

"Yes, thank you. That sounds great." He looked around at the quiet house then took the computer case from his shoulder and set it onto the coffee table. "Anyone else here?"

She started for the kitchen and pretended his question didn't startle her. "No, but I expect Helene any moment."

He followed her into the kitchen and looked around as she filled the kettle and set it on the stove to warm. He wore the same style of casual slacks he'd worn on the flight and a heavy navy sweater worn over a button-down shirt. It was an attractive look but it wasn't office attire. He must be off today.

"Pull up a seat," she said gesturing to the stool under the counter. "How have you been?"

It was a ridiculous question considering she'd only met him five days prior. She considered just how little she actually knew about the man sitting across from her. Now that she gave it some thought, his name, and the fact that he drove a Budget Rent-A-Car, were the only two things she actually knew.

"Just working mostly. I took in an art show last evening in the *Freihaus Quartier*, in the Fourth District. Have you been there?"

She shook her head.

"A new Italian artist. Too contemporary for me. Other than that, nothing exciting."

Camille poured two cups of raspberry tea and set one in front of Stephen. She set out the sugar bowl and poured milk into a pitcher. The image of it wedged in between a cup and box of crackers in the heart of the tower made her inwardly cringe. "What is it you do here in Vienna, Stephen?"

"Actually, Camille, I'm not at liberty to say. Let's just say I work for the United States government."

She could believe that. He fit the profile of an agent in a Tom Clancy movie. Tall, smart, a bit on the secretive side. It wasn't the answer she'd prefer to hear. Something calm and neutral and middle of the road, like a teacher or banker, would have been much more to her liking.

"Oh." She tried to think of something clever to add but she was drawing a blank.

"You're not in class today," he stated, an interested look in his eyes.

"No. I took a day off." Irritation rippled within.

"How is the German coming?"

"*Gut*," she said and smiled. "It's fun and we do a lot of social things too. I've enjoyed this week immensely." That was if she didn't count the unnerving encounters with

Branwell, almost being run down by Father Florian, and now this mystery with Sasha.

He slouched on the stool and rested a forearm on the counter. "There must be a lot of interesting people in your class."

Was he being friendly or just plain nosy? "Interesting in what way?"

"I don't know. Different from what you're used to in Portland."

She sipped her tea and savored its pleasant flavor. This conversation was becoming a bit of a struggle. She tried to remember when she had told him that she was from Portland. "The class is full of eccentrics, so to speak. Revolutionists, heirs to Swiss castles, along with a self-proclaimed princess. Nevertheless, I like it. It seems I've been ready for a change, *this change*, all my life and didn't even realize it. I'm taking one day at a time so I don't waste a minute. Enough about me. Where do you live when you're in the US?"

"Sorry…" he began.

"You can't tell me *that*, either?" She lifted an eyebrow and laughed, but cautioned herself to measure her every word from here on out. "Okay. Then tell me something about yourself that you *can* share."

He winked. "I'm just teasing. I was raised in Richmond but live now in DC."

The phone rang. It was Helene. They were taking Sasha to a clinic in another town. Camille wasn't sure of the town or where it was but scribbled down the name and several phone numbers.

They were leaving the twins with Helene's mother in *Perchtoldsdorf*, a small village twelve kilometers southwest of

Vienna. Helene asked if Camille would be okay alone for a few days without them. She reminded Camille to use the moped or anything else in the house she needed and apologized for the upheaval.

She hung up.

"Problem?" Stephen asked.

"No, not really. You were saying?" She wasn't going to share personal information.

"I've been traveling for work to Vienna for the past seven years. I know the city very well and wanted to know if I could take you to dinner some night soon? This weekend, actually."

Camille could feel the shocked look on her face.

"I hope I'm not rushing you," he continued. "The fact is, I know some really fine restaurants here in the city that only the locals know, and I'd like to share them with you. Since you are only here for two months, I don't have time to waste."

He had her over a barrel now. She could hardly turn him down without saying outright that she didn't like him. He knew she didn't know anyone and had an open calendar. And it wasn't that she didn't want to go, it was just she didn't really know if she wanted to go. She was ambivalent.

"Well, tonight is impossible." It was. With everything up in the air with Sasha. She wanted to stay right here by the phone.

"Tomorrow then. Six o'clock."

He certainly was persistent. She ran it over in her mind. By then, she would have heard from Helene and things would be a little more settled. She looked at him again.

"Come on. Even old-fashioned girls have to eat."

That made her laugh.

He smiled.

"Okay," she accepted. "Since you put it like that."

He brightened. "I thought that I had offended you. I'm glad that's not the case."

"No. Not the case at all. But I'll meet you at the restaurant because I have a busy day tomorrow." That was sort of the truth.

"Fair enough." He took a pen from his breast coat pocket and wrote down an address on a piece of scratch paper she handed him. He slid it over the counter so she could read it. *Bohème, Spittelberggasse* 19, Seventh District.

"Is six good?"

"Six should be fine."

The phone rang again and Camille quickly picked it up and greeted the caller.

"It's Stephanie. About time we talked," she said in a playfully curt tone.

"Steph. You won't believe everything that's happened. I've lived a lifetime in one week. I have so much to tell you."

Camille darted a quick look at Stephen. When the phone had rung, he'd gotten up and went into the living room where he was meandering around. He looked engrossed in some photographs on the wall, and then gazed thoughtfully into the office from its threshold.

"Like?" Stephanie asked.

"I have a visitor here at the moment so I can't go into all the fun details. But I'm healthy, with no problems."

"You're taking your low-dose aspirin every day?"

"Of course."

"Exercising?"

"You bet. Today's the first day I've missed. Maybe I'll go out a little later for a speed walk. But then again, maybe not.

It's clouding up and might start to rain. I'm having a wonderful time, though. How's Kristin?"

"Good. But she misses you. She has a crush on a boy who just moved into town and is new in class. Scott Taylor. I told her she can't do anything with him until you get home."

"A boyfriend? Wow, that's a milestone." Sadness at missing such an important moment in her daughter's life gave her pause.

"Camille? You still there?"

Camille glanced at Stephen. He was now looking out the front window. If she didn't know better, she'd think he was casing the place.

"How's Mom?"

"Fine. She's been working at the store regularly to help on the busy days. The girls say she's an angel and a fantastic help. I think even after you're home she'll want to be a regular."

"That's an incredible idea. It'll be great to have her there with me. I really hate to cut this short, Steph, but I better go. I'll call you back later."

She hung up and joined Stephen, who was now flipping through a magazine he'd picked up from the coffee table.

"Sorry about that."

"Not a problem. I have to run. Thanks for the tea and conversation."

"Well, there wasn't too much conversation, but you're welcome. I'll see you tomorrow night at *Bohème*."

He was standing in the open doorway, keys in hand and his computer case handle slung over his shoulder. "Looking forward to it. See ya then."

She shut the door and took the paper from her pocket that had Günther's cell phone number. Returning to the kitchen, she sat where Stephen had been and dialed the number.

"Günther Christove," his message began.

The instant she recognized it was his recorded phone message, a jolt of disappointment made her sag. She waited until it finished and left him a message about Sasha and what Helene had told her. Of course, he'd still be in class. It was only one o'clock.

Camille folded her arms on the countertop and rested her forehead. She closed her eyes. A light smattering of rain pitter-pattered on the dormered roof in the living room. As she relaxed, Camille thought about her heart attack, recovery, and what it meant in the big picture of her life. How far she was from home. Kristin and a boyfriend. Were they all anxiously awaiting her return—or learning to get along fine without her? What was happening at Chocolate Blossoms? She'd had very little news, making a conscious effort not to think about it, worry, or call the girls to ask about things. She'd been tempted a few times to look up the website online, but decided not to, giving it a clean break for the time she was here.

Slowly her thoughts turned to Günther in class, giving a lecture or relating some amusing anecdote. Günther laughing and smiling into her eyes. Father Florian, little Johann, troubled Sasha, Stephen Turner, and even Branwell. All the people and things that had made her first week in Vienna noteworthy. In such a short time, she had morphed from the woman who had boarded that plane almost one week ago to someone very different.

A clap of thunder sat her bolt upright, all mental musings now forgotten. She dashed up the stairs quickly to shut her window. She closed it and locked the latch.

Camille sat on her bed as darkness slowly enveloped her room. It felt unfamiliar and a bit unnerving. Outside, the normally busy neighborhood looked deserted and quiet. She clicked on her bedside lamp and turned on the radio, dispelling the quietness of the house. The rain started coming down in force.

Her light winked and went out.

Chapter Fifteen

Florian and Günther stood when *Frau* Blutel, the rectory secretary, showed Elizabeth Roth, the head of the Child Protection *Büro*, into his office. Florian steeled his resolve. He'd had many dealings with this woman and was not looking forward to today.

The stern-looking, middle-aged Englishwoman crossed her legs and smoothed her black skirt as she sat in the chair opposite his desk. Günther took the chair against the wall.

From the doorway, *Frau* Blutel asked if anyone would like anything, tea or coffee? Ms. Roth shook her head as she pulled a packet of papers from her briefcase.

"*Nein, danke, Frau* Blutel," Florian responded. His secretary nodded politely and quietly closed the door.

"I have meticulously reviewed Johann's file, *Herr Pfarrer* Christove. Until Johann's uncle, Bernhard Wernfried, is found, and agrees to waive his guardianship for Johann to another responsible party as you think he should do, the boy must be moved to the group facility immediately."

Florian knew Johann would founder in the overcrowded boarding school located in Augsburg, the small German city just north of Munich. Florian had been there on several occasions. It was cold and drafty. Scant rations were routine and it was woefully understaffed. No. It was no place for Johann, even for a short time.

She homed in on him with her hawk-like stare. "The family from your parish that is caring for him now is not in the foster care system. He cannot remain there."

The woman was only doing what she must, following the law. Actually, he'd expected to see Ms. Roth yesterday, the same day that he'd made the call to her office. He'd worked with her on several occasions and knew that she followed the book to the letter.

But they needed time to locate Bernhard. If Johann fell back into the endless cycle of temporary homes, moving every few months as he had done before coming to live in Vienna with his uncle, it would break his spirit. And more than that, Florian was certain that this time it would also break his heart.

It would be worse still if the agency left him with Bernhard. It was only a matter of time until something terrible happened. Disappointingly, not a trace of Bernhard Wernfried had been seen since his disappearance two days ago. He had called Günther demanding Johann back but hadn't left any information on where he was living or where he could be reached by phone. And now Wolfgang, who was handling the case personally, was gone for a few days and had had to turn the case over to one of his captains.

"A little time is all we're asking for, Ms. Roth," Florian said. He leaned forward in his chair so he looked straight into her eyes. "Johann is happy with the Weissmans. They're a loving family with a mother and father present in the home. He shares a room with two other boys. He's able to stay in his class, with the same teacher he's had for the past year. His grades have made a dramatic improvement since coming to Vienna and working with Günther. His life is stable, so to speak."

"I understand, *Herr Pfarrer* Christove. I've been by the Weissmans' this morning."

Ms. Roth looked unmoved.

"Packing him up and relocating him now could be very damaging. One more week. That is all that we ask," Günther added. His tone was flat. Temper controlled.

"*Herr Pfarrer* Christove," Ms. Roth began again, totally ignoring Günther's comment. The two had a strained relationship, at best.

"Can you give us that?" Günther pressed.

Florian flashed Günther a pointed glance. He'd given him explicit orders to let him do the talking. Elizabeth Roth didn't like Günther. They'd had two disagreements regarding Johann, and Günther, pushed to his limit, had not handled the situations well.

"*Herr Pfarrer* Christove—" Breaking off her sentence, she sat looking at him for several long moments. Her expression hardened. "*Herr Pfarrer* Christove," she began again. "I suppose you are only trying to help Johann. But haven't we been through situations similar to this before? Several times, as I recall. I understand that you think what you are doing is best, but we have procedures. Rules are to be followed and not broken."

Günther made a sound in his throat.

"One week?" Florian asked.

"And in that week, if something happens to Johann, you will be responsible. Are you able to accept that liability?"

He nodded.

"Your bishop, he would approve?"

That was a good question. One he would rather not think about right at this moment.

She didn't wait for him to answer her question. She looked at her watch and stood. He and Günther followed. She gathered her papers and put them back into her briefcase.

"I don't like you, *Herr Pfarrer* Christove," she said looking down her nose at him, "or your sanctimonious brother. Your kind always believe they know more than a trained professional, one who works with cases like this one, day in and day out."

Without looking, Florian could feel Günther bristle, imagine his face flushing.

"These *cases* have *names*, Ms. Roth," Günther said, his voice low.

"Since I do not have a place to put Johann at the moment, I will give you until Monday to locate his uncle, *Herr* Wernfried. Until then, I will leave Johann where he is with the Weissmans. When *Herr* Wernfried is located, it will be best if you remember that he has every right to take Johann wherever he wants. He is the boy's legal guardian. Do not plan any more dramatic rescues."

"That man is a menace and danger to Johann. How you close your eyes to his drinking and drug abuse is criminal," Günther challenged.

"Prescription drugs. I've told you that before, *Herr* Christove." Her tone fairly sizzled.

Florian came around the desk to stand between them.

"Thank you for the extra time, Ms. Roth." Actually, Florian was stunned at this turn of events. At least they had a few extra days. He had not expected it. They walked together into the reception area.

"You're welcome. Be assured, it is not because of your bleeding Catholic hearts," she said sarcastically, her mouth pulling down at the corners. "Just don't make me regret my decision."

"No. No. Of course not," he quickly said. "We will watch Johann very closely."

Florian and Günther watched her go.

When she was gone, *Frau* Blutel looked up from her work, a pained expression marring her normally pleasant face.

Florian smiled and gave her a thumbs-up. At least they had the weekend to find Bernhard. It wasn't much time, but it was far better than nothing.

Florian turned and drilled his brother with an ice-cold stare, ready to reprimand him for challenging Ms. Roth, but Günther ignored him and snatched up his jacket. "I have to get back to class. I'll talk to you later."

Günther gazed through the classroom window at the dark clouds surrounding the city like a sodden black blanket. The streets below were relatively empty, save for a few brave souls running for the restaurant across the street before the clouds let loose.

The affairs of late had him down. First it was Camille's troubling news about Sasha, and now Johann.

It was crucial that they locate the boy's uncle before the coming week. That may prove to be impossible given the man's seedy connections and his ability to disappear into the inner workings of the city's heart.

"*Herr* Christove, is something troubling you?" Stena von Linné asked, her brow furrowed in worry. She looked over his shoulder and through the window to see what he was looking at. Her hair hung freely around her shoulders.

"*Nein*, Stena. Just watching the goings-on outside. It'll rain soon." She wrinkled her nose, presumably, he thought, over the possibility of getting drenched on her way home.

"Tell me, how are you getting along this term? You are staying at the *Pension Pertschy*, are you not?"

"Yes." She seemed pleased that he knew this fact about her. He made it his business to see to all his students' comfort.

"How do you like it?"

"Very much. My room and board there is a gift from my Uncle Fran. He wanted me to enjoy myself to the fullest while here in Vienna. My room has a wonderful view of the courtyard."

"I know it well."

She raised her brows.

Their tête-à-tête was drawing the attention of the other students, who were supposed to be working on a writing assignment. Konrad Larroux and Mark Marslino watched them with interest.

"And The *Graben*. Are you discovering the social diversity and cultural richness of the famous street?" he asked.

If it was possible, her face brightened even more. "It's marvelous. The shopping is splendid and the restaurants are to die for. It's impossible not to love the car-free street with all its treasures. I'm having so much fun."

She stopped suddenly as if an idea had crossed her mind. "*Herr* Christove," she began, her expression beseeching. "My uncle is coming for a visit to Vienna next week. I want *very much* for the two of you to meet. Can you make the time to have dinner with us one evening?"

When Günther didn't answer immediately she continued, "Do you remember? He's the head of the United Nations Monitoring Verification and Inspection Commission."

"We'll see, Stena. It'll depend which night and what I have on my schedule." Günther lowered his voice and said, "You should take your seat now. If you remain here much longer, you will cause an uprising from all the young men in this class. They can only stand so much."

She laughed lightly, then made her way back to her desk, much to Mark and Konrad's relief. And his too.

Camille stepped carefully from the tiny shower stall, chastising herself for being so skittish. Ever since the lights had gone out and stayed off for ten minutes, her nerves were on edge. She grabbed a fluffy white towel from one of the recessed nooks and wrapped it around her wet body.

As she dried one leg and then the other, she smiled, thinking about Günther and the fact that he'd helped build this area. The bathroom was steamy. With her washcloth, Camille wiped off the hand-painted oval mirror.

A shriek ripped from her throat.

A woman's face reflected in the mirror as if she stood behind Camille. It was gone in one fleeting moment, but not before Camille lunged in fright, knocking her hairbrush and blow-dryer from the pedestal sink, clattering to the floor.

Still shaking, she knew if she didn't confront her fears now, she'd never make it through the night. She turned around slowly. Only the picture of a chalet perched on a flowering mountainside hung on the wall. It had black and white cows and was actually very charming. The windows did resemble eyes. If she stretched her imagination, perhaps the tail of the tiger-striped cat looked a bit like curving lips. She paused and listened to the rain on the roof, willing her pulse to slow down. The storm was getting the best of her.

For goodness' sake. Stop acting like a ninny. She finished with her toiletries and slipped into her pajamas and robe. All done, she closed the door to the bathroom and sank down into the chair in the corner. She clicked on the reading light.

The house was so quiet.

So empty.

Without Wolfgang, Helene, and the children it felt strange. *For the first time since arriving in Vienna, I'm lonely.* She sipped her lukewarm tea and tossed around the idea of reheating it downstairs.

Keeping busy all day had been a test. She'd updated her journal. Reviewed vocabulary words so she wouldn't be behind in class. She'd searched the house for candles, just in case the power went out again later on. She wouldn't get caught unprepared this time. Around three, she had bundled up, took Helene's umbrella, and went out for a walk. She'd made her way through the driving rain to a small corner store and picked up a few things for supper.

She glanced at the phone, wishing that Helene would call and update her on Sasha. What on earth was wrong with the child? She wished Stephanie were here now for support and help. She read stacks of medical journals and was excellent at diagnosis. Maybe she would have some ideas.

It was only nine o'clock, but Camille's eyelids sagged. She clicked off the reading lamp by the chair, leaving on the tulip-shaped light on her nightstand.

Discarding her robe and slippers, she climbed into her blankets, leaving the light on. She felt odd. She searched for the root of the feeling but couldn't put her finger on it. She was forty-four years old. The thought was shocking. Where had the years gone? More importantly, where had her life gone?

A small, unfamiliar ache made her face warm. She almost sat up, surprised. She realized she was longing for something. A man? Someone warm and alive, lying with her in this small bed. Someone to show her she mattered. Someone to prove that yes, she was indeed alive.

She'd never done that before. Not even once in the eight years since Bret had been dead. Why now?

The image of Bret chased away the glow of the warm feelings she'd been experiencing, replacing them with hot, vivid bitterness. Bret Ashland, her husband, had robbed her of so many years of her life. And Kristin's life.

For what? Living for the world, for things, for adventure. What did any of that matter in the big scheme of things? Nevertheless, responsibility lay at her doorstep too, she admitted. She had willingly followed his lead. First by ignorance, and then by apathy and pain. A million images flitted through her mind. Life was meant to be so much more.

A flash of lightning lit the room, followed by a powerful crack of thunder. The sound jolted her from her thoughts. Rising to her elbow, she made sure the candle and matches were still where she'd arranged them and within easy reach on the nightstand. She took up her pulse-monitoring watch and fastened it around her wrist. Excruciating slow moments ticked by. The number on her radio clock flipped over to nine fifteen.

The phone rang.

Chapter Sixteen

Camille jumped at the sound. For a moment, she stared at the phone in disbelief, then realized it must be Helene calling to report on Sasha.

She hurried to catch it on the third ring. "Hello?"

"Camille, it's Günther. I apologize for calling you so late. I've been tied up all evening and this was my very first opportunity to return your call."

A warm glow slid through Camille and the lonesome feeling vanished.

"Thank you for calling me to let me know about Sasha," he continued.

"You're welcome. And it's not late at all. I was just lying here with the light on…thinking."

"Oh, you've already retired. I'll let you—"

"No, no," she said, cutting him off. "You're not disturbing me at all. I'm the one sorry to report I haven't heard another thing all night. I'm worried sick about Sasha. I was hoping Helene would get another chance to call, but she hasn't. I have her cell phone number but I'm reluctant to disturb them. I think she's just busy with the whole sad situation, and I know she'll call when she can."

"You're right," Günther agreed. "We'll just have to be patient."

"Yes—patient. That's the key word here."

There was a moment of silence.

"How was class today?" she asked, not wanting him to end the call and say good-bye. "Did I miss anything important?" *Did you miss me, like I missed you?*

"It was a good day, all in all. We didn't do anything out of the ordinary. I'm sure it won't be a problem for you to catch up next week."

Over Günther's voice, Camille heard the small meow of a cat.

"We did a mock luncheon date," he said, "with several different scenarios. You know, in case something you've ordered is not to your liking and you have to send it back to the kitchen."

"I'm sorry I missed that. It sounds like fun. Who's that I hear there with you?"

"With me?"

That stumped him for a moment.

"Oh." He chuckled. "That's Flocki. She's hopping into my lap as we speak."

Camille laughed. "I'll bet she's black and white."

"She is. How did you know?"

"By the sound of her voice," she teased.

Günther's deep, rich laugher rewarded Camille and she couldn't stop her smile from widening. It felt so good to be happy, truly happy from the core of her being. A breeze floated over her and she pulled the covers and comforter up to her neck. She felt warm and snuggly.

"By the way," Camille continued. "How is Johann? What's happening with him?"

Günther sighed, a long, frustrated sound. He told her about a meeting he and his brother had with a social worker. And about the extra time they had been granted to locate Bernhard Wernfried.

"We do have a problem there," Günther continued, "because Ms. Roth is trying to line up a place in case Bernhard relinquishes his custody. That could land him just about anywhere—Austria, Switzerland, Germany. But thankfully there aren't any homes available now."

"Heard anything from Bernhard?" she asked.

"Only one call to my answering machine. He may have tried to call my brother, but we are not sure, because the caller didn't say anything or leave a name."

"Is it possible he might try to take Johann out of Vienna again?" Camille asked.

"Anything's possible. We've warned everyone with instructions to keep a very close eye on him. He's not to be alone, at least until we find Bernhard and get him into rehab."

"What will happen now?"

"If we can't find him, Ms. Roth will move Johann to the state institution in Germany to await finding his uncle, or a foster home. If Bernhard never surfaces, he'll be put into the foster care system until he is eighteen. On the other hand, if we can find Bernhard, we hope to persuade him to sign papers giving me guardianship over the boy."

"Günther, that's wonderful. I didn't know you wanted to take him in and care for him."

There was a moment of silence.

"I do. Very much."

Günther's voice was full of emotion. "Johann is very special to me. And he's also very gifted. I don't want him to go the way so many disadvantaged children do. I want to help him be all that God meant for him to be. I've tried for custody before but since Johann has a living relative—"

When a crack of thunder exploded above Camille's roof, she gasped in surprise. "Did you hear that?"

"How could I not? It sounded like it was right there in your room."

"I can't believe this storm. It's like it came out of nowhere today."

"It's actually the season for them. This is moderate. They can get really nasty.

How about you? What did you do while you were playing hooky?"

"I took down Sasha's bizarre tower and hung around waiting to hear from Helene. I walked to the market in the rain and picked up something for dinner. Oh. I almost forgot. I actually had a visitor. Remember Stephen Turner, the man I introduced you to at the bottom of the steps on Wednesday evening? The one I met on the flight here. He came by. He wanted to see how I was doing."

"That was thoughtful of him," Günther replied. "He knew the address where you are staying?"

Mortified, she continued. "Actually, yes. I'm embarrassed to admit it but when we landed in Vienna, I had a snafu with my bankcard. I didn't have any cash with me. The brainless advice of my travel agent was that I shouldn't bring any with me, that I should just withdraw when I landed. Then I couldn't get any after the ATM ate my card. Wolfgang and Helene thought I was coming in the following night so they weren't there to pick me up. Stephen was kind enough to offer me a ride. I had no other option but to take him up on it."

Another long moment.

"All's well that ends well."

"I guess so." Were these escapades only last week? It seemed like a year had passed.

Camille could feel the conversation winding down. She wished she could think of something more to say, something to ask him about, but maybe he had other things to do and she'd taken enough of his time already. Since he'd called her, she waited for him to make the move to say good-bye.

"Well, it's late," he said.

Camille looked at her bedside clock. They'd talked for half an hour. Keyed up, she knew she wouldn't fall asleep for a long time. "Yes. Thanks for calling."

"You're welcome. Remember to call if you find out anything more about Sasha."

They said good-bye and Camille hung up the phone, clicked off her light, and laid back into her covers. Her mind went over their discussion from start to finish. What a small thing. A simple conversation. And yet, so much more.

Did Günther mean something to her? Something more than a friend or teacher? It had been so long since she'd thought about anyone in a romantic way. However, when the feeling was there, there was no mistaking it.

Camille rolled to her side and tried to get comfortable. Having no luck, she shifted again and rolled to her back. Since coming to Vienna she'd been becoming increasingly conscious of something important taking place inside her inner self. She'd tried to avoid thinking about it, hoped the feeling would go away. She'd never have thought this about herself before this trip and yet seeing the struggles and hardships of people in their everyday lives was telling.

In comparison, her life back home was trivial. Superficial. She hated to admit it, but it was fact.

"It's true," she said into the darkness of her room, as if trying to convince herself of the certainty in her conviction. The realization made her cringe.

She was off track. She'd put herself first, only taking second seating to Kristin and her business. Her mother and Stephanie. Her close family unit was the only thing in her life that was important to her. Besides them, her biggest decision was what model car she wanted to buy this year and which rooms in her home to refurnish next.

Shame filled her. Was she really so shallow?

She thought about Günther wanting to adopt Johann, forgoing his own dreams and desires for someone else's welfare. And Wolfgang and Helene, barely scraping by, taking in students to supplement their income so she could stay home with their kids. Work at a soup kitchen. Volunteer.

For two hours, Camille struggled with her thoughts, feelings, and convictions. They were all jumbled up in her mind. Exhausted, she finally cried out into the darkness of her room, "Please, Lord, let me go to sleep. I can't figure it out tonight."

Günther relaxed on his bed, reading glasses perched on the bridge of his nose and *The Liturgy of the Hours*, opened to the Friday night prayer. Lying on his side, he held his head propped in his hand. Flocki purred contentedly, a little round, furry doughnut by his stomach.

At the sound of a knock at his door, he looked at the clock on his bedside table.

Ten fifteen. Was Aggie feeling poorly again? Florian? Perhaps it was Bernhard. That was an exciting thought.

Günther carefully extricated himself from the side of his purring cat. When he opened the door, surprise filled him. Günther recognized Stephen Turner immediately, the soft glow from the porch lamp illuminating his tall figure. A gust of wind blew a smattering of rain into Günther's face. Stephen held his wool coat firmly around his throat as he hunched his shoulders against the storm. Günther was glad Camille had refreshed his memory on his name during their phone conversation.

"*Herr* Christove," Stephen Turner said matter-of-factly over the howl of the wind.

"*Herr* Turner."

Turner shifted his weight but never took his eyes off Günther's face. "I'm sorry to barge in on you at this late hour, but it is important that I do. I wonder if I could speak with you for a few moments." His mouth was a hard-set line.

Günther was mystified why Stephen Turner would be initiating a conversation with him. He could only speculate that it must have something to do with Camille. He held the door open. Once in, Günther moved quickly to his sofa, picked up yesterday's newspaper, and tossed it into a pile of others in the corner. With a sweep of his arm, he cleared a spot for his visitor to sit down.

"Can I get you anything?"

"No, thank you."

Günther sat in his chair across from the man. "What brings you out on such a tempestuous night? It must be important."

"I'll get right to the point. I'm investigating a couple of students in your class, *Herr* Christove. I've been watching them for a few months." He reached into his coat pocket for his wallet. He flipped it open to show Günther his CIA badge. "My agency is working in tandem with your government on this matter."

Günther was shocked. "Camille Ashland?" A spy?

Turner smiled and a light brightened his eyes. "No, not Camille. But at this point I'm not at liberty to say who they are." He stretched out his legs and leaned back into the sofa cushions. "We've had reports of security leaks on an international level. We've followed leads to the school, and even to your class. You have been thoroughly investigated."

Günther's eyes narrowed.

"And cleared."

After hearing his life had been scrutinized under a magnifying glass, Günther didn't feel quite as accommodating to his guest.

"I can see what I've said has put you off. I'm sorry. I hope you understand that it couldn't be avoided."

Flocki came from the kitchen area and mewed at Günther for some food. When her request went unanswered, she meandered over to him and rubbed against his legs.

"And what are you expecting from me? To talk to you about my friends? My students? Give you private information?"

"Dissidents, *Herr* Christove."

"Alleged dissidents, *Herr* Turner."

They sized up each other.

With a sudden flex of muscle, Flocki bounded up the back of the sofa and began sharpening her claws directly behind Stephen's head.

"No, I'm not asking you for that," he replied, ignoring the cat. "Can you tell me though if you've noticed anything peculiar about any of your students? Any unusual behavior or patterns?"

Günther mentally scanned down his list of students. Branwell always displayed unusual behavior, but that was just him, poor kid. Possibly the self-proclaimed freedom fighter, Maria Glibrov, from the Republic of Macedonia. She looked like she fit the mold of a mole. Or Mark Marslino, importer living in Rome. He'd have access and means in passing information if he so desired. Now that he thought about it, many of his students seemed suspect.

"I really can't say. At this point I think it wise for me to think and not speak."

"I appreciate your candor, *Herr* Christove. I'm sure after tonight you will have a lot to consider."

Turner stood and Günther followed suit. He handed a card to Günther.

"Here is a number where I can be reached at any hour. It's secure. You can leave a message and I will get it. I'm sure you understand that what I've told you tonight is highly confidential and not to be shared with anyone. I can't stress that enough."

Chapter Seventeen

*C*amille turned in surprise, taking in the mysterious room. It was large, vacant, and filled with glistening silver light. The walls and windows shimmered brilliantly as if made from an opulent mother of pearl or water and yet, she could see nothing of the place outside. She realized she was able to see, or rather experience, the entire circumference of the space without turning an inch.

Happiness flooded. She felt magnificent and not frightened in the least. Where was she? Where was everyone else? Without a sound, the walls slowly began to move, revolving around her, the center of the room the exact point where she stood. Their momentum increased to the speed matching a merry-go-round, and faster still, until it was like being in the eye of a tornado without the intensity of the wind. She lifted. Swept up toward the tiny apex at the top of the funnel.

She soared like an eagle, a rushing sound traveling along with her, her hair flying free.

For one brief moment, Camille glanced down and was shocked to see the place was no longer bright with light but had grown darker, and was darkening still. She was either the source of the light, or the light itself, for it was traveling with her.

Beyond the white room, she looked at the street from a height matching that of the Empire State Building. Chocolate Blossoms! She could see inside her store, crowded with people. They gathered around *her discarded shell of a body, industriously trying to revive her. Her heart swelled with love for all of them. "Godspeed, my loves," she whispered. "Godspeed."*

What was happening? Did she die again in her sleep? If so, why had she seen her friends in the store? Was she now on her journey to the place of her particular judgment?

Things she hadn't thought about in years, her catechism she'd learned in her youth and thought she'd forgotten, were all still inside her, not gone at all, just set aside, waiting to be thought about, lived, made incarnate.

Without any problem, she landed softly on her feet in an open meadow. The place was verdant with loveliness and light. Was there no one here to meet her? The meadow looked deserted. How would she know where to go, what to do?

Over the sound of softly flowing water, tiny birds, in a multitude of colors, swooped over her head in the glittering sky. It was as if a rainbow of canaries had been splashed across a painter's canvas in one fluid movement. Camille laughed at their playful display.

"Camille." Her name was called softly from somewhere over the rise. Beyond the hummock, someone was waiting.

A stark light flashed past her eyes. It was nothing like the beautiful, soft light that had enveloped her before. She glanced around. Tried to see where it had come from.

Kaboom!

Thunder exploded, jolting Camille up in her bed. It was a moment before she got her wits about her. With trembling hands, she reached for the light switch and clicked it on only to have the darkness remain.

The matches!

Where were the matches?

In darkness and panic, she knocked them from her bedside table, clattering to the floor. She leaned over and grasped about madly in the blackness until her fingers touched the box.

She fumbled. Fought to steady her hands. Lightning flashed again and she waited until the thunder passed.

It took her two tries, but finally she had the candle burning. The small glow was some comfort as she struggled to slow her breathing. If she didn't get it under control, she would hyperventilate and pass out. Pain gripped her chest, radiating out, squeezing taut and sending her heart on another high-speed gallop.

She didn't need to put her fingertip on her pulse-monitoring watch. She could feel every twisted beat of her tortured heart as it ricocheted around her chest like the silver orb in a pinball machine.

"You're okay. You're okay. You're okay," she chanted over and over. Tiny beads of moisture slipped down her neck to pool between her breasts. As she calmed, her voice gradually grew slower, softer, but she didn't stop. "You're okay. You're okay. You're okay," she whispered.

"*Pfarrer* Florian?" A knock at the door brought Florian out of his papers where he worked on his message for this week's bulletin. "Florian, are you still up?" It was *Pfarrer* Schimke's soft voice from the other side of the old oak door.

It was a quarter past midnight, and Florian's eyes burned with fatigue. The rain had pummeled the window for hours as time slipped by. He set his pen down atop his papers and crossed the room to the door.

"*Ja, guten Abend*," he said, opening the door so his pastor could join him. The man wore a thick woolen sweater over his clericals, his protection against the damp halls of the rectory.

"I hope I'm not disturbing you, I know it's incredibly late. I noticed the light shining under your door."

Florian gestured for him to come in and sit down. Both men took a seat on the sofa.

"I have good news." *Pfarrer* Schimke, fifty-eight, was ten years his senior. Always clean and neat, he insisted everything in his parish be the same.

"Good news?" Florian rubbed his eyes to clear them.

Pfarrer Schimke settled back into the soft cushions, getting comfortable. "Yes. I had a call from the chancery today. I talked with Bishop Vonnegut personally."

Not often did priests or even pastors get a call from their busy bishop. The grounds must be significant. "And, how is Bishop Vonnegut?"

"Doing better. Almost fully recovered from his surgery. He sends his greetings. He says he's very anxious to get back on his feet and back on track with his parish visits throughout the archdiocese."

Florian knew this couldn't be the news his pastor had felt compelled to relay to him at this late hour. Always gracious, his pastor never failed to take a moment or two for polite conversation before jumping into the heart of the matter.

"And…I'm very pleased to tell you that he says he has a parish opening up for you. St. Anthony's. He'll be mailing out your letter of appointment in the next few weeks. He wanted me to tell you first so you could warm up to the idea."

A parish. Of his own. He didn't know why, but he hadn't expected *that* to be the news.

"St. Anthony's? But *Pfarrer* Mitchell has only been there for a year. Change again will be hard on the parishioners."

"That's true. And he is well loved there. But his order in the Philippines has need of him, and has called him back into their service. This will be difficult for him too."

Florian had settled in well at St. Elizabeth's. He'd been serving the Lord here for six years. That was a long time in one place. After the fourth year passed without being assigned to a parish of his own, Florian had accepted this was where he'd be staying for a while. He *liked* it here. It suited him. Big parish, lots to do.

"Florian, are you distressed?"

The older priest watched him closely.

"Nothing to be distressed over. God's will be done," he replied quietly.

"The parishioners here will miss you greatly. I will miss you even more. Your dedication to your vocation has been a blessing to me."

Without warning, a bright flash of lightning lit the room, dramatizing *Pfarrer* Schimke's statement with flair. Both priests looked to the window and the storm brewing outside.

"Thank you. I will miss everyone here also, very much." The boom followed quickly behind.

"Any news about Bernhard?" *Pfarrer* Schimke asked, the subject they'd been speaking of signed, sealed, and delivered.

"I've made numerous calls to everyone I can think of. To all of his old haunts. Not a trace. I have the feeling though, he is nearby."

"I will pray for a quick resolution to this problem."

"Thank you."

Pfarrer Schimke rubbed his arthritic fingers for a moment and stood. "I won't keep you any longer." He looked over to

Florian's desk and the array of papers and books stacked alongside. "Rest is important too. Why not finish up in the morning when you're fresh?"

Florian forced a smile. "Good idea." He saw his pastor out and leaned against the closed door, his room quiet again.

He didn't want to go. Six years was time enough to forge strong relationships, friendships, important ones. Not only that, but he'd started activities and groups for his parishioners. Scripture studies. Growing them from a mere few to fifty and sixty and seventy strong.

That was hard to give up.

He cooked with them, ate with them, laughed with them. Prayed with them. They were his family. His sisters and brothers. His children.

No. No, they aren't.

They are God's children.

He was the laborer of God's vineyard.

But then, there was Günther and Johann. He was a part of their life now. St. Anthony's was two hours away.

He could tell Bishop Vonnegut he was happy here at St. Elizabeth's. That he'd rather stay put. His superior was an understanding fellow. If it were doable, it might be arranged.

Perhaps.

His gaze landed on a picture of Jesus carrying His cross up to Golgotha.

But…what about obedience?

And sacrifice?

He crossed the room and went into his bedroom. Slowly, he sat on his neatly made bed, creasing the green and brown plaid coverlet. He removed one shoe and then the other, and scooted them painstakingly under the bed. Disregarding the cold, he unbuttoned his shirt and pants and stripped down to his shorts. In the bathroom, bare feet on the cold slab floor, he splashed his face and chest with ice-cold water and toweled dry. He quickly brushed his teeth and slipped into bed.

It felt good.

Cold, but good.

He closed his eyes. Usually his mind was restless, thinking, solving the problems of the next day. Tonight he was exhausted. Tonight he was asleep as his head hit the pillow.

Saturday morning came quickly. Florian hurried through his morning office, with thoughts of last night's announcement encroaching on his every prayer. He rushed through his toiletries and descended the steps into the rectory kitchen. *Frau* Kleimer was already there, working over the hot stove, wisps of her salt and pepper hair sticking to her damp brow.

"*Guten Morgen, Pfarrer* Christove," she said cheerfully. "*Wunderbarer Tag heute.*"

"*Ja, Gott sei gepriesen,*" Florian answered, agreeing with her on the beautiful day and praising God for it.

He'd already set up the meeting room adjacent to the kitchen the night before for the group he was expecting. A small table with the coffeemaker in one corner and alongside, a long table covered with a nice white linen tablecloth and a small vase of flowers. It was for the danish and other morning sweets he would offer after Mass and before the beginning of the English class. The chairs were neatly set in rows and there was a chalkboard in front, next to a podium.

Everything was in order. He switched on the coffeepot and the coffeemaker filled with water for the hot chocolate, then joined *Frau* Kleimer in the kitchen.

She muttered merrily as she dusted the top of some strudel with powdery white sugar and set the confection on a doily-covered platter. She worked swiftly, a baking and cooking machine, and an element of St. Elizabeth's rectory for the past twenty-five years. She'd been here longer than any other person.

A buzzer sounded from the small shelf above the butcher-block counter, sending her rushing to the old stove. She cracked open the oven door and, being careful not to get burned, peeked inside.

Saturday mornings were a favorite for all the rectory's inhabitants. *Frau* Kleimer never disappointed. There was always something scrumptious to take pleasure in along with a hot cup of fresh coffee.

Pfarrer Blauberg, being retired, spent many an hour chatting away, drinking coffee and watching her bake. He washed dishes for her sometimes and even set the table. They were a good team.

It was six forty. He bid *Frau* Kleimer good-bye, knowing she'd have all the necessary things set out when the service was over. He watched her for a few seconds longer than necessary, his heart a bit heavy and sad. This cheery little person had been a big part of his life for the past six years.

She must have felt his stare, for she looked up from her labor, a question in her eyes. She knew him well.

"*Ja, Pfarrer* Christove?"

He smiled and nodded reassuringly. "*Danke, Frau* Kleimer. *Danke sehr, für alles.*"

She blushed in her usual way and went quietly about her duties.

Chapter Eighteen

Günther arrived in St. Elizabeth's sacristy exactly at the same time as Florian. On his way there, Günther had picked up Johann, as the child was on the schedule to altar serve. As Florian prepared, Günther opened the lectionary to the correct readings and set the hefty volume on the ambo. He gathered the chalice, paten, purificator, and corporal and set them on the small table next to the wall in the sanctuary. He filled the wine and water cruets a third of the way, lit the two altar candles, and turned on the lights.

With everything in place, Günther took his place in the pews. As he knelt in prayer, he was surprised after a few minutes when Camille slipped in beside him.

"Good morning," he leaned over and whispered into her ear. His delight in seeing her vanished quickly when he looked into her eyes. "Are you okay? Is it Sasha?"

Her face was flushed from her walk to the church in the cool of first light. Her hair, clipped up haphazardly, was uncharacteristically messy. She looked like she hadn't slept at all.

"I haven't heard from Helene, or anyone yet this morning. I just wanted to come to church. I want to go to Communion."

What had her so rattled? What had taken place to cause such anxiety? There was something she wasn't saying. She looked very distracted.

"If you hurry into the sacristy, Florian can hear your confession. But you must go now for there is only a minute or two before the service will begin."

"Oh my gosh, I can't go *now*. I haven't been for years." Upset, she looked away. "Another thing I've forgotten about."

He smiled, trying to ease her anxiousness. "You know better than to be frightened. There is absolutely nothing you can tell a priest that can shock him. They've heard it all before and more than once. We're all sinners."

She looked at him now like he had an answer to every question she'd ever had. Like her whole world depended on his next word. She chewed her lower lip, trying to decide if she should take his advice.

"I don't remember how."

He took one of her cold, quivering hands into his own. "I have a better idea. I think you need a little time. Think about it, pray about it, and then go to reconciliation after the English class this morning. My brother hears confessions from ten until twelve every Saturday morning."

"Saturday?" she asked, looking a bit more relaxed now that she didn't have to run up into the sacristy this moment.

"Yes."

She looked at him intently.

"He can *never, ever* reveal a thing you've said to him. You know that, right? He can't even ask you about it later."

She nodded. "I'm *still* nervous."

He chuckled softly. At least now she was smiling again. "I know. We all get nervous. I get nervous. My confessor is my *brother*, so you see, you don't have it so bad."

The service was over in thirty minutes and Günther gave the announcement inviting all those interested for sweets and coffee to the meeting room in the rectory. The gathering room came alive with people, *Frau* Kleimer in the mix, giving orders and hugs.

There were eight children present that came faithfully to class every week, and two new young women he'd never seen. Günther had heard about them from Florian and was glad to see they were brave enough to show up. They stood in the back of the room, eating and keeping to themselves.

This was the social time before class started. *Pfarrer* Blauberg, now up and moving, was talking with Camille who seemed composed now, relaxed and laughing. Still, Günther wondered at what had had her so spooked this morning when she'd arrived. It wasn't just the thought of revealing her soul to a priest, he was sure. There had to be something more. For now, he was just pleased to see her enjoying her time with them.

Frau Kleimer approached with a tray full of strudel slices. "*Herr* Christove," she offered Günther, holding the tray out so he could take a slice.

"*Vielen Dank*," he replied, taking one. He shoved the whole slice into his mouth, experiencing the flavor. He swallowed the delicious treat and meandered through the children until he was standing by Camille and *Pfarrer* Blauberg. One look from Camille, and he knew he had done something funny. She laughed and brushed at the powdered sugar goatee that was left behind on his chin for all to see.

"Oops, sorry about that." He laughed. "It's just so good I can't control myself."

"Ah, it's the English teacher," *Pfarrer* Blauberg commented. Günther wondered if the old priest realized that he said that exact same thing every time they met.

"Are you staying for class?" Günther asked Camille.

"Yes, I think I will."

"Good. And then reconciliation at ten?"

Her brows scrunched. "Yes."

"Even better."

Camille approached Father Florian. "Good morning," she said, still feeling a bit shy around him. "Do you think I could use your telephone for two quick calls? I haven't yet had a chance to get a temporary cell phone."

"Of course. You can use the one in my office. It will be quieter for you there." She followed him down the hall. They passed the kitchen and a room that resembled a library. He stopped at the last door.

"Here you are." He pointed to the phone sitting on his mahogany desk and pulled out his chair. "Make yourself comfortable." He paused as if a thought had struck him. "Do you need help with the call?"

Camille dug for her address book, squirreled away somewhere in her backpack.

"Oh, no thanks. I think I can manage it on my own. And both calls will be local, I won't be calling overseas," she said so he wouldn't think she was charging up a costly phone bill.

His expression said he hadn't given that idea even a moment of thought. He closed the door and was gone.

Now alone in his office, she set her address book down and looked around. A picture of Günther and Johann with Father Florian in his vestments was next to his computer. They stood with big smiles and she thought it must have been taken at Johann's First Holy Communion. Another photo had Father Florian surrounded by six young women, two holding babies, and all looked very happy.

The whole room was very orderly. It smelled good. Like books. In the quiet, she could hear laughing and talking coming from the meeting room down the hall. On the back of the door hung a poster of old rice parchment, the sentiment written in calligraphy with Mother Teresa's Rules for Humility.

Camille read it twice, amazed by its wisdom. She wanted a copy for Chocolate Blossoms when she went home. Flipping her book open to *W*, she looked up Dr. Williamson's private number he'd given her on Wednesday. She dialed the number.

"Dr. Williamson," he answered.

"Doctor. This is Camille Ashland, from the United States. Stephanie's sister-in-law that you saw on Wednesday. I'm sorry to disturb you on the weekend."

"Yes, Camille. That's not a problem. Is everything all right with you?"

"No. I had an episode last night. I'm not sure if it was another heart attack or not."

There was silence for a few seconds. "Where are you now? And why didn't you call right away? How many hours has it been since you experienced the first pain?"

"I'm at St. Elizabeth's Church in town. I didn't call right away because I had something important I needed to do." *Mass.* "It's been about five hours since it happened."

"You should have called me immediately." Annoyance laced his tone. "I'll meet you in my office in half an hour."

"I'm sorry, Dr. Williamson, but I can't be there that soon." She knew she was sounding overly assertive and boorish. "I can be there around noon."

His tone switched from friendly to stiff. "That's *not* advisable. But if you insist, there is nothing I can do. I just hope you aren't putting yourself into more danger. Will you have a ride there?"

She knew she'd made him mad. "Yes, I'll take a cab. And, thank you so much."

They hung up.

Now, she needed to call Stephen Turner and cancel for tonight.

Her first real date in eight years.

Oh, well. She wasn't too disappointed. Hopefully, he'd take a rain check. Until she talked with Dr. Williamson, she had no idea what she should and should not be doing.

The number rang three times and then his voice mail picked up. She left a message canceling without going into detail, guaranteed to tick him off too.

She hung up and relaxed in the chair, glad that that was over. She'd wait to call Stephanie at home until she knew something definite. No use getting her all up in arms without first having all the facts.

Now that she'd warmed up to Father Florian's office for a few minutes, she felt right at home. She liked its sense of balance and its holy knickknacks.

Standing, she went over to his bookshelf where row upon row of heavy-duty theological books waited, the kind that would take a lifetime to read even one. Some were in English and others in German. She ran her fingertip down the shelf and scanned the titles looking for ones she could read. *The Confessions*, St. Augustine. *The Dolorous Passion of Our Lord Jesus Christ*, Anna Catherine Emmerich. *History of the Church of Christ*, Henri Daniel-Rops. *The Divine Romance*, Fulton J. Sheen.

The list went on and Camille was deeply moved. All these books and she'd never even heard of one of them. How could she be so ignorant about her faith? What had she been doing all these years?

Drawn to a volume with a bright red binding, *Saints Are Not Sad* by Frank Sheed, she took it from the shelf and opened it, flipping through the pages. She recognized a sketch of St. Francis only by the animals that surrounded him, but still, she felt a diminutive burst of wonder for that one small accomplishment.

Camille gasped when the door opened up without warning. In the alcove stood the rectory cook, the one she'd seen passing around the apple strudel.

"*Oh, Entschuldigen Sie bitte*," the old woman apologized, looking startled.

Camille held her hand to her chest as if she could hold her heart inside. She felt the compelling need to explain her presence here. "I'm using the phone," she said quickly. "Father Florian said it was all right."

The woman shook her head, not understanding.

Camille replaced the slip inside and set the book back on the shelf. She hurried to the desk and pointed to the phone. "*Telefon*."

The German woman nodded demurely but the look in her eyes asked, "What then, are you doing at his bookshelf? Going through his things?" She slowly backed out of the room and closed the door behind her.

Camille listened to the woman's retreating footsteps as she scuttled down the quiet hall, probably going to report. Camille gathered her address book and was about to put it back into her backpack when she thought about Helene. Would one more call be taking advantage? Had Father Florian sent the cook to see what was taking her so long?

Quickly she looked up Helene's number. She agonized for a few minutes whether to call. She didn't want to intrude, but then, she was going to be out most of the day and Helene had told her that she would call and let her know what was going on with Sasha.

Better to err on the side of thoughtfulness, she decided, and dialed.

The phone rang five times without answer. Camille was about to disconnect when Helene picked up.

"Hi, it's Camille."

Helene's voice wavered slightly when she returned the greeting.

"I'm sorry to intrude on your morning but I've been worried. How is Sasha?"

"We are not sure yet. They think..."

Helene started to cry. Camille could hear Wolfgang in the background trying to comfort his wife as she struggled to compose herself. "After all the tests, the doctors believe that Sasha is—autistic."

Chapter Nineteen

Now that ten o'clock had arrived, Camille wished she'd listened to Dr. Williamson and had taken his advice. If she had, she'd be in his office right now, instead of sweating nervously in this long line of people. The procession silently snaked down the right side of St. Elizabeth's and ended in the vestibule.

Günther was three people behind, probably there just to make sure she didn't get cold feet and bolt for the door. They'd gone over the procedure and how she should begin. When she was finished, she would see that it was really very simple and that there was nothing to be anxious over. That may be so, but she still felt like she needed a crowbar to dislodge her tightly wedged heart from between her ribs.

The confessional door opened and a man came out. The older woman in front of Camille went in. The light above the confessional blinked on.

Camille wrung her hands self-consciously and glanced back at Günther. It was true; if he weren't there, she *would* leave. In only a few short minutes, she'd be inside.

She searched her thoughts trying to remember all she was going to say. What were her sins? It'd been so long since her last confession, she knew she had more than a score of them. She'd gone carefully through her mind, like Günther had told her to do, and yet now she was having a hard time remembering even one.

On the other side of the church was another line where Father Schimke was hearing confessions too. From that line, Camille saw the rectory cook gazing at her across the church nave. Uncomfortably, Camille smiled briefly at the woman and looked away.

She took a few deep, relaxing breaths.

The door opened. The woman exited and politely held it open for Camille. Camille hesitated for an instant and then went inside. It was dark and very cool. A bit musty, but not unpleasant. There was a small crucifix lying on the shelf directly under the small curtained window and she picked it up and held it tightly.

As she knelt down, she recalled how the pressure on the kneeler turned on the light above the door outside. As a little girl, on occasion, she used to make it wink at her mom who was waiting in line.

She could see Father Florian through the semi-transparent screen. A dim light from above illuminated his profile, revealing the purple stole over his shoulders and a bible resting open on his lap.

"*Im Namen des Vaters und des Sohns und…*" he began in German. When he heard her saying it along with him in English, he switched to that.

After the sign of the cross, there was a moment of awkward silence before she began. She knew full well that he could recognize her voice without a bit of trouble.

"Bless me, Father, for I have sinned. It's been approximately twenty years since my last confession."

If he were going to die of shock, now would be the time.

She continued. "These are my sins. In those years I've hardly been to Mass. Only for Christmas and Easter, and I missed a few of those too. I've used the Lord's name in vain and anger too many times to count. I've been harsh and impatient with my daughter, when I should have been loving and patient."

She stopped, thinking. A few moments passed.

He shifted. "Are you finished?"

"No, not really. I know there's more."

"The fifth commandment says that we shall not kill."

She was relieved. "I've not killed anyone, Father."

"Unforgiveness, hatred, grudges, termination of a pregnancy, hurting others with our speech, killing yourself through excessive drinking, are all part of the fifth."

She stared at the crucifix in her clenched hands, thinking. "I've been drunk a few times. Probably a dozen."

She stopped. Hesitated. *Unforgiveness?* "It's about my husband. He's been dead for eight years. He loved the thrill of danger more than he loved life itself. More than he loved our daughter or me."

As her anger began to build, Camille had to work to soothe her tone. "I'm *still* angry with him. Sometimes I even hate him." She glanced around the little room for something besides Jesus to look at.

Father Florian waited silently.

"I'm sorry for that," she said. She was sincere. She *was* sorry. Sorry for all the time she had wasted hating instead of loving. It felt good to finally say it. *To mean it.*

"You need to forgive him *everything*, so God can forgive *everything* of you."

The tiny room grew warm as the minutes ticked by. Camille thought of the line of people waiting.

It was as if the priest picked up on her thoughts. "Not to worry about the others. It is a good exercise in patience. They may recall some sin that they would have forgotten, leastwise without the extra time of contemplation you are affording them."

She closed her eyes and tried to relax. "There is something else." She cringed inside, wondering how she could have put this totally out of her consciousness. "Once, many years ago after Bret died, I met someone at a gift expo. We had a few drinks." She had never told this to anyone. Not her mother. Not Stephanie. After the guilt had worn off, she'd filed it away never to be thought about again. How she had forgotten it now only showed how deeply she'd repressed it. "We spent the night together." She swallowed, gathering her thoughts. "I never went to confession. I wasn't thinking along those lines then."

"Yes. Sometimes it takes us some time to understand that the things we think are small are actually of great importance to God."

"Yes, Father."

"Anything else?"

Camille thought for a moment.

"Yes." Her throat tightened up. Tears pooled, then trickled down her cheeks and she brushed them away. "I cannot express how sorry I am for all the time I left God out of my life. Even after all of my blessings. I let my daughter's religious education fall through the cracks. Everything else came before catechism: riding lessons, shopping, homework. As a result, she is missing some of her sacraments and knows little about her faith. This past week, when I've begun to think about God, has made me very aware of all the years I've wasted." She took a tissue from her pocket and softly blew her nose.

"Yes," he said softly, soothingly. "I can hear it in your voice. Do not worry over the lost years, only look to the future with joy. For your penance, I want you to say a rosary each night for one week, offering it for the soul of your husband. Now make an Act of Contrition."

Camille sniffed. She said the prayer the best she could, needing more help from Father Florian along the way. When she finished, he said the words of absolution, ending in "…and I absolve you from your sins, in the name of the Father and of the Son and of the Holy Spirit. Now, go in peace, your sins have been forgiven."

At once, Camille's sadness was gone and she was filled with happiness. "Thank you, Father. Thank you so much."

She opened the door. Everyone in the line was staring at her as if they thought she'd died inside, never to come out again.

Günther's eyes met hers and she wanted to fly into his arms and thank him too. Instead, she walked slowly, quietly, but when she got to him, she was unable to mask her happiness a moment longer.

"You were right. So right about everything. Thank you."

He chuckled softly. "Let us thank God, for His love and mercy are endless."

Her enthusiasm was getting the best of her and the people around Günther were all smiling too, knowing well a sinner was experiencing the goodness of God's love and forgiveness.

"Praise God so much," she said looking around at them all.

"*Ja, ja,*" said one man caught up in her delight.

That made Günther and Camille laugh together, sharing the special moment. She looked at her watch. "Oh my gosh, it's late. Thank you for being there for me."

"Where do you have to go?"

He looked so earnest standing there.

She opened her mouth to say something, anything but the truth, anything but the doctors because she'd suffered a heart attack, but she couldn't tell a lie.

"Back to the doctors." She could see he wanted to ask her why.

She picked up his hands in the same way he'd held hers earlier in the pew when she'd been so scared, when he'd tried to soothe her frayed nerves and calm her quaking heart.

"Not to worry." She smiled into his eyes. "I've been to confession. Nothing can harm me now."

Camille took a taxi downtown, rocketing through the semi-crowded Saturday morning streets, taking in all the splendor of Vienna. Regardless of the exciting scenery, her thoughts kept coming back to Sasha and autism.

Oh, please don't let it be that, Lord. There must be another reason she is acting so oddly. A chemical imbalance of some sort. Something that can be cured.

"Cabbie, stop please," she called. "I need five minutes to run into this store. Please wait here." Camille ran into the electronics store that had cell phones on display. This was not a luxury, but something she needed. The young techie showed her phones, rang her up, and programmed a snappy ring tone. He showed her how to use her phone card for overseas calls. She felt much safer and self-reliant now with her new gadget.

There were no nurses today at Dr. Williamson's office, only one young woman taking calls. Dr. Williamson gave Camille a thorough exam to see if any damage had been done to her heart muscle the night before.

"Well, you were very lucky," he said when he was finished. He leaned against the cabinet and crossed his arms.

She sat on the end of the exam table, clothed and more than ready to get going.

"This time," he added in an "I told you so" tone. He was still bent out of shape that she hadn't called him the second it had transpired.

"Lucky?"

"Yes. You didn't suffer a heart attack last night, but an anxiety attack. Have you ever experienced those before?"

"No. Never."

"Did you eat anything unusual last night before bed, anything spicy? Chinese food? Pizza? Did anything startle you?"

Well, there was the evil-looking tower Sasha had built that morning, Branwell and his devious ways weighed heavily on her mind, and then, the face in the mirror and the relentless storm. Or, maybe it was the fact that she'd had a heart attack, died, and been revived back to life only a month before.

"I'm not sure, Dr. Williamson. There've been a few things on my mind lately. I was a bit spooked by the storm before I went to bed. Maybe that was it."

"Perhaps." He took the pen from his pocket and scribbled on his prescription pad. "I'm going to give you a sedative, something to calm you before bed, for when you feel yourself tense and edgy."

"I don't take drugs. Not even aspirin or Advil. Only when I absolutely have to."

"Well, you *may* absolutely have to. I don't want you having another bout of alarm getting you so riled up that it triggers a heart attack. I want you to remain calm, Camille."

Camille took the square of paper from his hand. "So, how should I take this?"

"If you feel anxious and unable to unwind. Take it with a cup of tea and allow yourself a little reading time. Wait until it gives you the desire to want to go to bed. Sometimes just the contemplation of the possibility of not being able to fall asleep will work someone up."

She got down off the examination table. "Thank you. Can I get this filled somewhere today?"

"On the ground floor, in the lobby next to the elevators, is a small *Apotheke*. You probably passed it on your way in." He paused. "And Camille."

"Yes?"

"I'd appreciate it if you just rested tonight. Stayed home. Read a magazine."

Chapter Twenty

Günther lay wide awake in his bed. Midnight had come and gone. He rolled out, knowing better than to lie there agonizing over his inability to fall asleep. He pulled on some pants and a sweater, grabbed his phone and wallet, and headed toward the door. Flocki, ever awake and watchful at night, pounced at his feet from somewhere in the darkness, tripping him up. She mewed incessantly with the sorriest of voices.

"I've fed you already. No more for you," he grumbled affectionately. His words didn't affect her in the least and she meowed all the louder.

The air was cold and brisk and walking felt good. The streets weren't completely empty yet and every so often he'd pass a couple of lovers walking hand in hand down the street, as if they had nowhere in particular to go and all the time in the world to get there.

Their whispers were felt more than heard, as sure as a hammer blow, and the magical lilt of their quiet laughter burned in his stomach. He looked away, unable to endure the sight. He closed his mind to his loneliness and concentrated on the moment at hand. He didn't deserve love, not one like that. Not after what he did to Katerina and Nikolaus. Never again, he promised himself.

Knowing he wasn't going to get any sleep tonight anyway, he veered into a café and made his way through the tiny, crowded room. On Saturday nights the place stayed open into the early morning hours, catering to the after opera and theater crowd.

"*Einen kleinen Braunen, bitte*," he said to the man working the espresso machine, ordering a small coffee with cream. "To go."

Back on the street, the cup of coffee forced Günther to slow down a little and sip and enjoy. The night was dark, except for the street lamps and the amber glow shining through the windows of the open businesses. A police siren sounded somewhere far off in the distance and he wondered what had caused it. He felt alone.

He found himself at *Michaelerplatz* on the flagstone steps just in front of the school. Opposite him, St. Michael's steeple pierced the darkness of the night and acted as an anchor for his sanity in his agitated sea of restlessness.

He wasn't tired at all. Too many things on his mind. He'd go into his class and work on some of the online assignments he'd been neglecting since the beginning of the week. A couple of uninterrupted hours could get him caught up and even set him up for next week. With purpose now, he moved easier.

The building was pitch black. Sometimes, during the week, professors would stay late working into the night, or meeting and helping students. There could be study groups in the library, or heated debates over coffee in the lounge. A glow from one or several of the rooms made the building feel inviting in a scholastic sort of way.

But that was very rare on the weekends. Günther made his way down the dark, empty corridor, the sound of his footsteps the only sound in the still, massive hallway. Being careful with his coffee, he took the stairs two at a time until he was on the third floor.

He unlocked the door to his room and turned on the light. Something about light was second nature to the soul. It felt good. His window shades were drawn and curtains pulled, keeping the glow from the overhead fluorescent tubes inside the room.

He took a seat at his desk and made himself comfortable. He clicked on his computer. Logged in. Opened his e-mail. Scanning down the list of correspondence, he looked for things of importance. It had been a couple of days since he'd checked, so there were thirty-nine new messages, but nothing that needed urgent attention.

He clicked into the school's online site and logged in with another password, allowing him access to the work sent to them by students from all around the world. There were thirty-six course works to be corrected.

Before opening them, he looked down the archives of students, clicked into 2010, the first year Camille Ashland had begun sending work to the school. Günther scanned some of her earliest assignments, empathizing more clearly now that he knew her, how she'd struggled. She'd come a long way since then. Her childish responses and simple sentences brought a smile to his lips. He took a sip of his coffee. He glanced at her student profile, her address, phone number, and contact numbers and the like.

He clicked onto the link to her store, something he'd never done before, and waited for the site to load. There were pictures of the store, Camille, Camille and her employees. Her display windows outside. Camille and her daughter Kristin, who amazingly looked nothing like her.

There was a short zip clip message of Camille to her customers. She promised them the highest level of service and quality of product. He gave her credit for her honesty, enthusiasm, and hard work.

Günther clicked out of Chocolate Blossoms' website and returned to the waiting homework assignments. He opened to exercise twenty-one of verb conjugation. He quickly read the list of ten verbs then began with the first, *kommen*, to come. He scanned down the pages, rapidly making corrections.

The next exercise was to practice making polite requests. He read down the first ten sentences with no mistakes. It was tedious work. Time passed. He continued until he heard the clock in *Michaelerplatz* chime four. Yawning, he signed out and turned his computer off, satisfied with the work he'd completed.

He was groggy. He'd have no problem falling asleep. After locking up, he made his way back down the hallway in a sleepy daze. As he was about to descend the stairs a sharp rap, like metal hitting metal, echoed around. Something had dropped in the stairwell two floors above him.

Chapter Twenty-One

Günther stopped. Fatigue gone and mind alert. He'd spent time in the Armed Forces, as was expected of all young Austrian males. Florian had too, almost making it a career. It took more than a noise in the dark to rattle him.

The sound had been sharp but not loud. Definite. Not outside, not a mouse, not in his head. Günther gazed up the dark stairwell. It curled around and around, ascending into a long black hole. The hair on the back of his neck prickled at the thought of someone looking down back at him.

He wanted to go on home, say it was nothing, but he knew better. A noise like that didn't just materialize out of thin air. He'd been walking pretty quietly. If someone hadn't known he was in the building or had been aware of his presence, they could have missed his approach to the stairwell because of his sneakers.

Could it be Stephen Turner's mole?

A muffled whisper, a response, and then light, descending footsteps on the landing directly above made him jump into action. Without thought, or sound, Günther slipped into the alcove next to the drinking fountain. He pressed his back to the wall and listened. Whoever was there was trying to be quiet. It wasn't like someone working late and leaving. There was definite purpose in stealth.

The sound grew closer. In the next instant, they would be making the curve on his floor landing before descending to the second floor and below. Curiosity got the best of him and he leaned forward, squinting into the darkness. He wanted to see who it was.

There were two. Both wore black, with hoods pulled up over their heads. They moved carefully. Stephen Turner's words came back to Günther, making him wonder if either of them could be a student from his class. They were almost around and down the staircase when the taller of the two stopped abruptly. He turned and searched the darkness as if he felt Günther's presence hiding in the alcove.

For a split second, Günther held his breath. He never took his eyes from the black hole where the person's unidentifiable face was. Unfortunately, because of the hood, it was impossible to see anything.

Slowly, they continued.

When he felt enough seconds had passed, he followed them down the stairs. They'd be near several exits by now. He needed to hurry.

Going with his instincts, he proceeded cautiously to the far exit, the one that opened into the alley. He crept along slowly next to the wall, with no idea if he was going in the right direction or if he'd come upon them suddenly.

He arrived at the exit but didn't want to open the door in case they were still in the long alleyway. If he could get into one of the rooms, maybe he'd find a window. All the doors were locked. He doubled back, hurrying to the front entrance. With his key, he unlocked the massive door and slipped out thankful he'd worn his black sweats and sweater.

Michaelerplatz was totally deserted. Günther jogged down the front of the long building and rounded the end toward the alley, already sensing that it was too late, they'd made their escape. As he got closer, he slowed and ducked behind a tall hedge, and continued on. He stopped and listened.

He looked between the branches of the shrub. There was no movement in or around the alley. Suddenly he felt very tired. And disappointed he hadn't been able to follow the pair and find out what they were up to. If they were somehow trafficking or selling sensitive information that put the United States or the world at risk, he wanted to help put a stop to it.

He took the cobblestone street in the direction of his flat. He passed the nursing home where Aggie slept. Turning the corner onto his street, he saw a person sitting on the steps to his building. As he got closer, he recognized it was Bernhard.

"About time you got here," Bernhard grumbled. "Been waiting most the night."

"Bernhard," Günther said in surprise, as he pulled his key out of his pocket. "I'm glad you showed up. We've been looking for you. Come in." Günther unlocked the door and held it open for Johann's unkempt uncle.

At that moment, the paperboy came jogging down the street, doubled over by the large cloth satchel filled with *Wien Heute Zeitung*, Sunday edition.

"*Herr* Christove," he said, handing a paper to Günther.

"*Danke sehr.*"

Inside, Günther tossed the paper onto the counter with his keys and turned on some lights. Bernhard looked sober. His hair, tousled and long, fell haphazardly into his eyes.

"You want some food?" Günther asked.

"What've you got?"

"Nothing gourmet. How about some rolls and cheese?"

"Good. Any beer?"

"No." He wouldn't give him any even if he had some.

"So how's your girlfriend?" Bernhard asked, as he took the proffered plate of rolls from Günther's hand. His face twisted in a knowing smile. "You've been out all night. What else am I supposed to think when you come sneaking home at sunrise?"

Günther's gut twisted with irritation. He didn't owe this man any explanation.

"Come sit. Eat in peace," he said, as he put the chunk of cheese onto a plate and grabbed a knife. He wanted to keep Bernhard in an agreeable mood. He was known for his hot temper. Much like his own. "In case you're wondering, Johann is fine. Doing very well, actually," Günther said as he watched Bernhard eat. "What are your plans?"

Bernhard swallowed. Took another bite and looked at Günther as he chewed. "You know it's funny," he said over a mouthful of bread. "You'd do just about anything to get custody of my nephew." He belched and wiped his mouth with the back of his hand. "Even sit here and make polite conversation with me."

Stay calm, Günther told himself. Stay cool. Just like he is. Wait and see what he has up his sleeve. "What do you mean?"

Bernhard laughed a spray of crumbs. "What do I mean? I couldn't have said it any plainer, could I?"

Bernhard was right. But his eyes were gritty and he needed some sleep. It had been years since he'd felt the temptation to beat the stuffing out of someone. Now was not the time to crumble. "What are your plans for Johann?" Günther asked again.

Taking his time, Bernhard cut a healthy corner off the Bavarian blue brie and shoved it into his mouth. "I'm going to keep him with me. I have some business to finish up and then we'll be leaving this wretched city. Just like we were trying to do on Tuesday."

"Don't you care about him at all, Bernhard? Or want what's best for him? What would your brother think of the way you're raising him? I could give him so much more. A stable home. A good education…"

"I can give him that too," Bernhard retorted. "Soon."

"Think how much easier your life would be without him tagging along with you. Kids are always hungry, tired, sick, and the agency is constantly looking over your shoulder, checking on what you're doing. Without him, you could do anything you wanted. Or go into rehab. When you are out, I could help find you a job."

Günther couldn't tell if the man was listening to a word he was saying. "Johann needs so much of your resources, time and money. It's hard for any single parent. Nobody blames you, Bernhard."

He wasn't making any headway. Günther's gut said to change tactics. "When are you picking Johann up?"

Bernhard gave him a sidelong glance. "In a week, maybe two."

"That's too long. If you don't check in with the *Büro* on Monday, *this Monday*, and take Johann from the family he's with now, she's moving him to the state facility in Germany. You don't want Johann to go there, do you?" Bernhard had pushed back in the chair and was rubbing his belly. Anger surged in Günther at the fool's lack of empathy. He slammed his hand down on the table and Flocki ran into the other room. "Don't you understand? There are no temporary foster homes available to put him until you're ready to take him. Unless, that is, you sign over your custody to me."

"Never!"

It's like talking to a brick wall. "Bernhard, be reasonable. Johann wants to stay here. He's afraid to go with you. Doesn't that mean anything?"

"It matters little what the boy wants. He may as well learn that you don't always get what you want in this life."

"What about somebody else? Would you give custody to another family?"

Sated, Bernhard got up and walked over to the sofa and stretched out. "Maybe."

Bernhard had a problem with him personally. It went all the way back to the time he'd reported Bernhard to the police for pushing drugs on the school grounds. He'd been arrested and served a light sentence. That's when he and Florian had gotten to know Johann. It was a grudge Bernhard wouldn't let go of.

"I know a family. A good family. And they have some kids and a stable mother and father." Günther was speaking as he was thinking. The only one he could come up with was Wolfgang and Helene. And possibly Bernhard was just stringing him along. Playing with him. Enjoying his power to make him beg.

Bernhard excused himself and went to Günther's water closet. When long minutes passed, Günther went looking for him but only found a window in his bedroom open and Bernhard gone.

Camille knelt in prayer, fifth pew from the front on the left side, the same pew she'd joined Günther in yesterday morning. She'd hoped to find him here today. All around her, St. Elizabeth's filled quickly for the eight thirty a.m. Mass. She was excited. Joy coursed through her body. She tried to keep her mind on prayer. On God. On what was about to happen. But the excitement of this day and the friendly smiles of the people around her kept pulling her out of her thoughts.

Today was special. She'd dressed carefully, choosing a charcoal cashmere sweater-coat over a matching cashmere short-sleeved sweater. Her calf-length skirt was black and white tweed. Taupe hose coordinated nicely with her sophisticated T-strap leather pumps that tapered at the toe. The look was completed with petite soft pink pearls at her ears and around her neck.

She felt wonderful.

And prepared.

She'd prayed her rosary last night with love. As she did, she wondered again how she could have stayed away from her faith for so long. Plus this morning she was rested. That felt glorious too. After the frightening dream on Friday night, she'd decided at the last moment before bed to take the medication Dr. Williamson had prescribed. *But only this once.* She'd slept like a baby all night, waking refreshed and clearheaded. As she looked at her watch, a man slipped in beside her. Thinking it was Günther, she turned.

"Good morning," Stephen Turner whispered, his freshly showered scent, mixed with a spicy aftershave, wafted her way. "I hoped I'd find you here."

Her mind raced over the vague message she'd left him yesterday morning on his answering machine canceling their date that night. He didn't seem annoyed.

"I know it was a crazy idea but I just felt like seeing you. I hope you don't mind," he said in a low voice. "It's been some time since I've been to Sunday service."

"Not at all," Camille said, regaining her composure.

He gazed around the nave of the church, taking in its splendor of saints and angels. His gaze landed on the life-sized statue of St. Elizabeth opposite their pew, her arms laden with a basket overflowing with bread for the poor.

Stephen turned and looked down into Camille's face. "I hope God doesn't mind that I have an ulterior motive for being here. Or, you, for that matter." He laughed quietly.

"Ulterior motive?"

Stephen exhaled. "Isn't it obvious? I wanted to see *you*."

Chapter Twenty-Two

Günther rushed into church eight minutes late, just as the first reading was almost over. He instantly spotted Camille sitting in the exact spot where they had been the day before. As he started up the center aisle to join her, the back of the man sitting next to her caught his attention. *Stephen Turner.*

Stopping abruptly, Günther genuflected and slipped into the first available pew. So what if Stephen Turner was here. That was good. The body of Christ was growing. There was always room for hearts to expand.

But *why* was he here?

Was it to worship?

Was it because he was interested in Camille?

Or, was he working? Hunting for information?

Günther had a good view of the two. Camille looked intent on what the lector was reading. Stephen Turner was another story entirely. He wasn't looking at the ambo. Or the stained glass windows. Or anything else. He was staring straight at Florian, who was seated on the right side of the altar, between a deacon and an altar server.

Florian?

Did he suspect Florian of espionage?

Could that possibly be? Did he think Florian was involved in some way with his conspiracy theory? That was completely and totally absurd.

Günther's brain kicked into high gear as he worked at putting this puzzle together. Damn. He wished he'd been able to see who it was in the school, sneaking around in the dark. That would have solved the problem here and now. He'd been so close.

Maybe he was totally off track. Perhaps Stephen was just here to see Camille. They were both Americans, close in age. His being attracted to her made much more sense. Until proven differently, the least the man deserved was the benefit of the doubt.

When the lector finished, he went back to his seat. Günther tried to stay ambivalent but Stephen's gaze was riveted on his brother. If Günther read him correctly, he had little interest in Camille; it was Florian he was here for.

When realization dawned, Günther almost groaned aloud. Florian's years in the Armed Forces. His high degree of clearance. That had to be it. If whoever was involved with this new espionage escapade was looking for someone to hang it on, Florian would be the perfect scapegoat.

Outside the church, Günther waited for Camille in the crisp morning air. When she appeared she was all smiles, aglow with happiness. Stephen was right behind.

After greetings were made Stephen said, "Do you have plans today, Camille?"

There was indecision in her eyes. She turned to him. "I'm not sure. Günther, I was hoping you might have a little time right now. There's something I'd like to talk to you about. But only if you didn't mind and it wouldn't be an inconvenience for you."

Stephen's gaze never ventured far from his brother as he greeted the parishioners. "Would you like to go over to my office at the school?"

She turned to Stephen. "I hope you don't mind. You came to church. Were you looking for me for a reason?"

The CIA agent looked around nonchalantly, but Günther could tell he wasn't happy with the outcome of the morning, or this conversation.

"Well, we did have an engagement last night that you canceled. I was hoping I'd get a rain check today." His smile didn't reach his eyes. "I thought I'd take you to brunch."

"That sounds really nice, Stephen, but there truly is something really important I need to discuss with Günther. If he's willing to see me now, then that's what I want to do."

Günther masked his delight. Perhaps Stephen thought they were plotting some top-secret reconnaissance or something. Whatever he believed, it didn't matter. Camille had wormed her way into his heart, he admitted to himself with surprise. A forgotten emotion he hadn't experienced since Kat, and he liked it very much.

"Tuesday night then," Stephen said bluntly. "Dinner. Anywhere you choose."

Chapter Twenty-Three

Camille felt uneasy making a date standing between the two men. It shouldn't matter; she was free to do anything she chose. Günther was her teacher, not a boyfriend. Whatever he was, he looked utterly handsome this morning. His hair glistened in the sunlight and his warm smile was thoughtful and knowing, making her insides warm. He looked completely at ease and comfortable in his clothes, a trait she wished she possessed.

"Okay, Stephen. I'll look forward to it."

She tucked one side of her hair behind her ear, then fingered her earring. "Sorry about yesterday, and leaving you the message canceling our dinner. But it really couldn't be helped. I appreciate your understanding."

"You pick a place and I'll call with a time." Stephen smiled and looked around. "Plus, I'll keep the theater tickets intended for yesterday, for next Saturday." He turned to leave. "Günther, good to see you again."

Günther smiled. "Likewise."

Fifteen minutes later, Camille sat back in her chair and relaxed. This was her first time in Günther's office. It was spacious and, unlike Father Florian's, books, magazines, and other stuff was everywhere, in no special order.

The wall opposite the window had pictures and mementoes. There was a ceramic stand in the corner that held several well-used umbrellas. It was everything you'd think a man's office would be.

Today, being Sunday, the building was virtually empty, making it feel quite poignant and lonely without the chatter and laughter of the students. She loved her new friends from class. Well, all except Branwell and Stena. She would work on trying to like them too, even if it wasn't enough to miss them when she left. Why did they dislike her so much? Enough that she had to watch her every move around them.

She refused to let them spoil this moment. Instead, she turned her attention to a picture on the wall of Günther, Father Florian, and someone she didn't know.

Günther had disappeared down the hall to get them a cool drink. He'd unlocked his office, invited her to make herself comfortable, and promised to be back in a jiffy. She heard the approach of his footsteps.

"So, how are you feeling today?" he asked, handing her an opened can of sparkling water.

"Wonderful." She willed herself not to blush like a schoolgirl. It was so hard. She wanted to jump up and hug him. Instead, she took the can from his hand and smiled.

"I can never thank you enough for encouraging me back to my faith."

"It wasn't me," he replied with a small grin.

"The Holy Spirit, I know." They laughed in unison.

"You laugh," he said as he sat in his big swivel chair behind his desk. He leaned forward, setting his drink on the shiny glass top. "But it's true. There is a reason for every meeting that takes place on this earth. God," he pointed up, "brings people together on purpose. It's no coincidence that brought you here to Vienna."

"You're an amazing man, Günther Christove."

It was his turn to blush. Camille could hardly believe her eyes. She was pleased that her words could affect him too.

He cleared his throat. "So, what is it you needed to talk to me about? It sounded important."

This was her moment of truth. She wanted to share the dream she had Friday night, see what his take was on it. But to do so, she would have to tell him everything.

It felt awkward. Stephanie had said she shouldn't feel embarrassed, but still, she couldn't change her feelings. She took a deep breath. "It is important. Very." She took a sip. "It's kind of hard to share."

"No worries."

Camille gazed into his honest eyes and took another cleansing breath. "Okay, here goes. Before coming to Austria, I suffered a heart attack. During it, I had an experience where I watched the EMTs resuscitate me. I don't remember much about it except the time in my shop while the rescue workers hooked me to a machine."

She took another sip, realizing this wasn't going to be as hard as she'd thought.

"My sister-in-law is my doctor. She thinks stress, due to my work habits, was the cause. So she and my mother cooked up this idea and actually forced me to take this holiday."

Günther listened patiently, gazing at her over his tented fingers.

"At first I resisted. I've never left my business before for any length of time. Or my daughter, Kristin. She's at a crucial age, where she doesn't think she needs me but she really needs me a lot."

"How is your health now?"

"According to Stephanie, with diet and exercise and managing my stress, I should be fine. My father died at forty-nine, so that's also a factor for me. But all this medical history is not really what I wanted to tell you about."

"No?"

"No," she replied, slowly shaking her head. "You see, Friday night after I talked to you, well, the storm kept me awake for a rather long time.

"It was quite the storm."

Camille repositioned herself nervously, trying to get comfortable. "Let me back up an hour." She put up her hand, finger on her lip. "This is going to sound rather...strange."

"Go ahead. You've caught my interest."

"If you remember, I was home alone. When I was getting out of the shower, it was quite steamy in the bathroom. As I wiped off the mirror so I could see my reflection, I was terrified because it looked like there was a person, actually a woman, standing behind me. It was so real. When I turned around, it was just a picture of the Alps hanging on the wall."

She paused and took a drink of her water. "I was a complete basket case. After our conversation, I finally fell asleep, but experienced this dream, or it was more like a reoccurrence of the day before Valentine's Day when I had the heart attack and left my body. I'm sure it was something I had experienced at that time and was just now remembering. Or, and this sounds even stranger—that I was actually experiencing it again in reality? I don't know. But"—Camille felt her face brighten—"it was wonderful. I was weightless and it felt so right. I went flying past all the people I loved, not even worried that I wouldn't be seeing them anymore. I ended up in the most beautiful place."

Günther was smiling now, too, a captivated look on his face. He came around his desk and took the chair opposite her.

"Go on, *please.*"

"It was dazzling. I won't even try to describe it, except to say, I'm sure it must have been heaven, or a place before heaven, paradise, or something. I don't know. What I *do* know is that it was not of *this* world."

The jarring sound of Günther's office phone rent the stillness of the air, making Camille jump. It rang three times, but Günther chose to ignore it. The answering machine picked up and the caller left a message.

After it was quiet again, Günther prompted, "And?"

"I was alone. At least, that's what it seemed like at first. I didn't see anyone around me, but soon felt a presence of someone. I wasn't scared, but happy and I knew in my heart that I'd died, and was on my way to my new destiny. Suddenly, out of nowhere came a voice. It was a woman's voice, coming from over a small hill. I couldn't see who it was. The woman called me by name. Before I could see her, I awakened."

Günther sat forward, his elbows resting on his knees, his chin perched on his folded fingers. Wonder gleamed in his eyes. "How marvelous. Is that all? You can't remember anything else?"

"Isn't that enough?"

"Yes." He laughed. "And no. One can never get enough firsthand experience of heaven. We can try to understand our true destinies, the best we can through our hope and faith, but actual eye witness…"

When he stood, Camille did too, although a little shaky. They embraced. "Don't worry. You were given a great gift," he said next to her hair, then stepped away. "You have been chosen for something wonderful."

Yes, that was how she felt. She just wanted to know what it all meant. "What about the face? Do you think that was just my imagination because I was edgy from what had happened with Sasha and then with the storm?"

"I don't know."

Günther took her drink and set it next to his on his desk. "Now, let's go celebrate your big day. I know a little neighborhood spot that serves a wonderful Sunday brunch. It's close. Just around the corner. You must be starving by now. I know I am."

He opened the door and waited until Camille exited.

This wasn't a date, Günther told himself. They would just enjoy a meal together. Drink some coffee. Pass an hour in conversation.

Chapter Twenty-Four

They were just exiting the building when the tower clock chimed ten thirty. Clouds had gathered, covering the sun, and the air had turned frosty. As they walked along his phone rang again, bringing a moment of annoyance. "Christove," he answered. "*Ja. Ich verstehe. Ja, OK.*" He disconnected and slipped it back in his pocket.

"I'm very sorry, Camille, but I have to cancel our outing," he apologized. "Something very important has come up."

Camille looked lovely standing there with the breeze ruffling her skirt. Instinctively, she pulled her soft-looking wrap closer around her body. He could see the disappointment in her eyes, and felt his all the more.

"Please, don't be sorry," she said. "Bob and weave, I always say."

He reached out and gently squeezed her elbow. "You can get home then?"

"Of course. I walk this every day."

Günther glanced down at her fancy heels. "But normally with your athletic shoes. It will be quite a different matter in those. Let me call you a cab."

She made a silly face. "Günther, stop worrying. I'll take it slow. Do a little window-shopping. Stop and have a cup of coffee. If I find it's too unbearable," she reached into her purse and pulled out her own cell phone, "I'll call a cab myself. I am capable, you know."

"That you are." He was reluctant to leave. "If you insist then."

"I insist."

He backed away a couple of steps. She *was* disappointed. Her eyes looked sad to see him go. He would make it up to her before her two months were over and she left for home. They'd do something fantastic. Something she would remember for the rest of her life. The coming Bonbon Ball, held at the Vienna Symphony *Konzerthaus*, popped into his head making him smile. "Don't talk to any strangers."

She laughed.

The sound of her happiness fueled him, making him want to stay a moment longer.

"I'm totally serious." He grinned broadly, taking pleasure in teasing her. His reward was a defiant stance and pointed finger.

"Go on now," she chastised. "I'll see you tomorrow."

"Indeed you will. Bright and early."

Camille quashed her disappointment as Günther disappeared down the street. She wanted to have brunch with him, get to know him better. See if this feeling growing inside her was real.

She felt relieved she'd finally told him about her heart attack. He hadn't thought her weird at all. In fact, he'd seemed in awe of her.

She would use this Sunday morning to learn more about the city. She would have fun on her own. What should she do? Nobody had returned to the house yet, but Wolfgang had called and left a message on the answering machine telling her he'd be home sometime today. Helene was staying with Sasha; the children were still with their grandmother. They had no answers yet concerning Sasha. He said he and Helene were sorry about leaving her alone.

The street was much less crowded today than on a busy weekday, but still the Viennese filled the eateries and coffee houses with laughter. All the retail shops were closed but the restaurants, pubs, and bakeries were taking up the slack.

For a change of pace, she'd take an alternate route home. See something new. Her sense of direction was getting quite good, and after just the few days she'd been here she felt she was getting to know the area well.

Was it too late to call Kristin? She didn't want to wake her. Besides, the cell phone charge would be astronomical. Deciding to Skype when she got back to the house, she started off.

After several more blocks, Camille sank onto a sidewalk bench. These shoes *weren't* made for walking. A blister had already formed on her heel, and both toes pinched cruelly. Not only that, but the temperature had dropped and it was bitterly cold. She looked across the street to a sports shop and the blue Nikes on sale. If only the store were open, she'd march right in and purchase them. As much as she hated to admit it, Günther was right. She needed to call a cab.

"Cabbie, stop here."

Camille rummaged around her purse for her euros. They'd only gone a few blocks when she spotted a darling restaurant tucked between two brick buildings. It was especially busy, a good sign that the food was worth sampling.

She was starved. If she went home now, no telling what there was to fix. Besides, it was Sunday, a day she usually went out to brunch with her mother and Kristin. She would show her independence and go alone.

After a completely scrumptious breakfast, Camille set her fork into her empty plate and sighed. She was rejuvenated. The strawberry torte and several cups of coffee had revived her, but still she sat. In actuality, she was avoiding getting up on her sore feet. Even the walk to the curb to get in a cab was too long. Under the table, she wiggled her shoeless toes and decided to have one more cup of coffee.

Camille had her coffee cup halfway to her mouth when she noticed Johann hurrying past the restaurant window. His cheeks were candy apple red in contrast to his bright yellow jacket. A mountain of worry marked his face. He glanced back quickly, and then darted away, making her think someone may be following him.

Chapter Twenty-Five

Adrenalin shot through Camille. Instantly, she gulped down the remainder of her lukewarm coffee. With a grimace, she pulled on her shoes and jumped up, bumping the table in the process. Dishes rattled dangerously and water sloshed over the rim of her glass onto the white tablecloth. Ignoring the razor-sharp pains in her feet and the waiter's flabbergasted expression, she limped as fast as she could out the door, thankful she'd already paid the bill.

On the sidewalk, she grasped a flower-basket-topped pole for support. She searched down the street. Johann was gone.

No way was she going to be able to follow him anywhere in these blasted, feet-mangling heels. She kicked them off, then stuffed them into her bag, running to the corner of the block.

"Johann," she called loudly between cupped hands. Too late. He was rounding the next corner, too far away to hear her.

"Oh my gosh. I'll never catch him," she said to no one in particular. She didn't care now how many people wondered why a woman was running down the street in her stockings. The boy had looked distressed. She was sure he was in some kind of trouble. Günther had said he was not to go around unescorted. Maybe Bernhard was trying to steal him away again. She had to help.

Leaving the business area behind, Camille noticed the blocks had changed into a neighborhood. Her feet were cold and numb. She wondered if she was still going in the right direction.

From of the corner of her eye, she caught a flash of yellow as a small figure climbed several steps of an old home and disappeared inside.

It had to be Johann. She wondered now at the wisdom of following him on such a goose chase. What if he was fine? Just out visiting or going home? She didn't know where he lived. Could this be it? He was already suspicious of her. She'd seen the distrust in his eyes as he'd looked at her. Well, there was only one way to find out. She'd never sleep tonight unless she knew he was okay. Let him be mad. Better angry with her than abducted, never to be seen again.

Before she stepped onto the porch, she paused, and as gingerly as she could, put her shoes back on. She took the stairs very slowly, each sending shooting pains up her legs.

She knocked.

An older woman wearing an apron opened the door. "*Kann ich Ihnen helfen?*" She asked if she could help her.

Oh dear. She needed to put her German to the test. "*Ja, bitte.*" Her mind went blank. Each second felt like an hour. All she could remember was, I am American. "*Ich bin Amerikanerin.*"

The woman waited patiently.

Feeling pressured, Camille blurted out in English. "I'm looking for a small boy." She held out her hand waist high. "I saw him enter here. Can I talk to him, please?"

The woman was trying to understand what she was saying. Camille could tell she wasn't getting any of it. The woman shrugged.

Camille paused, then said, "Johann." She put her hands out again and pretended to give the imaginary boy a hug.

The woman's eyes lit up. "*Ahhh, Johann. Ja. Ja. Bitte, hereinkommen.*" She opened the door and stepped aside, motioning for Camille to come inside.

The entry was small and cluttered with a coat rack and two straight-back chairs against the wall. It certainly wasn't Helene's home, smelling of fresh-baked bread and apple strudel.

The woman retreated down the hallway. "*Einen Moment, bitte.*"

Camille felt like an intruder. What would she say to Johann when he appeared? I thought you were running from an abductor. Is your drunken uncle chasing you? Compared to her German, Johann's English was excellent. He was much more accomplished than she. He'd have no problem understanding anything she would say. But would he appreciate the intrusive behavior in his life?

Her stomach clenched with nerves. She glanced down at her feet. The bottoms of her stockings had worn through during the pursuit, and the dirty, tattered ends were now pulling up around her calves. If there were a bathroom handy, she would hurry and take them off. She glanced around. Too late, the door was reopening and the woman was on her way back.

"*Bitte.*" The woman motioned to one of the chairs, then disappeared into another room.

Camille nodded and took a seat. Muffled voices floated down the hall. A long, rattling sentence followed by a shout startled her. Was that cursing? Camille fidgeted, seriously regretting coming here at all.

The door opened and Johann appeared. Not a step behind was Günther.

Stunned, Camille stood. She wanted to evaporate into thin air. Their walk down the hall seemed to take a lifetime as she felt her world spinning. As sure as she knew the nose on her face, Günther was *not* happy to see her.

She waited for them to reach the entry before trying a wobbly smile. Johann's face was dark and foreboding, and Günther's? She couldn't tell. His eyes were masked. But it was the first time she'd seen him without a welcoming smile and friendly "hello."

For a moment, they all stood staring at each other. Without a word, Günther went into a side room, and motioned for her to follow.

"What are you doing here?" His tone was harsh.

"I-I," she stammered. Hurt. She hadn't meant to intrude into Günther's private life but that was exactly what she'd done. If he didn't mean so much to her this would be a lot easier. "I saw Johann," she began again, "from a restaurant window where I was eating. He looked like he was running away from someone, or in some sort of trouble. So I followed." She glanced at the boy, not wanting him to know Günther had shared with her the circumstances about his uncle. He stood a few feet from the adults, listening.

Another shout came from the room down the hall. Günther jammed his fingers through his hair, perturbed. He turned and stared out the window.

"Günther, I'm sorry. I didn't mean to intrude."

Günther turned to Johann and gave him a curt order in German that Camille couldn't understand. Johann just stood there, his face defiant, and she knew he was disobeying whatever it was Günther had told him to do. After a moment of Günther's hard stare, the boy hurried back down the hall.

"I really thought Johann needed me. I would *never* have imposed on you like this had I known he was coming to see you," Camille said, trying to get it all out before he interrupted.

"The boy called me soon after I left you this morning," Günther replied, annoyance still written in his face. "He wanted to come with me. I told him no. He disobeyed and slipped out of the house."

When he glanced down at her feet, she swallowed nervously. She ignored the angry clenching of his jaw and said, "You were right. I should have called a cab right away. Running after Johann didn't help."

Shouting was followed by another loud crash. A nurse ran down the hall to the room.

When Günther turned, she placed her hand on his arm, stopping him. "Günther, who's in there?"

Günther looked at her for a long second. "Aggie. My *wife's* mother. I'll be right back." He moved away and her hand fell, leaving her insides cold.

Chapter Twenty-Six

Camille gathered herself together and quietly left the house. She was not sorry for following Johann but she was desperately sorry she'd stepped into Günther's private world, upsetting him. Even though the blunder had been totally accidental, it didn't make her feel any better.

Mother-in-law?

Where had that come from?

Had he actually said his wife's mother?

It was too hard to believe. Where was his wife? He'd never even hinted that he had one. He didn't wear a wedding band. Although, by no means really had he *ever* done anything out of line with her even if he *were* married. She certainly would not have let her imagination run wild concerning him if she had known.

Mrs. Günther Christove.

A horn blared, and Camille almost fell as she jumped back and scrambled to the sidewalk. A little red Porsche careened down the lane and was gone. She didn't even see the car that had almost hit her. The pain of her sore, blistered feet was dull compared to the pain in her heart.

Another horn beeped, and a green compact pulled over.

"I thought that was you," Wolfgang called out the passenger window. "I was horrified when you stepped into the street in front of that Porsche. Get in. I'm on my way home now."

"Thank you." Camille opened the door and climbed in. "I don't think I could have walked another step."

"I guess not." His tone was tinged with incredulous humor as he took in the sight of her feet. "What happened to your stockings?"

"I bit off a little more than I could chew."

He snickered.

"Okay, a lot more. It wouldn't have been a problem in my comfortable shoes. How's Sasha?"

His face clouded. "Not good. I guess Helene told you that the doctors suspect some level of autism."

His expression tore her heart.

"That is what they're basing their tests on. We really don't know much yet."

"I'm so sorry, Wolfgang. How are the twins taking the news?"

He put on his signal, made a right turn into a circle change, and sped past a truck. "We haven't told them. But they're old enough to know something is going on. They are good kids though, and are waiting patiently, giving us time before demanding an explanation. We'll have to give them one soon."

"If there is anything I can do to help. In any way. Please, you must let me."

"Thank you, I will. At the moment, I really can't think of anything."

Two minutes later, they were pulling into the small garage.

Wolfgang put the car in park and switched off the ignition. He turned and looked at her. "Actually, there is something. Just be a friend for Helene. She's going to need someone she can talk to when they return. Woman to woman."

"Of course. That goes without saying." They sat in the dark garage as the door had closed. "Can I go to her now? Be a support for her?"

"That is very kind, but no. When they get home will be soon enough."

Wolfgang opened his door and collected his things off the backseat. "We're sorry to have all this emotional upheaval happen to spoil your holiday. Leaving you alone much of the time," he said over the hood of the car as they walked inside. "It is not our usual hospitality."

Before entering the house, Camille took off her shoes and dangled them from her index finger. "I've been doing just fine on my own. Don't give that another thought. Now I'm going to run upstairs."

He raised an eyebrow.

"Okay, I'm going to limp upstairs, change, and then come down and fix you something to eat."

"No, no. I ate on my way home. We'll think about that later."

"You sure?"

"Positive. Unless you're hungry. Have you eaten today?"

Camille wished she were still in her newfound favorite restaurant. Another cup of coffee would have been heavenly. If only she'd opted for that instead of following Johann. "Yes. I had brunch after Mass."

"Alone?" His scrunched brow told her he was again sorry.

"I enjoyed the solitude."

"I don't believe you. Anyway, get a pot in the kitchen on your way upstairs and go soak those feet. You'll find antiseptic and bandages in the medicine cabinet. If you need anything else, just call down."

After a good, hot soak, Camille flopped down on her bed. Today *was* Sunday, after all. A day set apart for rest and rejuvenation.

She'd call Kristin in an hour or two, or get her online. It was still too early on the west coast to call now. She missed her daughter. Missed her happy-go-lucky ways. Her insatiable laughter. She missed her great big bear hugs desperately, and wished she could feel one right this very moment.

Camille rested back on her pillow and opened a travel magazine. Would Günther call? Most likely not. *He's married*, she reminded herself. The other calls he'd made to her had been out of courtesy when she hadn't come to class. And then about Sasha.

She closed the magazine and flopped her arm across her eyes, feeling physically and emotionally drained. Every bone in her body seemed to sink down into the mattress. What a day. So much to figure out.

She tried to analyzed her feelings truthfully. She *was* sorry Günther was married. She would be a liar if she said she didn't care. How had she been so wrong? She'd thought that he was interested in her. At least a little. She'd felt the chemistry. The bond. She yawned and closed her eyes for a moment. Was it all in her head? Her head, it must be. Must, must be all in her…

Startled, Camille cried out in delight when she found herself back in the garden, the beautiful place she'd told Günther about today. Thinking about him now brought a profound sadness. But his image seemed to intensify the colors surrounding her, the feelings, the sounds.

She strained to focus on the trees, the flowers. There was so much to see. She headed in the direction of the hill where she'd heard the woman's voice before.

"Hello?" she called out softly.

Just like the first time, her heart filled with a joy so deep it almost hurt. "Is anyone here with me?" Camille turned a complete circle, noticing her feet felt perfectly fine. In awe, she strolled past a brook and under a canopy of blossoming trees, enjoying their lovely fragrance. Each one was unique, as different as snow is to the sun. Where the bark on one was shining with a pearlescent coppery color and had twinkling silver flowers, another was a deep coral shade with periwinkle and gold blossoms. Inside the trunk, some sort of liquid pulsed in rhythm with the soft breeze. Unable to control her curiosity, she reached out and gently ran her finger over the strange bark. The tree quivered and a slight tinkling sound surrounded her.

Camille pulled back in alarm. "Oh, I'm sorry."

The tinkling came again. It was the breeze or the air or something else. The petals trembled and shimmered as if trying to communicate with her. Goodness radiated all around. From the plants, the sky, the ground.

"This is not possible," she whispered aloud.

"Are not all things possible with God?"

Camille turned quickly expecting to find someone behind her. "Where are you? Why can't I see your face?"

"You will see me when the time is right. For now, just enjoy the privilege you've been given."

Each time the voice spoke, it came from a different location. But it was, without doubt, the same female voice Camille had heard Friday night.

"Look more closely."

Feeling like Alice in Wonderland, Camille looked up into the branches, deeper into the blossoms, knowing there must be something magical there.

The miniature birds, which had been still and invisible until now, took flight all at once. They swooped down and surrounded her, enveloping her in a cocoon of love.

Camille opened her eyes when a knock sounded on her door. "What? Who is it?"

"It's Wolfgang. I heard you cry out." He paused. "Is everything okay?"

Camille rolled from the bed and opened the door. "Yes, I'm fine. I fell asleep, that's all." She glanced at the clock. An hour had passed. It felt more like a few moments.

"Good. A little nap is what you needed."

The phone next to her clock rang. "Oh, I'll leave you to that," Wolfgang said as he turned and started down the stairs."

Günther, she wondered?

With trembling hands, Camille lifted the receiver.

Chapter Twenty-Seven

"Mom, it's me. Kristin."

Camille's heart stopped its crazy thumping and was replaced with delight at the sound of her daughter's voice.

"You must have picked up on my vibes today because I wanted to call you an hour ago, but it was too early. I didn't think you'd appreciate me waking you up. How are you, sweetheart?"

"Super good."

Kristin's voice was a bit too chipper.

"Kristin?"

"Mom…I really *miss* you. I didn't know I would so much."

"I miss you too. I was wishing earlier today for one of your big hugs. It's only been a week since I left. I don't know how I'll make it without you for two months." Camille wondered if there was something else Kristin wasn't telling her.

Silence filled the line. Camille waited. She heard Kristin sniff a few times and thought she heard her crying softly.

"Kristin, honey, what is it? Has something happened?"

Kristin sniffed louder into the phone. "No."

Camille doubted that missing her mother was all that was troubling her, but she didn't want to push her daughter. "How are Grandma and Aunt Stephanie?"

"Grandma is…Grandma, you know. She's well. And I like staying here. I've been helping her with all her chores. I even cooked spaghetti the other night."

"Good girl."

"And Aunt Stephanie, she's great and all but…she's not you, Mom. She doesn't understand me at all." Kristin blew her nose. "She's pretty bossy too."

Camille's stomach tightened. A nodule of guilt blossomed, taking root. How else was a young teen supposed to feel when her mother runs off all the way around the world? And for something as frivolous as to study a foreign language, for goodness' sake. She and Kristin were like two peas in a pod. They had been inseparable since Bret died. They did everything together. Biking, running, skiing, and she even let her friends see them going to the movies together. They were best friends.

"Yes she does, honey. Give her a chance. You know they both love you very much."

"I know that, Mom, but…" Her voice faded off into silence.

Camille glanced at the wall calendar. "I can arrange to come home, Kristin. I knew when the three of you gave me my going-away gift that two months was a *really* long time. I can easily change my plans."

Something inside Camille rioted. Her heart was rising up against her better judgment.

Günther is married.

She had to stop this crazy fascination with him. Better to leave now before she fell deeper, before her heart got completely broken.

"No, don't do that," Kristin screeched. "I feel a lot better just talking with you. I don't want to spoil your trip."

Going home a month early was probably the smartest thing she could do. She was falling in love with a married man. She was having crazy dreams and visions and doing fanatical things like running down the street in only her stockings. She worried about the outlandish lengths her possibly unbalanced study partner was willing to go to make her life miserable. He was a hard one to figure out. Going home early would actually be very smart.

"But I'm homesick too. Can't I please come home? If I came home after a month, then maybe next year I could come back for a refresher course. I wouldn't mind doing that at all. I'll look into it tomorrow."

"Mom, no! Aunt Stephanie will absolutely *kill* me. I'm sorry I said anything to you. I'm just being a big baby. I'll be fine." Kristin sighed. "Really. Mom, promise you won't do anything to change your ticket."

"Now, stop panicking. I won't say anything to Stephanie or Grandma just yet. First, I'm going to find out if it's even possible, without a huge loss of the money you all spent. Oh, by the way, how's Scott?"

"Scott?"

"Yes, Scott," Camille said, laughing. She wanted to cheer Kristin up.

"He's really nice. Did Aunt Stephanie tell you about him?"

"A little birdie flew all the way around the world and landed in my window."

"No, Aunt Stephanie told you. See what I mean?" Her voice was back to normal.

Camille could hear Kristin's cell phone ringing in the background.

"Aunt Stephanie is supposed to tell me. She wouldn't be doing her job if she didn't. Now, be sure to be nice to her. And be a good help too."

"I better go now, Mom."

"Okay, sweetheart. Thank you so much for calling. I'll call you back in a couple of days with some news. Don't worry about anything. Remember I love you, sweetie. And Jesus loves you too."

"Mom?"

"What?"

"That just sounded like Grandma, not you."

Camille laughed. "Grandma's a pretty smart lady."

They said their good-byes and Camille hung up the receiver and smiled.

Boy trouble.

All the way around.

Florian was worried. He sat at his desk staring blindly at his calendar. *Pfarrer* Schimke had the Sunday evening Mass and he could hear the congregation singing in the church.

Two days had passed since the meeting with Elizabeth Roth in regard to Johann. Just yesterday, Bernhard had called on Günther with his late-night visit at his apartment, which was totally out of character for the man. If only he could find Bernhard and speak with him, convince him to sign over custody. But to whom? Wolfgang, who was working on

Johann's case, had said that he and Helene would somehow take the boy. Make it work. It was a generous offer, but might prove impossible for them on Wolfgang's salary, with the three children they already had. And now there was the troubling news about Sasha, and whatever that would play out to be. The family had the room and intention, but lacked the means with which to carry it out.

How long did they have? Ms. Roth had said the weekend. That was almost over. It seemed impossible. Florian's gaze moved up the wall to the crucifix hanging there. *Impossible for us, but not impossible for You.*

Florian closed his eyes and rested his head in his hands. "It's up to You, Lord. Use me in any way that You need me but…help us find a home for Johann. So he doesn't have to leave everything that he loves. So he won't be trapped by his uncle into a life of hopelessness and crime."

There was a cough outside his door and then a knock.

"*Ja, bitte kommen Sie herein.*"

Old *Pfarrer* Blauberg tottered in and closed the door behind him. "Guten Abend, Pfarrer Florian."

Florian returned the greeting and motioned for him to have a seat on the chair facing his desk. His old friend took his time getting comfortable, and then shared with Florian his congratulations on how successful the Saturday English class was becoming. The number of students was growing each week. It was good work. Important work.

Florian got comfortable too. Once *Pfarrer* Blauberg got it in his mind to visit, he could easily carry on for an hour as if it were only a minute. Not getting out much anymore, he was a bit lonely. He'd lived his vocation loyally, working hard, and Florian was happy to visit with him when there were no pressing matters at hand and when time allowed.

A time like now.

Pfarrer Blauberg went on saying he'd enjoyed very much meeting the young American woman. She was intelligent and had an air about her. She looked extremely prosperous, in her American sort of way…

The rest of what the elderly priest said faded out as an idea took hold in Florian's mind. Turning, tumbling, picking up speed.

Is this your way, Lord? He glanced at the crucifix. *Are You speaking to me through* Pfarrer *Blauberg, as providence would have it?* His visitor had just said something funny and was laughing, as he slapped his knee. He got up.

"*Gute Nacht, Pfarrer* Florian."

"*Gute Nacht, Pfarrer* Blauberg." Florian stood too, feeling a bit guilty over not paying closer attention to his words. He walked with him to the office door and assisted him up the tricky stairway to his room.

Was he putting the cart before the horse?

Could Camille Ashland have been sent to them for a reason? A very important one, at that?

In the darkness of the quiet house, Camille got ready for the Monday of her second week of class. An hour earlier, she'd heard Wolfgang banging around in the kitchen and then watched his taillights as he left for work. She was much more nervous today than she had been last week, and dreaded seeing Günther after their encounter yesterday.

The circles under her eyes attested to the fact that she had gotten little sleep. Robotically, she pulled on a pair of

Levis and donned a chocolate-brown sweater over a camisole top.

After nine days here, she was much better at judging the unpredictable weather that could be bright one moment and cloud up with rain the next, and was familiar with the idiosyncrasies of the old school building with its drafty halls and cool rooms.

She studied her reflection in the mirror as she brushed her hair. She'd lost a little weight. She added a touch more blusher to her drawn, pale face. She looked intently at her mirror image, remembering how different she had looked lying on the floor of her shop. Life was such a mystery. She felt sorry for the people who couldn't bring themselves to believe in the supernatural or afterlife. It seemed amazing to her.

What was going on anyway? Again last night she'd had another very short vision, or dream, or whatever they were. Camille felt sure they were real, in some way, the remembrance of her three and a half minutes in...eternity?

It was so uncanny. If it were God she was seeing or angels, saints, or some other known heavenly entity, she would feel a little bit better in thinking it was some sort of afterlife experience.

But an unknown woman? She'd actually gotten a glimpse of her for the first time last night, with her long brown hair and striking face. Obscure to say the least, but she'd seen it. *Very close to the face she'd seen in the mirror.* She'd tried to talk to her and ask her what she wanted. Why she kept coming back time and time again as if she wanted—no, *needed*, to tell her something important.

Before she'd gotten a chance to get close enough, she'd awakened in the darkness of her room, alone and bewildered. She lay there awake for hours until she heard Wolfgang below.

Camille made sure the house was locked up and made her way toward the school in the comfort of her Nikes. Her feet still hurt, but with the Band-Aids she'd brought with her and plush socks, they weren't too much of a problem.

She needed a cup of coffee. Time was short this morning and she hadn't put forth the effort to make a pot at home. Helene usually took care of that and with her gone, she and Wolfgang would need to take up the slack.

She ducked into a pastry shop in the middle of the block. The women behind the counter hustled back and forth as they helped customers.

Branwell stood at the front of the line. As if subconsciously sensing her presence, he turned and saw her enter the store. She hadn't seen him since class on Thursday, and what he'd done to her on Wednesday morning still rankled.

She pasted a smile on her face, and waved.

He waved back and smiled, although it didn't reach his eyes. He signaled for her to come forward to where he was. "Let me buy you a cup of coffee?" he said.

"You sure?" *What's this about?*

"Of course." He smiled warmly.

"Okay. That's very kind of you." She was wary. Why now?

"What would you like? Espresso? Latte?"

"Plain coffee will do," Camille said.

"Two black coffees," he voiced when it was his turn. "Would you like a pastry, Camille?"

Camille was looking over all the wonderful offerings while they were waiting for their drinks. "Oh, no. Just fantasizing. I don't usually eat breakfast." *Stephanie would be horrified at the thought of me eating one of these sticky delights crammed with cholesterol.*

"The marzipan rolls are good."

"No, really. You go right ahead, though. I don't mind."

He shook his head.

The woman handed Branwell two cups of coffee in sturdy cardboard cups. Camille took one from his hands and walked over to the condiment table.

As she dumped some coffee off the top to make room for her milk, she inwardly cringed. This was so awkward. She searched for something to say.

She wanted to ask him about their walk on Wednesday, but then, didn't want to bring up bad blood, so to speak. He was only twenty. She would treat him with respect. Like she wanted him to treat her. She should be able to handle someone his age, but there was just something about him, something very different. He made her nervous.

"You missed Friday."

It was said matter-of-factly but she could see he was very interested in what she was about to say. Did he think she was filing harassment charges with the school? *That's what this is all about.* The thought had crossed her mind.

They walked out of the shop and down the street. She took a sip, making him wait for her answer. "I had business that needed some attention."

Now it was his turn to sip. He looked around nonchalantly. Smiled at some schoolgirls passing by. "We had a couple of handouts. I picked some up for you."

This was a Branwell she didn't know, and made her even more suspicious.

"Well, thank you again. That was good of you."

Stephen suddenly appeared out of nowhere and began walking along with them, falling into step. Relief flooded and she felt tiny between the two tall men.

"Good morning, Camille. I hoped I would see you on my way to the office."

On his way to the office? Right. His appearances were getting uncomfortably frequent. He was showering her with more attention than she wanted.

"Hi," she replied. "Fancy meeting you here. You're on your way to work, then? Somewhere that you can't name?"

He laughed and gave her a wink. "You mad at me?" He put his arm around her shoulder and squeezed before letting his arm drop. "Have you decided where you'd like to eat tomorrow night? I was very disappointed Saturday when you canceled."

Chapter Twenty-Eight

Oh, brother! Branwell was soaking this up like a sponge. She could see him mentally filing away each and every word that came from Stephen's mouth. Delight beamed from his eyes and he could hardly keep a straight face. Camille looked around and said the name of the first restaurant she saw.

"There," she pointed, wanting to put an end to the discussion as quickly as possible. "I've heard the food is *really* good."

Stephen scoffed. "No way. You can go there anytime. This has to be special."

He put his hand out to Branwell as if just noticing him.

It was so blatant, Branwell couldn't do anything but take it.

"Branwell Rothshine-Millerman," Stephen said, having no problem with the very long, unusual last name.

Startled, Camille looked at Stephen, trying to remember when she'd told him about Branwell.

Stephen laughed. "Come on, Camille. You don't remember telling me about your study partner? Friday afternoon ring any bells?"

"Pleased to make your acquaintance," Branwell responded. His put-out expression was most likely a result of the thought of Camille discussing him with friends.

Camille *knew* she hadn't said anything to Stephen about Branwell, the class, or about *any* of the students. But then, that had been a very upsetting day.

"Branwell, this is Stephen Turner," Camille offered. "He's from the States also." She refused to give him any other explanation.

They'd reached the steps of the school, and stopped. Out of the corner of her eye, she noticed Günther approaching from the other direction. His hands were deep in his pockets and his shoulders were hunched against the cold. He looked devilishly handsome and her heart did a somersault before she looked away.

"We better get to class, Stephen," she said and tried to move away from him without seeming rude. "We don't want to be late."

He nodded. He glanced up at the doorway.

Branwell downed his coffee.

"Allow me." Stephen took Branwell's empty cup from his grasp, not giving the younger man a chance to refuse. Branwell's eyes narrowed. "There's a trash can right over there," Stephen explained. "I'm going right past it."

Camille still held her half-full cup between her palms. What was Stephen up to, anyway? She'd never before witnessed him acting so peculiar. Günther avoided them completely and took the steps two at a time. There was no doubt that he'd seen her here with Stephen and Branwell, but chose not to stop and talk.

She wasn't surprised. She desperately wanted to make things right with him again. Regain the easy camaraderie they'd shared before yesterday afternoon when she'd blundered into his private affairs. Even if Günther was married, she didn't want to lose his friendship.

Three days passed quickly. Oddly enough, Günther had not returned to the classroom since Camille last saw him entering the building, and his fill-in, Stena von Linné, was enjoying her newfound position of authority.

On the first day, she'd informed them that *Herr* Christove had a pressing matter he had to attend to and would not be in class for a few days. He was sorry if this presented a problem for any of them, but she assured the class that he was monitoring their lessons closely and would be going over all their work personally.

Camille's enchanted balloon burst. Günther's absence was her doing. She wasn't sure why, but feel it she did. She'd caught passing glimpses of him in the hallways, but he was always too far away to get his attention. If he wanted to talk to her, he had her number.

With Stena in charge, Branwell took on a completely new persona. He was her right-hand assistant and between the two of them, they were making Camille's classroom experience nerve-racking to the point she considered dropping out. One or the other was always calling on her for the answers to the most difficult questions, embarrassing her time and time again.

She decided she would check with the office today about canceling her two-month enrollment for a refund or credit for another year. She hated to give in. To let them win. But what did it really matter. Her heart was begging her to do so.

After class, Camille went upstairs to the administration office to make an appointment to see the placement counselor the following day.

Florian turned his ignition key to Off and pulled his motorbike onto the kickstand. Straddling the seat, he slipped off his gloves and placed them on the dash. He slowly went about unbuckling his helmet.

It had been a quiet Wednesday evening in the rectory and he'd felt the growing need for speed. He needed a diversion, something to take his mind off the looming approach of Friday, when Elizabeth Roth came back with all the necessary papers to take Johann from the Weissmans and enroll him in the institutional home in Germany. She'd been busy and granted them a few extra days. All because he and Günther had failed miserably in finding the child a permanent home.

After riding for an hour through the winding roads of the hillsides, he'd come back into the city and now found himself parked in front of Wolfgang and Helene's home. The temporary home of the American, Camille.

He couldn't get the idea out of his head. It had taken form on Sunday evening and grown until he was forced to come here and see if it held any merit. He got off his bike and carried his helmet under his arm as he approached the door. *Lord, this is up to You.*

He rang the bell.

Camille answered a moment later. She was wearing a light gray sweater and jeans, and had her phone in her hand.

"Good evening, Camille. Is either Wolfgang or Helene home?"

Her expression was one of surprise. "Father Florian, hello. Please come in. Wolfgang is working in his study. I'll get him."

Florian stepped inside the house and Camille closed the door. On her way to Wolfgang's office, she clicked off the television, where she must have been watching a show.

"*Pfarrer* Christove. Come in. Sit down," Wolfgang called out as he hurried into the living room.

Florian sat on the sofa opposite Wolfgang, putting his helmet at his feet. Camille hovered by the kitchen, watching. He turned to her. "Please join us."

She looked a bit uneasy. "You sure? Don't you want to talk in private?"

He laughed. "No, no. This is social."

"Well, in Helene's absence, may I offer you anything? Tea? Water?"

He shook his head.

"Homemade peach pie with vanilla ice cream?"

His taste buds sprang to life.

Camille laughed lightly, making her hair swing around her shoulders. "I made it today after school," she said. "Wolfgang needed something to cheer him up. I'll admit now that I had to use frozen peach slices, but still it's good. I'll cut you a slice."

"Small, please."

She glanced at Wolfgang.

"How can I resist? I had a piece after dinner but I'll throw caution to the wind and have another."

"Okay, three peach pies à la mode, coming right up."

Florian could hardly repress his smile. Camille had looked like she had been called into the principal's office when he'd first addressed her. Now in her element, she fairly flew around the kitchen getting the dessert ready. A bit nervously, she served him his pie, warmed, with a healthy scoop of ice cream on top. She sat on the sofa next to him.

Wolfgang and Camille watched as he took a bite. "Ummm." He chewed and swallowed. "The angels couldn't have done a better job. This is delectable. Thank you."

Camille took her first bite. She hadn't had a piece after dinner, wanting to save hers until later. It was good. It was her mom's very simple recipe that she knew by heart.

"So," Wolfgang and Florian started at the same time. They chuckled and sat back. Wolfgang gestured for Florian to proceed.

"I needed a port in the storm," Florian began, resting his fork on his plate, "that's why I came here. I'm still struggling with this problem with what to do with Johann Wernfried. The time allotted by the Child Protection *Büro* is about to run out. On Friday, in fact. They are going to end up taking Johann since I haven't been able to find his Uncle Bernhard, or a place that would be willing to take him in permanently."

He contemplated his pie as if answers could be found there. "I just needed someone to talk to tonight."

Wolfgang straightened. "I totally understand. I'm glad you came. Let me tell you that among other things this week, I have been poring over our financial accounts. Unfortunately, with Sasha and the unknown state of her condition, we just can't commit to this blessing at this time. I'm so sorry. Any other time or circumstance, we would."

Camille watched the conversation as it went easily back and forth.

"Helene and I both wish we could. Johann is a good boy and gets along fine with our three. But we exist on a pretty tight budget as it is." He turned and looked at Camille. "That's why we remodeled the upstairs seven years ago into an apartment. With the income from the student renters that the school sends our way, we are able to get by and put a tiny amount away for the children's college educations. Now with unknown medical bills coming up, that makes it even more impossible."

Camille listened intently. She hadn't known the Eberstarks were considering adopting Johann. This was news to her. Father Florian was clearly torn at the thought of Johann being placed back into the system, with his final destination unknown.

The Eberstarks' home would be a splendid place for Johann. Helene and Wolfgang were wonderful parents. He would even have a brother and two sisters for support. And he would also stay close to Günther, who was doing so much to help him, and loved him. They were meant to be together.

How devastating to find people willing to sacrifice so much to help, and yet not be able to make it work financially. Wolfgang actually thought of it as a blessing.

Suddenly, her heart began to beat faster. The conversation faded out as she thought about Saturday. Hadn't she just told Father Florian she wanted to make a difference in this world? *Well, didn't I?* Was that just something to ease her troubled conscience, or had she meant it? Truly meant it.

"Excuse me…"

The men stopped talking and looked at her.

Where had that come from?

"Yes?" Father Florian said, his face radiant with expectation.

Chapter Twenty-Nine

"I can help," Camille whispered slowly. Something inside her shrieked at her to stop. Be quiet. Forget what she was thinking. Her stomach churned and twisted, threatening to make her run to the bathroom and throw up. *What are you doing? Think this through. It's a lifelong responsibility. It will cost hundreds of thousands of dollars. Let someone else do it. It's not your responsibility!*

To contemplate taking on a commitment of this magnitude was one thing. To step up to bat, actually walk the walk and talk the talk, completely another. Her heart was willing, but her mind was trying its best to dissuade her with reason after reason why she shouldn't. But she wouldn't listen.

She bolted to her feet.

"Camille?" It was Father Florian.

Walking around the sofa, she rested her hands on the back, looking at the two. "I want to help. With Johann. I've thought about it and have come to a decision. I certainly have the means. I think this is why God brought me to Austria."

It was Wolfgang's turn to stare at her as if she had just done a backflip and landed in the splits. His expression was one of shock and disbelief.

"Forgive me, please, if what I say sounds rude or snobbish. That is not my intention at all. But the fact is, I'm a wealthy woman. It wasn't always like that. When Bret died, my daughter and I nearly had to go on welfare. And then, the first two years at Chocolate Blossoms were a struggle. It was very tough, touch and go. But now I'm established and make more than enough income to live on comfortably, put my one daughter through college, and support Johann here at the Eberstarks', if they are willing to take him in."

She glanced at Wolfgang. "It could be a joint endeavor."

Both men looked stunned. "Are you serious?" Wolfgang's face was all the encouragement she needed.

"I've never been more serious in my life."

"Camille," Father Florian began. "Think about what this means. Johann is only seven years old. That could mean eleven years of financial support. Not an insignificant amount."

Camille was picking up steam. Once she'd jumped in and made up her mind, shushed the voices trying to dissuade her, she was definitely warming to the idea. "What could be a better way to spend my money? Johann needs you all." She said "all" because she was thinking of Günther too.

The men looked at each other.

Camille couldn't contain her happiness. "Will Helene agree to this?"

"No question. I'm sure she will be very excited," Wolfgang said.

Father Florian stood. He reached out, taking Camille's hand. "I don't know how to thank you. This means more to me than you could ever know."

She looked into his blue eyes, reminding her so much of Günther. "Trust me, Father Florian, I think I do. But now we must find Bernhard, right?"

Günther paced around his apartment. This had been a very frustrating three days. He'd taken time off from class to try to find some clues into the real spies so he could clear his brother's name, or any of his students, if Turner dared to draw them in. He'd spent time in the dean's office going through files. He used the ruse that he needed to research some personal items. He'd been there many years so the school was lenient with him.

He'd turned up empty handed.

Three days and he was no closer to finding the two mysteriously clad figures from last Saturday night, or what they'd been up to. He had no other choice than to call Stephen Turner.

On the second ring, Stephen picked up the phone. "Turner."

"Günther Christove here."

There was a moment of silence. "Günther, hello. I can't say that I'm surprised to get your call," Stephen commented. "What brings you my way?"

Günther considered trying to flush Stephen out. Unfortunately, he didn't have any information that would help.

"It's about the other night at my apartment. I've been thinking. Trying to figure out who it is you're after. Unfortunately, I don't have a clue."

"So why the call?"

Günther folded himself down into his sofa, anything but comfortable. Flocki jumped into his lap.

"Because on Sunday, I inadvertently noticed you had an unexplained interest in my brother."

There was a long silence. "You're quite astute. Maybe you should rethink your line of business."

"I am right then?" Günther was in no mood for games.

"Yes."

"He doesn't have anything to do with your case. He's a priest, for God's sake."

"That may be, but that doesn't mean he's above the law."

"No?"

"Absolutely not. Everyone that has any connection to the school is suspect. His connection is you. Besides, he had clearance to top secret codes and information when he served in the army, in case it's slipped your mind."

Günther's temper flared. He mentally counted to five before responding. "There's something else."

"Go on."

"Last Saturday evening, I couldn't sleep. I went for a late-night walk and found myself at the school. I went inside and corrected papers for a few hours. On my way out of the building sometime early Sunday morning, I encountered two persons sneaking out of the building."

"How do you know they were sneaking? Maybe they were just working late like you."

"Because they were dressed in black and were wearing hoods. And because they were being as quiet as they could.

They crept down the stairs, from above. When they got to my floor, one must have sensed that someone else was there and stopped for a few seconds before going on. They were definitely sneaking. I followed them but didn't get a look at either face."

"Damn it, Christove! Why didn't you call me right away?"

Stephen had every right to be irritated with him. He should have found some time to tell him on Sunday outside the church when they were talking with Camille. At the thought of her, his heart thumped a little harder, but he pushed the feelings away.

"Because I wanted to see what I could find out on my own. I was annoyed to see that you were investigating Florian."

"Well, the trail is cold now, thanks to you. Still, I'll go over there and see if I can't find some prints or something. How late do they work in those offices?"

"It varies on weekdays."

"Could one of them have been your brother?"

"I knew you'd ask me that. No. Neither one was Florian."

"How do you know? You said they were covered and you didn't get a look at their faces."

"I checked it out. He has an alibi. He was on call that night and had gone over to the hospital to administer last rites."

"Did you tell him what's going on?" Stephen asked hotly.

"You forbade me to, remember? I just asked how his evening was and he told me about his trip to the hospital. He has no idea you're looking into his past. I want to keep it like that."

Günther heard a long, exasperated sigh on the other end of the phone line.

"The next time you have any, and I mean *any* information, you better call. Control your Sherlock Holmes ambitions."

Flocki had abandoned Günther during his long conversation. She must have been agitated by his uncharacteristically aggressive tone, and jumped off his lap to find another napping spot. "Stephen," Günther began, "what are your intentions for Camille? I don't like to see people being used."

More than four seconds went by in silence.

"Who says I'm using her? What business is it of yours, anyway?"

"She's my student. And she's vulnerable right now. I don't want her going home with a broken heart. You just want to get close to the other students and she's an easy cover for you."

"Christove, this conversation is getting ridiculous. I'll be in touch in a day or two. And Günther," Stephen lectured, "I'm glad your brother has an alibi. I really am. Talk to you later."

That evening at the rectory, Florian spent extra time with his evening prayers. As always, the Lord had provided. If things went as planned, Camille would soon set up a trust fund for Johann. The Eberstarks would use it as needed for Johann's expenses. Wolfgang would put another bed in Patrick's bedroom and that would be that. With Wolfgang's background in law enforcement, the Child Protection *Büro*

couldn't possibly turn down the adoption. The only obstacle was Bernhard. They needed to find Johann's uncle, and soon.

Pfarrer Schimke and *Pfarrer* Blauberg had retired soon after evening prayer. *Pfarrer* Blauberg was noticeably slower, feebler, and grew weaker by the day. Florian felt sure his heavenly reward was not that far away.

Back in his room, Florian reread the letter he'd received today concerning his relocation. The bishop thought St. Anthony's a very good match for him and thanked him for taking on the challenge. The move would take place in July, a month after the annual diocesan priest retreat.

Folding it neatly, he slipped it back in the envelope and put it in the top drawer of his desk. Well, that was that. He hadn't petitioned the bishop to stay, as he thought he might. After praying about it, he decided to let God's will be done.

Günther would be fine without his big brother around. They just wouldn't get to see each other quite as often. Perhaps once a month he'd make the two-hour-long drive across the city for a visit. That wasn't much.

More importantly, Johann would be fine now, too. He'd wanted to call Günther right away to tell him the good news about Camille and her generous offer, but by the time he'd gotten back from Wolfgang's it was time for evening prayer, and then the chairperson of the church festival committee had called and kept him on the phone for almost two hours. After that it was too late. He'd save the good news for the morning.

Florian stripped out of his clothes and donned a pair of sweats, than lay down on top of his covers. In his reading glasses, he flipped the pages of a motorcycle magazine and let the tensions of the day ease away. He gazed at the beautiful red sports cruiser. It was a powerful machine.

From somewhere downstairs between the rectory and the church an unfamiliar sound filtered up to Florian. He pushed up on his elbow, listening. A moment went by, but he heard nothing further. He slipped off his bed and grimaced when his bare feet contacted the cold floor. Silently he went over to his window.

Chapter Thirty

All was quiet below. It was dark except for the one small light above the gate leading into the cemetery. The olive tree and the sycamores moved slowly in a gentle breeze, so different from the stormy night before. A white cat jumped from the wall between the burial ground and the rectory garage and ran into the blackness of the night.

Cold radiated from the bottom of Florian's feet and up his legs, giving him chills. "I need to get to bed," he spoke into his quiet room. "Günther will be so surprised to hear his student from America was heaven-sent. We must celebrate tomorrow."

As Florian turned, something moved down by the gate. A mere shadow drawing his attention back into the yard? No. Someone was standing up against the side of the building. Close to the garage door. His hand was on the doorknob.

Without a moment of thought, Florian turned and hurried from his room. He bounded down the stairs. He rounded the landing and breezed through the kitchen and stopped. He dropped his hand into his pocket and felt for his rosary, bolstered by the thought of St. Michael and all the angels. He knew the Lord was already by his side. As quietly as he could, he eased open the door between the kitchen and the porch, and slipped inside the large three-car garage.

He waited for his eyes to adjust to the inky darkness. Slight noises came from the far right corner of the cold, dank space. The scent of motor oil, usually very calming, seemed to put his nerves on edge. A flashlight came on and beamed across the open space, missing Florian by a foot.

Florian crouched and inched past *Pfarrer* Schimke's clunker, a dilapidated automobile always in need of repairs, and carefully hid behind the front tire. His heartbeat thundered in his ears.

He slowly edged his way around the front bumper and flattened himself against the blue Volkswagen sedan parked in the middle slot. A noise and then a low curse came from the invader as if he'd injured himself in some way.

Gathering his courage, Florian took one quick step to the far wall and hid himself behind the water heater. He peered through the darkness. The intruder hovered around his motorcycle, oblivious to Florian as he went about his business. He wore a dark sweatshirt and hood. What was he doing? Looking for something? The person felt the dash with his hand, then let it fall down the side, moving his fingers as he inspected every nook and cranny.

He jiggled the handle on the locked glove box, and then stopped. He glanced around behind him in Florian's direction. Florian's heart slammed against his ribcage as he flattened closer to the wall. Spider webs and something sharp jabbed into his bare skin.

The intruder mumbled angrily.

Florian, now certain the burglar was a man, sized him up. He'd been pretty sure before due to his stature; but then, size could be deceiving.

The thief, setting his flashlight on the seat of the bike, knelt down and reached up under the engine, as if to place something there.

Florian took three huge strides and leaped. He landed on the man's back. The man gasped in total surprise, then let go a string of curses.

Straining every muscle in his body, Florian wrestled him, grasping for his arm so he could twist it around behind his back. Unsuccessful, they rolled to the left and bumped a stack of boxes. Cartons of paper plates, cups, and plastic utensils left over from the church picnic rained down on the two.

The man was strong. And big. *Saint Michael, Saint Michael,* was all Florian could think as the intruder flipped over in his grasp, and tried to scramble away.

With strength Florian knew wasn't his, he reached out and grasped the man's leg before he could get away. He toppled him over.

Florian leaped up and put his knee square into the man's back with a force he felt sure would subdue a giant. From inside his jacket the man pulled a knife and sliced wildly as he rolled, making contact with Florian's neck. The pain was instant and intense but then went forgotten, as warm blood flowed freely onto his chest.

Lights blazed on.

"*Pfarrer* Christove, is that you?" *Pfarrer* Schimke's voice called out loudly.

It was just the distraction Florian needed. When the interloper looked up, Florian grasped his bicycle tire pump within arm's reach and brought it down hard over the man's head. He slumped over Florian, out cold.

Florian rolled the body off his own and tried to stand. "*Pfarrer* Schimke, over here!"

His pastor was at his side instantly, helping to steady him. "What in heaven's name is going on out here? I heard noises and came down to see. Oh, no!"

Florian pulled the hood from the man's head, revealing a man they both knew well.

Bernhard!

"Florian, you're bleeding." Concern laced the older priest's voice. "Let me get you inside."

Florian put his hand over the ugly red slice that started under his left ear and continued down an inch, trying to stop the flow of blood. "I think it's only superficial. I'll be all right. First let me tie Bernhard up before he comes around."

Pfarrer Schimke went to the tool cabinet and took out a length of twine that was part of the banner for vacation bible school. He returned and gave it to Florian. "What on earth do you think he was up to?"

The loss of blood was clouding Florian's thinking. It was a moment before he said, "I'm not sure. Something to do with my motorbike." He swayed. "We best not touch anything though until we call the authorities and they come and check it out."

"Yes, yes of course. This is just like that crime show that's on every Friday night," *Pfarrer* Schimke said. "Who would have thought?"

"*Pfarrer* Schimke? *Pfarrer* Florian? Is that you? Is anyone out here?" *Pfarrer* Blauberg's sleepy voice called from the kitchen. "Are you there? Brr, it's cold in here. *Pfarrer* Schimke? Anyone here?"

"You go take care of *Pfarrer* Blauberg while I tie up Bernhard," Florian instructed as he knelt down. "I'll be right along to get myself cleaned up. And if you can, call Wolfgang and Günther. Let them know we found Bernhard."

Wolfgang, Florian, and Günther sat around the kitchen table quietly talking. After all the commotion had settled down, *Pfarrer* Schimke had summoned *Frau* Kleimer and asked her to help with Florian until he could get to the hospital. The only one going back to bed tonight was *Pfarrer* Blauberg.

"What could this mean, Wolfgang?" Florian asked. "What would Bernhard want in the rectory? And more perplexing, what was he doing with my motorcycle?"

"He's not saying just yet and I can only speculate."

Günther sipped his coffee, feeling more than a little guilty that he couldn't tell his brother what he knew. He'd called Stephen Turner as soon as he'd received the call from *Pfarrer* Schimke waking him from a deep sleep. There was a very good possibility Bernhard was involved with the people Turner was trying to uncover. Stephen had stressed to him the importance that he not give anything away around his brother or any of the others. He'd said he'd had a small breakthrough yesterday and would be in contact as soon as he could.

"Günther, did you hear what I just said?" Florian asked, an incredulous look on his face. "I think you're still asleep."

"Sorry, no."

Belying the fact that Florian's face was a bit pasty from the loss of blood, it fairly shone with an angelic beauty. "God has given us a solution for Johann."

With a noisy clunk, Günther plopped his cup onto the wooden tabletop and coffee sloshed over the rim. "Say that again." He looked between the two men.

"It's true," Florian continued. "It all transpired last night. I had intended to call you but it became too late so I was saving the good news for today."

"Stop stalling, man, and tell me."

"Your American friend. Camille. She's offered to sponsor Johann until he's eighteen. She's wealthy, you know. Anyway, during a conversation last night at Wolfgang's, she offered to help. To set up a trust fund so Wolfgang and Helene could afford to legally adopt him."

At the mention of Camille, Günther had to stop and concentrate on what his brother was saying. He'd missed her terribly these last three days. He was sorry over the way he'd treated her when she'd come to the nursing home on Sunday. He understood her explanation, but his irritation had clouded his judgment. She deserved better than he'd given. She'd only been looking out for Johann.

But *this* news. It was astonishing. And wonderful. How mysterious were God's ways.

Wolfgang and Florian were laughing.

"This is the first time I've seen Günther dumbfounded," Wolfgang chortled.

"Yes. I'll admit that I am. This is unbelievable news. And now that we have Bernhard, and he's not in a position to dispute anything anymore, the way should be clear. Have you spoken with Ms. Roth yet? What does she say?"

Florian winced at the mention of their confrontational friend. "Not yet. I'm calling her today." He pressed his hand to the bandage on his neck. "Right after I go to the hospital.

I'm sure she can't have any objections to this perfect solution."

"One would assume," Günther added sarcastically. "What about Johann, does he know?"

Wolfgang ran his hand through his hair. He looked worn out. "No. We won't tell him until we have the definite approval from the agency. We don't want to get his hopes up just to have them dashed."

"You're right about that," Günther agreed. "What about your family, Wolfgang? How are Sasha and the twins? Helene?"

"We are taking one day at a time. Helene has stayed on with Sasha at the medical center while they are testing her. Helene and I agree that it is best if the twins remain with their *Großmutter* until things at home are stable and we know a little more about their sister's condition. It won't be so frightening for them there."

Günther nodded. "I think that's wise."

It was nearing eight in the morning and Günther had to get over to the school. He glanced down at his attire, looking a bit shabby since he'd rolled from his bed and rushed over to the rectory after receiving *Pfarrer* Schimke's call.

"I need to get a shower before class." He looked at Florian. "Call me after you see the doctor."

Chapter Thirty-One

Sitting cross-legged on her bed, Camille hung up the phone from an early morning call to the United States. Kristin had answered, just getting home from school. She was snacking on cheese and crackers while she waited for her grandmother to get home from the grocery store. She sounded much better than she had on Sunday.

Camille had wanted to shout the exciting news about Johann and how he would now be a part of their lives. But for now, she'd held back, a bit apprehensive since Kristin knew nothing yet about the boy and his struggles. Would she understand her mother's motivation at all?

Camille glanced around the quiet room. So much had happened since arriving in Vienna. It was almost like she was a totally different person. In such a short time.

Would Günther be back in class? She missed him. Not only that, but another day spent with Stena and Branwell in charge would make her scream. They were a formidable pair.

Yesterday when she stepped out to go to the ladies' room, Stena announced to the class that after the lunch break they would resume class across *Michaelerplatz* at the museum, where they would study Austrian impressionists for the rest of the afternoon.

This unbeknownst to Camille, as she'd spent her lunch hour upstairs in administration inquiring if it were possible to get a partial reimbursement, in case she decided to go home early. On her way back to class, she'd run into Stena on the stairs. If the devious vixen had wanted Camille to know about the change, she would have mentioned it then. But she hadn't. Camille had spent the whole afternoon alone in the classroom wondering where everyone was.

After school, she'd learned about the museum excursion—and how it came about—when she ran into Mark Marslino in the café on the square. Camille made a personal vow that enough was enough. She knew why Branwell disliked her, as trivial as his reason was. Why couldn't he let it go? She may be clumsy but he was unforgiving. He must have unresolved insecurities. It made no sense at all.

But Stena? What had she ever done to her? *Nothing*. Well, except everyone knew the off-the-fashion-page beauty had a huge crush on Günther. *She must sense my interest in him too.* Being truthful with herself, Camille admitted she had been romantically interested in him from the start. Was that it? *Am I that transparent?*

Had been interested. *Had been*—she reminded herself harshly.

The question was, did Stena know he was married? This was her second term. She must. Perhaps a small thing like a wife didn't matter to her at all.

Camille descended into the kitchen looking for some hot coffee. A quarter pot of yesterday's was all that was there. She glanced into the living room for Wolfgang. Not finding him, she looked in the garage and found his car gone.

Rinsing the pot, she filled it with spring water from the jug on the counter and added the grounds. While it brewed, she hurried back upstairs to get ready for the day. Twenty minutes later, dressed in jeans and a royal blue cashmere sweater set, Camille poured a cup of coffee and opened the morning paper she'd picked up off the front step. She glanced down the page, looking for something easy to try. Since her arrival, her German was much improved. She could understand a good percentage of what she heard and she could speak in simple sentences, proficient in getting her ideas across. But reading the paper or magazines, made up of complex sentence structure with three-inch-long words, was another story. Giving up, she flipped to the cartoons. She always did well there.

"Camille."

Camille jerked around in surprise, sloshing coffee everywhere. She was alone. Yet someone just whispered into her ear. *I didn't imagine it.* A shiver of apprehension tiptoed up her spine. Turning back, she took the kitchen towel and began dabbing at the counter and newspaper, her thoughts on what had just occurred.

It was the woman's voice. She was sure of it. The same woman from her dreams, or visions, or whatever they were. And yet, she wasn't dreaming now.

Her hand stopped, her eyes were drawn to a large cartoon in the middle of the page. It was the only one done in color. It was a depiction of heaven. A couple of angels were looking down from their lofty perch at the world, where mayhem on all accounts was breaking out.

Camille felt compelled to look. To study it. Could not drag her gaze away. She worked, trying to figure out what it said, and meant. Finally frustrated with her lack of ability, but completely compelled to find out what it said, she ran upstairs for her dictionary.

Back in the kitchen she diligently looked up the two words she was having trouble with, and then filled in the blanks. *Alles geschieht aus einem Grund.*

She slowly lowered herself to the stool. A peace stole over her as she took another look with the words tumbling around in her heart. *Everything happens for a reason.*

Günther watched out his classroom window as students hurried up the flagstone steps. Several from his class approached, but not the woman he was waiting for.

She was sponsoring Johann.

What a windfall.

Who would have thought?

His heart thumped several times when he spotted Camille with her black coat and chestnut tresses moving as she walked. Her face, the same color as raspberry ice, was drawn up in a smile as she observed a stroller-pushing mommy. She held a cup of coffee in one hand, the other clasped tightly on the strap of her backpack.

Why had he treated her so shabbily on Sunday, he asked himself for the thousandth time. Why? He knew the reason and it almost doubled him over. His guilt over his attraction to her. Her being there so close to Kat's mother. It felt like a betrayal of the worst kind to Katerina and Nikolaus. He'd vowed to himself the day that had taken his whole life that he'd never let himself enjoy the world that he'd robbed his family of. This was his responsibility. His alone to shoulder. His sin to expiate.

He was the one that should have died that day. Been in the accident that took both of their lives. If he'd done what Katerina had asked him to do, in a timely manner, it would have been him and not them. They would be alive. If only he could do it all over.

But he'd procrastinated. Kat had gone, taking their son with her, and been hit by a drunken driver. Every time he went to Aggie's, he relived it. Forced himself to remember.

Seeing Camille there, with his growing love, was too much to handle. He'd been mean. Hurt her feelings and crushed the fragile trust that had been growing between them. Now, after these three days, would she even talk to him?

When she was almost to the top of the steps, Stephen Turner joined her. They walked together, talking. She smiled at him and laughed at something he'd said. Günther's heart fell.

"She's a beautiful woman."

Absorbed in his thoughts, he hadn't heard Stena von Linné's approach.

He turned and looked at her. "Who?" That was a stupid question. She'd obviously seen who he was looking at.

A perfectly plucked eyebrow rose sardonically. "Camille Ashland."

Stena's face was hard. An expression he'd never seen before transformed it into a sneer of jealously and hate. He was surprised.

"Yes. I agree with you."

"It looks as if the other American finds her attractive too. I've seen him around here recently. Quite often, actually."

That was an odd thing for her to say. Or notice, for that matter.

Günther went over to his desk and sat down. He motioned for Stena to sit also. "How did it go for you? Did you have any problems?"

She sat, but looked troubled. Not the cool, composed person he was used to. She smiled. "It went well. The students seemed to like my methods. There was much class participation." She shrugged. "It was good."

"Thank you again for stepping in for me in my hour of need."

Students were filing in now, sitting or chatting. Camille came in, followed by Branwell. She took her seat quietly and avoided looking in his direction. She turned to Lena and complimented her on her sweater. This was going to be a difficult day.

It was. They avoided each other at every move. Others seemed to feel the tension in the air, for it was quiet and tempers were short. At lunchtime, Günther received a text from Florian. He'd been to see the doctors. They'd cleansed his wound, given him numerous injections, and he'd suffered through eight stitches. He'd have a scar to show for his bravery. Günther smiled. Ms. Roth was agreeable to the plan for Johann. *Probably glad to be rid of us*. Besides the fact that Bernhard was on his way to the penitentiary, her opinion of the thug had taken an impressive turn for the worse, especially after seeing the slash on Florian's neck.

At a quarter to three, Günther was glad the day was almost over. Some of the students grumbled when he handed out homework. He hadn't had a private moment with Camille all day.

She approached his desk now, her heart was in her eyes. "*Herr* Christove?"

"Günther," he reminded her quietly. He wanted to smile but a dull ache inside prevented it. He came around his desk and stood close. "I'm sorry about Sunday," he said sincerely. "I almost bit your head off." The apology just slipped out unplanned. "I scared you."

"No. No. I'm the one who is sorry. I intruded on you."

"Well, it was a shock. I just reacted badly. I've heard the good news about Johann. I can't tell you how wonderful I think this is. But are you sure about it? Have you given it enough thought? Enough prayer? This is an enormous step."

"Yes, I have. It's actually the first time that I feel one hundred percent positive about anything I've ever done in my life. It's for Johann. And God." *And you*, she thought.

He took both her hands into his own, holding them out in front of him. "Who would have thought that our student from across the ocean would—" His phone rang, cutting him off. As he shook his head in disbelief, he dropped one of her hands to look at the number.

A disappointed look crossed his brow. "I'm sorry, Camille, I need to answer this."

She smiled brightly, making his spirit soar. "That's all right. I'll see you tomorrow."

In *Michaelerplatz* Camille wandered around, too keyed up to go home. She went over to the church and looked at the relief of Christ on the side of the wall, thinking. "Lord," she said softly. "Thank you for bringing Günther and me back together as friends. I would have been so sad if we had parted without making up."

Just then the bell tower rang out. A bittersweet shiver slipped down her spine. She and Günther were friends. That was all they could ever be. But she was happy with that. That was better than nothing.

She strolled around a bit more, and then sat on a bench. She gazed at the sky with its wispy clouds and golden-brown birds swooping on the breeze.

She had a decision to make. Should she go home early for Kristin or try to stick it out for the full two months? The school was agreeable to a credit for the future. Was that what she really wanted?

In her heart of hearts, she knew she really wanted to stay.

But…should she?

Her health seemed fine. The shop was doing well, and today Kristin had sounded happier too. She was living her dream. Getting to know who she really was. Deep down. Somewhere where she had never looked before.

And better still, she was drawing so much closer to God. Learning about her faith. She knew a lot of the reason was because of Günther, but she couldn't help that. He had a natural ability to see God everywhere. It was hard for others not to be drawn to him. Who knew if she'd ever really get the chance to come back? Life took unexpected turns when they were least expected. Hadn't she learned that a few weeks ago?

She heard laughter and saw a couple coming out of a restaurant, hand in hand. They looked happy. They stopped and kissed. The man tucked a wisp of his sweetheart's hair behind her ear and then whispered something. The woman laughed softly and snuggled against his side as they walked away.

Love was a beautiful thing.

She wanted that. She wanted that with Günther.

Günther is married, she sternly reminded herself.

She could never have him—and that was a cold, hard fact. She glanced at the restaurant the lovers had exited. That may be so, but she *could* have a glass of wine.

Chapter Thirty-Two

"*Möchten Sie noch ein Glas Wein?*" Camille's waiter asked as he picked up her empty glass. She glanced at the plate of fresh fruit, nuts, and assorted crackers and wafers she'd ordered and he'd just placed on the pink and green floral tablecloth. It looked delicious, but the cheese and assortment of meats on the table next to hers looked even more appealing, making her mouth water. She shrugged, resigned to her lot. *What could one more glass hurt?*

"*Ja, bitte,*" she replied, smiling at him as if it was the most natural thing in the world to be drinking alone on a Thursday afternoon.

The place was bustling, loud.

Now, after one glass of wine she felt better about her state of affairs. Actually, she felt wonderful. Warm and languid. She delved into the colorful plate of goodies.

Günther was married. Period. End of sentence.

Her waiter was back with her second glass of Franz Prager Grüner Veltliner, 2006. When she'd ordered it, she hadn't really known what it was, except that it was listed under white table wines. Chardonnay was her usual choice, but none had been offered. Whatever this was, it was good.

"*Danke sehr*," she said as he placed it before her on the table. She glanced at her watch. She'd been leisurely taking her time. Enjoying being alone. She did need to call Wolfgang out of courtesy soon, or he'd be worried.

Camille placed a succulent strawberry on a golden wafer and placed it in her mouth. She chewed thoughtfully and washed it down with a sip of wine.

Her phone chimed signaling a text. From Wolfgang. *Call me*, was all it said. She put in his number and waited for him to pick up.

"Wolfgang, I got your message. What's up?"

"I need to talk to Günther and was wondering if he was with you?"

"No. I haven't seen him since class. Did you try calling him?"

"My call isn't going through. Possibly his phone is dead, or something. He lives close to the school. Are you still in the area?"

Camille knew where this was leading. At least she thought she knew. No way did she want to go over to Günther's house. He'd think she was following him again. She could fib to Wolfgang, but that wouldn't be right. Maybe it was important.

"Yes, I'm still in *Michaelerplatz*."

"Would you mind going over to his apartment and giving him a message for me? It's really quite close."

She almost groaned. "Not at all." *That's a boldfaced lie.* "Just give me directions and what you want me to tell him. I'll go over there right now." She paused. "Are you sure I won't be intruding?"

Wolfgang laughed. "On Günther? I don't think so."

He gave Camille the address and a few simple instructions to get there.

Camille stood in front of the apartment building for a good five minutes gathering her courage. *This is exactly what I deserve for feeling sorry for myself. If I'd gone home when I should, instead of imbibing indulgently on two glasses of wine, I wouldn't be in this predicament.*

How fast things change. A few days ago she would have marched right up to the door and knocked, unmindful of what Günther might be doing. Not so now. Forcing one foot in front of the other, she found herself at the door. Gritting her teeth, she rang the buzzer.

A few heart-stopping moments passed and then Günther answered. His brows shot up in surprise. And then he smiled. A beautiful, welcoming, cartwheel-producing smile. His shirttail hung loose and he was barefoot. A cat ran between his legs and out into the bushes.

"Camille."

"Günther, I'm *really* sorry to barge in on you like this— *again*," she began. She ran her fingers through her hair and pulled the mass over one shoulder. Her face suddenly warmed so much she wondered if it was the wine or something else entirely. "But Wolfgang is trying to get a hold of you. He's tried to call you several times but can't get through. He asked me to come over here and tell you to call him."

Günther moved aside and opened the door. "Forgive my rudeness." He swept his arm wide in a gesture to enter. "Please, come in. Do you have a moment to visit?"

She did. As a matter of fact—and after a final decision—she had one week short of two months. "I guess. Only if you're sure you're not busy."

"I'm not doing anything except relaxing." He looked down at his feet and wiggled his toes. They laughed.

The moment Camille stepped through the threshold, an intense dizziness bombarded her. She swayed to one side and Günther reached out quickly and took hold of her by the shoulders. He led her through the room to a burgundy sofa.

"Whoa, now. Sit. Are you feeling okay?"

"I was. All of a sudden I felt warm and then dizzy. It must be the wine." *Ouch. How embarrassing.* "I mean, when Wolfgang called, I was in a restaurant having a snack. I guess it went to my head."

"No more apologies. Let me get you a cool glass of water."

He disappeared from the room and soon returned with two glasses of water and some crackers on a small round plate. He placed all three onto the coffee table, then handed Camille her glass.

Camille wondered if Mrs. Christove would materialize at any moment. The place didn't have a woman's touch. Actually, and she felt completely uncharitable even thinking this, but it was quite messy.

"So, what's this about Wolfgang?"

"He didn't say. Only that he needs you to call him and he'd thought your phone may have died. It sounded important."

"That's exactly what happened and I've misplaced my charger." He looked around pointedly. "You can understand why."

Camille sank back into the cushions, closing her eyes. Vertigo swirled. It almost felt as if she was having that bizarre flying sensation when she'd had her near-death experience. The lightheadedness was getting so bad, she was afraid she was going to have to run to the bathroom and get sick.

"You're worse." Günther's tone was full of concern. "Lie flat." He plumped a pillow for her head and reached down to take off her shoes. With that done, he lifted her legs and covered her with a soft chenille throw. "Just rest. I'll be right back."

As he walked away, Camille's instincts warred inside her. She tried to stay calm, but the room tilted and spun. To make matters worse, Camille dreaded the thought of his wife walking through the door and finding her lying on their couch.

"Camille…"

That wasn't Günther. He was off doing something in the other room.

"*Camille.*" The voice was soft, inside her head.

Günther reappeared. He had his phone in his hand. Looking at her, he set it down and squatted at her side. "Camille, what is it? You don't look yourself."

"Something very, very bizarre is going on." Her voice wobbled. "I think I'm going crazy."

He put his palm on her forehead. It was comforting and she closed her eyes.

"You're not warm," he said, and she opened her eyes. "And you're certainly not going crazy. You're getting sick is all. No concern for panic."

"Günther, I've been hearing voices. No, not voices. A voice. *The* voice. The voice of the woman in my vision," she rattled off breathlessly. "I heard it calling my name this morning during breakfast and now I'm hearing it again here. And I have this all-consuming feeling like I had right after the heart attack."

"Are you having chest pains?" His brows drew down over his eyes as he searched her face. "Should we call your doctor?"

She pushed up to a sitting position and lowered her feet to the floor. "No. I don't feel like that. Rather, like something supernatural is going on. It happened the moment I walked through your door."

Günther handed Camille the glass of cool water. "Take some of this," he said, hoping to calm her down. Console her in some small way. Figure out what all this was about. The next time he looked into her face, it was as white as a sheet.

"Who...who is *that*?" she sputtered, as her body shook uncontrollably. She pointed across the room to a picture of Katerina on the bookshelf.

The portrait, one Günther had taken himself when they'd gone on an outing to Salzburg, was his favorite. The breeze from the steep mountainside had swept her dark hair back, showing her beautiful, heart-shaped face. There was no smile, only an expression of deep contemplation. Her brow was pensive and her mouth, soft.

"My wife. Katerina." He was surprised that it brought him no pain to say it.

Camille bolted up and ran to the bookshelf. She took the portrait and studied it intently. Her body shivered ferociously.

"Camille. What is going on?" He followed and took the picture from her hands.

"It's her. The woman in my vision." She turned and stared into his eyes. "There not a shred of doubt in my mind. Where is she now? I need to meet her."

Günther's insides twisted. "That will be impossible. Katerina has been dead for five years."

Camille sank to the floor and put her head into her hands. "Dead?" she said to herself softly. "Five years?"

He pulled her to her feet and they sat on the sofa side by side. Ten minutes went by without a word spoken. Both were lost in their thoughts.

"Do you believe me?" Camille finally whispered.

"What exactly did she say? In your vision, or whatever it was."

More time went by. At last, Camille began. "The first few times she only called my name. Then I saw her and she didn't speak, only I got a feeling of deep, abiding peace. And love. It was as if we were speaking through feelings. Then this morning she called my name and then had me read a comic in the paper." She grasped his chin and turned his face to hers. "I *know* that sounds totally ridiculous. But it's absolutely the case. I'm sure of it."

Camille looked around frantically. When she saw the stack of newspapers in the corner, she jumped up and ran over, taking the one off the top.

Chapter Thirty-Three

"**L**ook." Camille jabbed the paper with her finger, almost ripping it. "That's it. Right there." She flung the paper down between them, still pointing to a cartoon at the bottom of the page. Günther's hands were shaking so badly the paper jerked back and forth when he picked it up and brought it closer to his face. *What kind of a stunt is she pulling? It isn't funny in the least.*

"*Alles geschieht aus einem Grund,*" Günther read aloud.

"Everything happens for a reason," Camille continued, remembering the translation she'd had to look up to understand.

They stared at the cartoon of the two angels examining the crazy, haphazard, mind-boggling earth below.

"So, what could that mean? Besides the obvious." His tone was hard. Jaded.

Camille turned and took his hands. "How did she die?"

Günther ripped his hands from hers. He'd never discussed this before with anyone. Florian had tried, but they hadn't gotten very far.

"How?" she prompted insistently. "Please, Günther. Talk to me. I can see by your expression this must be very painful for you."

He allowed her to reach up and brush away some hair that had drooped into his eyes. "It's important that we get through this. I think she sent me here with a message. I think everything that has happened to me in the past month is connected to this. To you. I know it is."

That blow was below the belt. He stalked over to the window. Flocki was in the branches of the tree out front, climbing higher and higher. He wished he could follow.

"Tell me," Camille repeated from where she stood. He was thankful she hadn't followed him across the room.

"Katerina," he began in a gravelly voice, "and our son, Nikolaus, were killed in an automobile accident."

"I'm so sorry. Oh, Günther, that's horrible. I'm so very sorry…"

He couldn't bear to look at her, to see the revulsion in her eyes. He deserved to see it though, he knew, still that would be too much at once.

Her voice faded out on the last word and he was again grateful that she was giving him his space.

"That's very sad."

Moments ticked by. He wiped perspiration from his forehead. His heart felt like a block of lead, cast out and lost forever on the bottom of the sea. *It is time.* The instant he acknowledged the fact, he felt a tiny bit of peace edge inside.

He turned. Camille was still standing where he'd left her. Waiting patiently. He could see that she knew without him saying so, that he was going to explain. Her eyes, a whirlpool of darkness, looked tortured.

"I killed them."

"Why? Why do you say that?" It was a whisper, barely audible. "Were you driving the other car?"

"Kat asked me to go over and pick up Aggie, who was coming over for a visit. It was a twenty-minute drive from where we were living. I was watching a soccer game. My favorite team was playing. It grew late. She took Nikolaus and went instead. I knew, and yet I let them go." A huge sob tore from his throat. "I *let* them go," he shouted. "It should have been me. I should have died, not them!"

Camille rushed to his side. She pulled him to the sofa and down onto the seat next to her.

"I let them…"

"Shhh, it's okay." She held his head to her shoulder and let him cry. His pain came out in great gasps of sorrow. "It's okay. It's okay." They stayed like that for a long time. Finally, he lifted his head.

"Everything happens for a reason," Camille whispered and stroked his cheek. "While we were sitting here, I was trying to remember every tiny detail of my short time with Katerina. See if there was anything I had forgotten. I know now what she was trying to tell me and why she appeared to me in the first place."

Günther had no more tears. He was exhausted. Drained. He listened, hoping upon hope that Camille knew what she was talking about.

"She is truly happy, Günther. As hard as that might be for you to hear, she is more alive now than when she was actually alive here on earth. From the small part I saw, heaven is the most incredible place. No one in his or her right mind would ever want to come back after seeing it. She will meet you when it's your time to go there. You have to accept that she doesn't want to come back to earth. The only thing that makes her sad is your unending guilt and heartbreak."

He stiffened.

"You have to let it go. Forgive yourself. Forget the circumstances of the accident and believe that everything happens for a reason. God makes something good out of every situation, even horrible ones. She wants you to get on with your life."

He held tight to Camille's hands, absorbed every soothing word into his being. If only he could know for sure what she said was not some fanciful dream, or delusion she'd been having.

"And Nikolaus?"

"I don't know. I never saw him. I did feel something about him, or a child. Goodness and love always accompanied those thoughts."

"Was there anything else?"

"Just one smaller thing that didn't seem to make any sense at all."

"What?"

"*Süßkartoffel ist wunderbar*, Katerina said to me once. I wasn't familiar with the long first word, so I looked it up. Sweet potatoes are wonderful. I thought it curious she would talk about food."

Günther traced his fingers across the cold glass of the photograph still clutched in his hands. "No," he said slowly, joy rippling through his battered heart. "That is not the correct interpretation. *Süßkartoffel ist wunderbar*. Sweet potato is wonderful. *Süßkartoffel* or sweet potato was my nickname for Nikolaus."

The day grew late. Camille had gone home and Stephen Turner had called. Günther was expecting him at any moment. He was limp from the expenditure of emotion, still reeling from all he'd learned today.

A knock sounded on his door. Günther ushered Stephen in without a word being said. He closed the door behind him.

"So, Turner, what are the new findings?"

"The capture of Bernhard was really a boon. His involvement is small, though. I think he was just drawn in recently for the cash. The plan was for him to put a slip of phone numbers and codes into the glove box on your brother's motorcycle. My guess is, clues would have led me there next, and the heat would have been shifted to him."

"What *is* the case you're working on? Terrorism, stolen artifacts—what?"

"Of course I can't tell you everything, but you *have* earned some sort of explanation," Stephen said. "It revolves around numerous Swiss bank accounts that originated during the Second World War. It seems someone is leaking information just when we're about to make an arrest." He waved the subject away. "So much for shop talk."

Günther nodded. "And Stena? Where does she fit into all of this?"

"That's another puzzle. Bernhard confessed her involvement but as of yet we can't arrest her without some kind of evidence. Speculation is she's the one sending e-mail from the chancellor's office at your school to distract from the true spy—her uncle, Fran Smale. For now, she's run off home to Uppsala. An agent there will look into things. For some time, I've believed Branwell was also involved.

However, I was able to get some good prints off a cup and they don't match anything we have. Actually, I'm glad."

Questions filled Günther's mind. He'd work them out one answer at a time. Now he'd query a little information from his tall friend.

"And Camille? I've asked before about your intentions. You were evasive. Now I want to know."

Stephen's brows rose inquiringly, then he paced the length of the room.

"It's true. I capitalized on her being part of the class that held most of my suspects and suspicions. But…I wasn't using her. If she'd shown any interest in me at all, I'd continue pursuing her." He shrugged his shoulders. "But to her, I'm only a friend. Nothing more."

Günther realized he'd been holding his breath, waiting for Stephen's answer.

"You sure?"

"Would I tell you that if it weren't so?" His usual stern mouth curved up at the corners. "Unfortunately for me, it's the truth."

Chapter Thirty-Four

The next month was a whirlwind of activity for Camille. Günther helped her with all the paperwork involved with Johann and the Eberstarks. He accompanied her on several trips she was required to make to the Child Protection *Büro* for a lineup of interviews. Johann moved in with the Eberstarks, his bed placed in with Patrick's. The boy was a true joy and she felt blessed that he'd been dropped into her life. His distrust of her was virtually gone, replaced with respect and admiration.

Günther spent all of his free time at the Eberstarks' now, also. Wolfgang's running joke was that he was a little too old for adoption. Helene and Sasha were both home, adjusting to the knowledge and hope of her diagnosis.

Her pal, Stephen Turner, was off to other parts, working on gathering evidence to support their theory of Stena von Linné's involvement. He called every now and then with a question or favor and had turned into a true friend.

Günther still struggled with the news that his brother would be moving in July to another parish. Günther alone would be responsible for the English class on Saturday mornings at the church. It was sad but he was excited too for Florian. A new chapter beginning in his life book.

Through the activity, the only black cloud was the all-consuming knowledge that her time was running short. She felt every moment of the ticking clock.

Günther and Camille sat alone on the couch in the front room after a family dinner. Dread as thick as steel hung over their heads.

"I don't want to go," she said, her hands held firmly in his. "Next week will be here too soon."

"I know." It was a whisper and Camille wondered if it was because the children had already gone to bed or if his throat was as painfully tight as hers.

"If only there was a way of being in two places at once. Then I could take care of my mother and daughter and also stay here in Austria. Close to you."

When he looked into her face, Camille gasped. His pain was deep, his eyes tortured. He put his finger on her lips to still them.

"There is nothing we can do or say. You must go. I must stay. Kristin needs you. Aggie needs me. Now, I think, more than ever. I better understand the torment of the apostles when they learned of the Lord's departure."

"But," Camille continued, "we were brought together for a reason. An important one."

She studied his face, committing every detail, every nuance to memory.

"That is true." He stood and pulled her up into his arms. "But we also have very important responsibilities that we can't take lightly," he said against her lips. "Ones we cannot forsake."

"Of course. Of course." Her lips moved softly on his as she answered, her breath mingling with his. Heat coursed through Camille, sending her heart careening around her chest. This was Günther, her love, finally holding her close, kissing her breathless.

She knew he loved her. Wanted her. As much as she loved and wanted him. But they would wait. Bide their time until it was possible for them to work it out. She would either come back to Austria or Günther would come to America. He'd said that was a possibility too.

With a heavy heart, Camille stowed her carry-on in the overhead compartment and sank down into her window seat, trying to block out all feeling. The sun had set an hour ago. Far away on the horizon, the lights of Vienna were beginning to twinkle. Robotically, she buckled her seat belt, leaned back, and closed her eyes. It would be a long flight home to Portland.

The sounds of passengers boarding the 747 were familiar and a bit comforting. People scooted by and families talked. Somewhere in back, a baby started to cry. What would happen now? Would her life just pick up where she'd left it two months ago? As time passed, would Günther forget all about her? No. She'd never believe that. But…but…

A jumble of emotions overcame Camille, and a tear squeezed out between her clenched lids. She reached for her purse and pulled out her hankie. She discreetly daubed her eyes and then quietly blew her nose. She needed to pull herself together so she didn't scare the passengers that would share this row of seats for the next two hours to Heathrow. They'd think she had a cold, or worse yet, that she was an emotional basket case—which indeed she was.

Wadding her hankie back up, it fell to her feet when she went to put it away.

"It looks like a full flight," a masculine voice said.

She jerked up straight. A young man sat in the aisle seat and buckled up.

"Y-yes." Camille managed a halfhearted smile.

"Please take your seats as quickly as possible," a male flight attendant said over the intercom. "There are only a few passengers left to board and we will be closing the door momentarily."

Camille clamped her eyes shut, wishing she could do the same with her heart. The door swished closed with a muted *thump*. She stretched her jaw open several times until her ears popped. *Just get through this. One flight at a time. One flight at a time.*

Just when she expected to feel the plane begin to push back, voices sounded from up by the cockpit, talking excitedly. She didn't have the energy or volition to even try to see what it was about. After several minutes, she glanced over at the young man who already had his earbuds in and was reading a magazine.

She reached across the empty middle seat and tapped his arm. "Excuse me," she said quietly. "Can you see what the delay is?"

He leaned out. Shrugged. "Don't know. Looks like a late passenger."

She sat back. Frustrated. If she had to leave Günther behind, she wished the pilot would hurry up and take off. Get it over with. It wasn't more than a minute later when the plane rolled back. The 747's engines kicked over, droning softly. The soft vibration was comforting. *This is it*, she thought as they headed for the runway.

Turbulence rocked the plane. It had been a rough takeoff and hadn't let up since. As the aircraft climbed, it vibrated violently, causing all the passengers to sit in hushed anxiety. Camille didn't care. She stared down at the lights of Vienna transfixed, trying to imagine the school, *Michaelerplatz*, the Eberstarks', and everything else she'd grown to love. Where was Günther? What was he doing? Was *his* heart ripping in two, like hers? Finally, the jet evened out and all the bumping stopped. A soft *gong* sounded and the seatbelt sign turned off.

"I'm glad that's over," the young man said in an edgy voice.

She glanced over. His face was as white as a ghost. He unclasped his seatbelt and headed for the bathroom at the back of the plane.

The video screens popped down and Camille watched without sound. It looked like a commercial for an upcoming thriller.

"Is this seat taken?"

"Well, *that's* a silly—"

She gasped. Then gasped again. Günther slid in beside her and wrapped her into an embrace, finding her lips. The kiss was long. The young man, who had returned moments after Günther, stood in the aisle with eyes wide.

Camille laughed and pushed Günther back. "Oh, my God, *Günther*! Where did you come from? I can't believe it." That was all she could get out before the tears flowed.

"Shhh, don't cry. I just couldn't let you go."

"B-but how?"

"The term is over for two weeks. Added to the vacation I have coming, I have a whole two months. My colleagues were happy to fill in. That's enough time for Kristin to get to know me before I marry her mother and whisk her off to Vienna for good."

"What about Aggie?"

"Wolfgang and Helene have generously offered to fill in until my return." He picked up her hand and held it firmly between his own. When he spoke this time, his words were solemn and low. "I just couldn't lose you now, not after just finding you. I don't know, maybe it's time you opened a second Chocolate Blossoms in Vienna. I think Kristin, and your mother for that matter, would enjoy it. The way I feel right now, anything is possible. We'll work this out. We have to. I love you. I *can't* live without you." He glanced away for a moment and his face clouded up. "If it's important enough for Kat to send me a message from beyond, then I'm not going to question it. I want to live my life. Every second of my life. Make every moment count."

Camille, overcome with emotion, couldn't respond. Her prayers had been answered. Her life was beginning anew.

The young man, still standing conspicuously in the passageway, cleared his throat. "Uh, can I sit down now? I, uh…" He looked around confused, his face as red as the Austrian flag. "Sir, I could take the seat you left, wherever that is?"

Günther and Camille laughed together. "No, no. Sit down here," Günther gestured to the empty aisle seat. "We have an incredible story we'd like to share."

More Books by Caroline Fyffe

The McCutcheon Family Series
Montana Dawn
Texas Twilight
Mail-Order Brides of the West: Evie
Mail-Order Brides of the West: Heather
Moon Over Montana
Mail-Order Brides of the West: Kathryn
Montana Snowfall

~~~*~~~

Stand Alone Western Historical
Sourdough Creek

~~~*~~~

The Prairie Hearts Series
Where the Wind Blows
Before the Larkspur Blooms
West Winds of Wyoming
Under a Falling Star

~~~*~~~

Stand Alone Contemporary Women's Fiction
Three and a Half Minutes

~~~*~~~

To LISTEN to any of these stories in audio form click Caroline's link at Audible.com. Take your reading experience to another level!
http://adbl.co/192j6id

Sign up for Caroline's newsletter: www.carolinefyffe.com
See her Equine Photography: www.carolinefyffephoto.com
LIKE her FaceBook Author Page: Facebook.com/CarolineFyffe
Twitter: @carolinefyffe
Write to her at: caroline@carolinefyffe.com

About the Author

Caroline Fyffe was born in Waco, Texas, the first of many towns she would call home during her father's career with the US Air Force. A horse aficionado from an early age, she earned a Bachelor of Arts in communications from California State University-Chico before launching what would become a twenty-year career as an equine photographer. She began writing fiction to pass the time during long days in the show arena, channeling her love of horses and the Old West into a series of Western historicals. Her debut novel, *Where the Wind Blows*, won the Romance Writers of America's prestigious Golden Heart Award as well as the Wisconsin RWA's Write Touch Readers' Award. She and her husband have two grown sons and live in the Pacific Northwest.

Made in the USA
Middletown, DE
07 May 2020

93526801R00170